DIRE WARNING

AMAZON INTERNATIONAL
BEST-SELLING AUTHOR

Mary Rundle

A Dragonheart Story published by Dragonheart, LLC.

First Edition: October 2017

Photo by Alex Salgues

Dire Warning is a work of fiction. Names, characters, places, events, and incidents are either the product of the author's imagination or are used fictitiously and any resemblance to actual persons, living or dead, events or locales is strictly coincidental.

All characters depicted in sexual acts in this work of fiction are 18 years of age or older.

Dedication

To Lisa,
When I had a dream, you encouraged me,
When I despaired, you lifted me up,
When I finished, you cheered the loudest.

I owe you so much for all your help and support,
You are simply the best!
With All My Love and Appreciation!

Acknowledgements

My gratitude and appreciation go out to the many people who helped bring this book to life.

To Phil – my personal go-to guy for answers to my publishing questions and who saved me hours of time trying to figure it out myself.

To Jessica – my beta reader who went through the manuscript with her fine-toothed grammar comb and gave it back to me squeaky clean.

To Carla – my beta reader whose comments always made me laugh and whose eagle eyes spotted those pesky continuity bugs that sometimes creep in.

To Leah my beta reader who started me on this journey.

To Alex – whose image inspired my story and whose photography is simply nonpareil. Vive La France!

To Muriel – Without whose help I would never have connected with Alex.

To Dan – the fastest Photoshop gun in world, for his cover design skills.

And last but not least, to my husband, the editor. My book was the first romance story he'd ever read and it was a M/M paranormal one at that. His dedication to making my book the best it could be went far beyond anything I could have anticipated. You are a gem and I love you.

TABLE OF CONTENTS

BLACKWOOD PACK SERIES

Follow the journey of the Blackwood Pack, seven brothers who are wolf shifters in search of their fated mates – stories about love at first sight with twists and turns, angst and humor, romance and adventure. Each book has two main characters who meet, fall in love, mate and achieve an HEA but the stories also chronicle the continuing saga of the Blackwood Pack.

WHO'S WHO IN THE BLACKWOOD PACK

Fox River Pack (The Original Pack)

Striker Alpha of Fox River Pack. Younger brother to Josiah. Father to Jackson, Logan, Cody, Colton, Carson, Dakota, and Zane. Six other children were killed in the massacre.

Hope Alpha Mate of Fox River Pack. Mother to Jackson, Logan, Cody, Colton, Carson, Dakota, Zane; also six other children who were killed in the massacre.

Blackwood Pack

Jackson Alpha of the Blackwood Pack. Members of this pack are Jackson's brothers Logan, Cody, Colton, Carson, Dakota, and Zane, the sole survivors of the Fox River Pack Massacre. First-born son of Striker. Fraternal twin to Logan. Mated to Steel Valentin, a Dire Wolf. His story is told in **Dire Warning, Book 1**.

Logan Survivor of the Fox River Pack Massacre. Second-born son of Striker. Younger twin to Jackson. An interior designer.

Cody Survivor of the Fox River Pack Massacre. Third son of Striker. Oldest triplet.

Colton Survivor of the Fox River Pack Massacre. Fourth son of Striker. Middle triplet. A nurse.

Carson Survivor of the Fox River Pack Massacre. Fifth Son of Striker. Youngest triplet.

Dakota Survivor of the Fox River Pack Massacre. Sixth son of Striker. The pack's chef.

Zane Survivor of the Fox River Pack Massacre. Seventh son of Striker. Computer genius.

Dire Wolves in the Blackwood Pack

Maximus Alpha of the Dire Wolves. Guardian of the Dire Wolf Treasure. Chairman of Dire Enterprises. Fated Mate of Oracle. Father to Steel and Slate.

Oracle Mate of Maximus. An Oracle. The voice of the Fates on Earth. Mother to Steel and Slate.

Steel First-born son of Maximus and Oracle. Fated Mate of Jackson. Older brother of Slate. CEO at Dire Enterprises. His story is told in **Dire Warning, Book 1.**

Slate Second-born son of Maximus and Oracle. Younger brother to Steel. COO at Dire Enterprises.

Associated with the Blackwood Pack

Jimmy Known as Jimmy Blackwood. Fated Mate of Mystia. Friend and surrogate parent to the Blackwood Pack. After the massacre, the survivors of the Fox River Pack changed their name to the Blackwood Pack for security reasons.

Mystia A Witch. Fated Mate of Jimmy Blackwood. Cast an anti-scent spell on the brothers after the massacre to prevent enemies from discovering them. Friend and surrogate parent to Blackwood Pack. Friend of Oracle.

Penn Known as Penn Anderson. Personal friend of Steel and Slate. Attorney for Dire Enterprises.

Ian Dr. Ian Wallace. Worked for Frontline Doctors. The pack's physician. A Scottish Wolf.

Silver Point Pack

Josiah Alpha of Silver Point Pack. Older brother of Striker. Former member of the Fox River Pack. Challenged his father and lost. After being banished, formed the Silver Point Pack. Never found his Fated Mate. Mated with a Beta and had four children. Believed to have issued the Fox River Pack massacre order and subsequent kill orders for members of the Blackwood Pack.

Kahn Eldest son of Josiah. Cousin to Jackson, Logan, Cody, Colton, Carson, Dakota, and Zane. An artist.

Rudy Second in command for Silver Point Pack.

Dylon An enforcer for Silver Point Pack.

TERMS OF ENDEARMENT FOUND IN THE BOOKS

Mon petit loulou French, roughly translated means 'my small wolf'. Mystia uses it when speaking to the brothers.

Mo chroí Irish for 'my heart'. Steel calls Jackson this.

Chapter 1

The late afternoon sun blinded him as he woke on the soft ground and opened his eyes. *What the fuck...* Jackson groaned, as he remembered what happened to him. He closed his eyes and wondered if he was as stupid as his father always claimed. It would appear so, since he'd been robbed of everything, including his clothes; all because he'd stopped to help two dudes at the side of the road. "Engine trouble," the tall man drawled. "Can't find the problem," said his blond-haired buddy. And so, Jackson once again paid a price for always wanting to believe the best in people.

Attempting to get to his feet, he became aware of the pounding in his head. "I wonder what they hit me with," he mused. Luckily his aching head appeared to be the only lasting damage he'd suffered—except for his lack of clothes, money or car. Jackson looked down and shook his head. *Ouch! I better not do that anymore.* "I need to stop believing in people," he mumbled. Wasn't that what his father always said? No, that wasn't right—his father never spoke, he just yelled. Jackson ignored him during his teen years because trying to live up to his father's expectations was impossible. At eighteen, he left for college and finally escaped the daily fault-finding.

Standing in the lush orange grove, he could smell the sweetness of the ripening fruit, reminding him of his mother's scent. Jackson's stomach grumbled, but first, he needed to solve his immediate problem of no clothes. He looked around, hoping at least to see his pants, but no luck; all he found was a small, torn, pair of pants that some migrant worker left behind, half-buried in the ground.

Well, it would have to do—he could hold it in front of him in an effort to get a ride from a passing farmer. Walking through the grove and looking for the dirt road he'd been driving on when he'd stopped to help the two thieves, he started to worry about his brothers. He had to get home soon. After a short walk, he stood to one side of the road, bunching the ragged pants in front of his cock and threw his thumb out, hoping he wouldn't be waiting long.

~/~/~/~/~

Steel had been driving for several days now, coming to the end of a long trip, and couldn't get back home fast enough. He looked at the sun hanging low in the cloudless blue sky; it reminded him of his bedroom. He missed the solitude of his place in the country with no one near him for miles, where he was free to be himself. It had been too long since he'd shifted and run through his mountains and his whole body was antsy. Shifting would help settle his body down, but Steel had a strange feeling his wolf needed more than just a run; he just didn't know what.

During the drive, he thought about his life and the compelling need to find his mate. He'd searched for a long time and was disheartened about his failure to accomplish the goal that had eluded him for so long. Steel hoped the man he'd met in the city would have been the one, but during lunch all he could think of was how to escape. Oh, the man was hot enough but Steel's blood didn't boil in want and need.

After saying goodbye, he hit the road immediately even though he planned to stay a week to do some sightseeing. He just couldn't bring himself to do it alone because it would just reinforce his sense of failure.

Turning onto the short-cut dirt road through the groves so he'd get home by sundown, he once again found himself frowning. Trying to rid himself of his gloomy thoughts, he turned on the radio and, tapping his fingers to Boxcar Willie's version of "You Are My Sunshine," decided to be positive as he wondered where else he should look for his mate.

Steel glanced down at his phone to check for messages and as he looked up, he suddenly slammed on the brakes. There, in front of him, was his fantasy—a man with dark, curly hair and piercing blue eyes set in a beautiful face with a chiseled chin and full cock-sucking red lips. Steel's cock hardened instantly. *Holy fuck! Pierced nipples! And the man is naked, with miles of muscles, just ready for me to bend him over my truck and take him.*

~/~/~/~/~

As the dusty black truck approached, Jackson held his breath hoping it would stop for him. He couldn't see who was driving, but—hallelujah—it stopped. Jackson stood still, waiting for the driver to speak. The late afternoon sun was in his eyes and he wasn't going to say anything until he knew who his guardian angel might be.

Hopefully, it was someone who wouldn't object to having a bare-assed dude sitting on his seats. Jackson decided right then if that was a problem, he'd beg to ride in the back of the truck—not the most comfortable choice in his condition but far better than staying out here.

"Shit, I'm so fucking late. I just hope my pack doesn't do anything stupid," Jackson mumbled while waiting to see if he was getting a lift. He drew his dark eyebrows together when there was no sign of life in the truck.

Maybe whoever was in it was waiting for him to approach. He didn't want to do that until he had more information. *Yup, I need to be careful and wait for a sign the driver stopped to help me.*

As the seconds dragged on, Jackson considered his options. With no car, money, or clothes, it limited what he could do if this person meant him harm, so running away and hiding in the grove until they left seemed like his best bet. He knew if he shifted, he would outrun a human but what if they had a dog who could track him? That wouldn't be good, but it really didn't matter since he couldn't shift in front of humans anyway. *Gods, I hate feeling so vulnerable. If only home were closer, I could get there on my own four legs.* But he couldn't risk it because the Silver Point Pack hunters were in the area.

Jackson tilted his head, trying to listen but heard nothing. He exhaled the breath he was holding when he didn't hear a barking dog. *Although, the dog could be trained to be quiet. Oh, double shit—great, that thought isn't helping.*

Jackson hesitated, thinking about what to do because his gut was filled with turmoil and that was never a good sign. His wolf was dancing around as if he were just served the biggest, rawest steak ever. Nope, Jackson didn't understand his wolf today—and just when he needed him the most. "A lot of help you are," he admonished his wolf. Just as he began to turn so he could get a head start if he needed to flee, a window rolled down and a deep seductive voice asked, "Do you need a ride?" Jackson froze. That voice…

~/~/~/~/~

Steel stared at his fantasy and couldn't believe his luck. What a tasty morsel to make up for his shitty trip. He knew he had to fuck this man—right now if he could arrange it—because his cock was harder than it had been in a long time and he could feel his blood heating up. *Huh, that didn't make sense.* But he decided to ignore it for now since all the blood had left his brain, heading to the part of him that was demanding attention. Steel licked his lips and closed his eyes.

Every dream he'd ever had was right before him. He wanted to kiss this man; no, he needed to devour him. Yes, that's what his body was telling him while his mind envisioned softly touching those moist red lips, gently seeking access to his sweet mouth and then, the lips would part—just a bit—allowing Steel's eager tongue to enter to get his first taste of him. Oh yes, the taste would be so sweet—he just knew it. *Fuck!*

As the kiss grew in fierceness, he would grind his iron-stiff cock against his man's groin, feeling the hardness of his man and knowing he wanted it as much as Steel. Then he could feel the man licking his jaw and biting his neck while twisting his nipples. Holy Fates, he was being driven insane with the need and lust boiling through his body. Hell, yes! He knew what was coming next.

His man would lower himself to his knees and look up at Steel, eyes filled with lust, seeking permission to swallow the cock in front of him. Fuck! Steel could see those ruby-red, plump, luscious lips around his cock while he stared down at those darkening, passion-filled blue eyes. *Oh Fuck! That's right baby, suck me deep, take all of me!* Steel could feel that hot, wet mouth, running up and down his large manhood—sucking, licking, and nipping until he was on the edge of coming.

As the tingling at the base of his spine began, Steel's balls would tighten; he would pull out of that gifted mouth, grab his sexy man, spin him around, bend him over the tailgate of his truck, spit on his cock, part his cheeks and push in with a mighty roar. *Holy crap!* Steel nearly came instantly—feeling the tightness, the softness, the heat in his mind—making it nearly impossible to stop his cock from shooting his seed.

Steel's eyes flew open—he had to stop or he'd come in his jeans and that's not how he wanted to meet his dream man. He pinched the tip of his cock to kill his hard-on, while taking deep breaths.

As he was trying to calm down, Steel suddenly realized the time he'd spent imagining having sex caused concern and worry to furrow his man's brow. A slight shift in his man's posture signaled he was planning to run. No, no, no... do something now his wolf demanded. For a moment, Steel was distracted by his wolf's reaction but quickly began to roll down his window.

As the window rolled down, Jackson's cock grew long and hard and he knew in that instant, he'd met his mate. The addictive scent hitting his nostrils brought back all the happy memories of his childhood before everything had gone to hell. He closed his eyes and remembered his siblings and the love they shared. Just as quickly, though, the precious memories faded and his urge to run increased. *Run Now! My life is way too fucked up to have a mate. Nononononoooo! This can't be happening to me right now.* As much as Jackson was dismayed, his wolf was beside himself with joy and that wasn't helping.

Oh Shit... This man was a wolf—a very large one. But Jackson didn't recognize his scent. *Wait, maybe this dude won't realize I'm a wolf—or his mate.* His chest tattoo, given by a witch, masked his scent from other shifters. His brothers wore them too. Jackson's pack had been able to hide in plain sight for several years now. Mates knew each other by their scent and with no scent, no mating pull. *I should be safe.*

When the man spoke, a whole-body shiver consumed Jackson and his cock grew harder still. That voice—deep, smooth as a Macallan-40-year-old scotch—spoke to his wolf, causing him to roll over in submission. *What? His wolf was submitting? Huh? What was that about?* But before he could figure out why, there was a bigger problem. *Oh crap, how am I going to conceal my erection; that voice alone would cause my cock to stay hard. My wolf isn't going to like this, at all.*

The truck door opened, the man stepped out and Jackson's jaw dropped. *Holy shit on a shingle!* He stood way over six feet tall—Jackson bet it was closer to seven feet. The man's face was in shadow, but he could see the rest of him was all muscle□big muscles□chest, arms, and legs. Drooling over the sight of his fated mate, Jackson's hands tightened on the torn pants, frantic to hide his cock growing by the second. He could smell his arousal and felt the cloth grow wet. *Damn! The man would smell it, too.*

~/~/~/~/~

Steel stood next to his dirty truck while inside him his wolf was doing a happy dance. He could smell the man's arousal swirling in the air along with his. His wolf was demanding a claiming immediately, which he was all for, though something made him hesitate. He inhaled deeply—the man had no wolf scent. He must be human, Steel thought, but that didn't make any sense since his blood was boiling in want and need which could only happen when he found his mate. And then there was his agitated wolf—clawing to be let loose, demanding to claim the man. Steel was damned confused—he knew his future mate had to be a wolf, but this man wasn't a wolf. He wondered if the Oracle was wrong. *Was his mate a human? No, impossible.* He needed another wolf so his line would continue. *Oh hell! Now what?*

Chapter 2

Jackson inhaled sharply as the walking, living, sex god moved toward him. *Oh fuck, I'm in so much trouble*, as his mate's face became visible for the first time. *Sexy? Yes! Beautiful? Oh Gods! Yes!* If Jackson could have sketched his dream mate, this dude was it—tall, long dark silky hair, wide eyes, high cheekbones, full bottom lip, closely shaved beard and those muscles. *Shit! A mate who has the power to fuck me into the next room just as I always dreamed.* Jackson could feel his ass clench and his hole flutter, knowing his mate would send him out of this world with pleasure.

He pushed against his cock, trying to hide his hard-on from his mate's gorgeous brown eyes. But that wasn't the only problem he had—his wolf was demanding his mate and Jackson was fighting to control him. He had to, because his life and the lives of his pack members depended on it. *Better answer before his mate got too close.* "Yeah, I need a lift to the outside of the next town, if you can."

~/~/~/~/~

Steel's cock was now straining to be free from the confines of his jeans—that *had* to be his mate. That voice causing his blood to boil and his need for the man was driving him over the edge. But it made no sense. Something had to be wrong because he'd never had a reaction like this during his long life. Shit, he needed to get home and search the archives to see if there was a mistake as to who his mate might be.

Dammit, until that was sorted out, he wouldn't be able to touch this man. It would cause too much trouble and damage if he fucked the wrong one while his body was in its *toirchigh* period. *Shit, Shit, Shit! Think! Need to find out who this is and where he's from.*

"I'm Steel Valentin. I can give you a ride. Is that where your home is?"

"I'm Jackson. That would be great. I'll ride in the back, if that's okay," he said, not answering Steel's question.

Steel thought for a moment. His wolf wanted Jackson in the cab near him but he knew *that* would be a disaster. *No, better to keep some distance between them until he could do his research.* "That's fine," said Steel, "there's plenty of room back there."

Jackson gave Steel a wide berth as he headed for the rear of the truck. Steel was talking but Jackson was so involved with keeping his wolf under control, he missed most of it. *Oops!* Jackson suddenly realized Steel was offering him sweatpants.

"Oh man, that's great. Thanks," he said.

"Where're your clothes?

Jackson could feel himself blush as he remembered his stupid decision to help. "Uhhh, they were stolen," he said, not meeting Steel's eyes.

Steel thought how cute Jackson looked with deep pink cheeks and whoops, he *had* to stop thinking that way. He offered the sweatpants to Jackson and glancing at the torn pants Jackson was still holding in front of him, asked, "How did that happen?"

Jackson took the gray sweatpants, carefully avoiding touching his mate and mumbled, "I stopped to help these dudes. They had other plans because they knocked me out and made off with my money, clothes, and car." Jackson hoped this would end the conversation, and he quickly dressed, then climbed into the back of the truck.

Hearing that Jackson had been attacked, Steel's wolf demanded to hunt down the assholes and kill them. Steel braced himself against the truck and breathed deeply. His wolf was asserting itself and he was strong. Steel's mouth filled with fangs and the hair on his arms and chest started to elongate. His claws left scratches on the truck's door frame as he retracted them. He couldn't shift in front of this human no matter how much his wolf wanted to. It took several deep breaths but he pulled back his wolf. Anxious for it not to happen again, Steel climbed into the truck, put it in gear, and started down the road.

Steel kept glancing in his rearview mirror at Jackson, still puzzled why his wolf and body were acting as if Jackson was their mate. Why couldn't he smell anything? Nothing—no scent, just arousal but nothing else. That just didn't make sense. Well, maybe he'd have his answers after his research. Steel wondered what the chest tattoo on Jackson meant. He'd never seen one like it and hmm-m-m, yes—he'd take a picture of it with his phone, secretly. It seemed familiar but he just couldn't place it.

Steel could feel Jackson's anxiety and his wolf was telling him this man was in danger. But according to shifter laws he couldn't offer his protection to a human even though his wolf was demanding it. Any involvement in the affairs of humans was strictly forbidden. His wolf was more upset than he'd ever been, and he'd need an extra-long run tonight to see if he could quiet him down.

Tomorrow he'd start researching this man that both his body *and* wolf were insisting was destined for him. He hoped the answers were in the archives because he needed to cool his blood soon; once his body started heating in anticipation of mating, the only thing that would work was fucking and claiming his mate.

Jackson could feel Steel's eyes on him but he ignored them. *No sense in pursuing what I can't have. Crap! Why did this have to happen now when my pack is under attack?* They'd been through so much and still had so far to go before they could be free of the danger that threatened them. Jackson covered his face with his hands and tried to relax but it was hard as he thought about the massacre that killed most of the pack. He needed to call Logan soon or there'd be a search party out and he didn't want to expose the pack to more danger. As the truck ate up the dusty miles, he thought back to that fateful day when his world changed forever. Damn, he wished it never happened.

Jackson felt the truck slow down to enter the paved highway. Just another 20 miles and he'd be near the outskirts of the town where the remainder of his pack lived. While he enjoyed riding in the back of a pickup when he was younger, he now felt too exposed because he was afraid someone might see him and call Silver Point.

It'd been a long time—a couple of years for sure—since he was so out in the open and it was rattling his nerves. *Better to lie down and reduce the chance of being seen.* There wasn't much in the truck bed except a bag of rags which he used to rest his head on. Not very luxurious but he'd been in worse situations and at least he had a kick-ass man driving the truck—not that the man knew he belonged to Jackson but he just knew Steel was the kind of dude who would stand by his side. He fervently hoped it wouldn't come to that.

The last thing he needed was for Steel to get a whiff of his blood; the protection spell only masked his body scent—one drop of blood and Steel would have him pinned and ready to claim as his mate. And then Steel would be in danger—a target by association. *Fuck, I just can't take that risk because I'll be unable to protect both my mate and my pack if the fight comes.*

~/~/~/~/~

Steel saw Jackson lie down, at first thinking he was tired. "He's hiding from view," Steel said to himself. "Now why would that be?" Steel hadn't detected any deceit coming from Jackson—*right-t-t-t, stupid thought, why would I be able to smell deceit when I couldn't smell anything except Jackson's arousal. Duh... I must be more tired than I thought.*

He jolted himself back to reality, surprised to see he was about five miles from the next town, Blackwood Pass. Pulling over to the side of the road, he killed the engine and got out. Jackson lifted his head and looked at him with a raised eyebrow.

"I wasn't sure exactly where you wanted me to drop you off," said Steel. "Are you sure I can't take you home? It won't be any trouble."

Jackson shook his head. "No, it's all right. I'll be fine. Just drop me at Jimmy's gas station; my brother can pick me up there. You can't miss it. It has a big yellow sign on the roof."

"Sure, no problem." Steel didn't want to leave Jackson at all but it was too dangerous to stay close until he had some answers. He stared at him, hoping to see something in his face that would tell him Jackson felt a mating pull. He knew he'd been aroused by him but that wasn't enough to guarantee Jackson was his mate. However, if he *wasn't* his mate—and since Jackson obviously was attracted to him—maybe they could hook-up once his *toirchigh* period had passed, assuming he hadn't found his mate by then. Damn, just that thought got his blood boiling again. He turned quickly and got back into the safety of his truck. *Shit! It is going to be a long drive home with my cock weeping pre-cum down my leg.*

~/~/~/~/~

Jackson lay back down and nearly cried as Steel started the truck and drove toward Jimmy's. His mate was so sexy up close and, as shown by his willingness to help a naked-ass man without asking too many questions, was a kind and caring soul. A mate he'd be proud to have by his side—one he could love and be with the rest of his life. As he closed his eyes the picture of Steel pounding his ass caused his cock to rise again. Jackson rolled to his side away from Steel, reached into his pants and stroked his rod as his fantasy continued.

Oh yes, he could feel Steel in his ass, as his cock twitched in his hand. It was so real and Jackson was so lost in his fantasy that he nearly came. *Shit! No can do*, squeezing his balls to stop his orgasm. *Shit! Fuck and fuck again! That was too close.* He thumped his cock several times to deflate his erection while trying to clear his mind of the sensuous picture of Steel's cock in his ass.

Jackson heard the truck change gears, and raised his head. On the left side of the highway, he saw the familiar billboard-sized sign on top of a single-story concrete building. As they drew closer, Jackson smiled. Jimmy's looked like it was frozen in time; faded yellow paint covered a Spanish mission-style store with antiquated red gas pumps out front. "Something I would see in the 1940s," he mused. A wooded mountain loomed behind it and nestled among the trees was a small, white, Victorian house.

Thank the gods, Jackson thought as he felt the truck slow down to make the turn. As soon as it came to a stop, he jumped out and stood on the opposite side from where Steel was getting out. “Thank you very much for the ride.” He spoke quickly, wanting to send his mate away as fast as he could but saw Steel flare his nostrils and heard him discreetly inhale deeply, trying to get his scent. He had to get away from his mate quickly or he wouldn’t be able to keep from shifting. “I hope I didn’t delay you too much,” Jackson said, backing away from the truck.

Steel just stood there, watching him, before finally saying, “Nope, no delay at all. I still have further to go before I get home. Are you sure someone will be able to pick you up? I feel bad about leaving you here with no money or car.”

Jackson could feel the look of panic form on his face before he quickly schooled it to impassiveness. “No really, I’ll be all right. My brother will pick me up. Everything’s cool, man.”

Jackson saw Steel’s face harden and knew his panic had been noted. A mate’s instinct was to protect, but Jackson prayed his scent blocker was enough to stop the man asking any further questions. Steel hesitated, as if he were going to ask more questions but then with a nod and a heated glare, he got back in his truck and drove off.

Chapter 3

Watching Steel pull away, Jackson fought to control his urge to run after him and claim his mate. *It's for the better—this is the only way I can protect him from Silver Point.* Grabbed from behind, he felt a shot of fear racing through him and his body started to shift. But as a familiar scent wafted to his nose, he pulled back his claws and the hair on his arms slowly receded. "What the fuck are you trying to do, Jimmy," he growled, "trying to create a shit storm by having me shift?" Jackson quickly looked around and saw no one watching.

"Naw, I was just so relieved to see you. Where've you been?" Jimmy asked. "I've been fielding calls from Cody and Logan, wondering if I'd seen you. You better call 'em because they're planning a search party." Then Jimmy added, "What happened to your clothes and your car? You didn't have a run-in with Silver Point, did you?"

"I'm fine, Jimmy," Jackson said, hugging his friend. "I'll tell you everything but first let me call my brothers."

"Go into my office where there's some privacy."

"Thanks, could I have a bottle of water? I'm thirsty as hell."

"Go ahead and grab one—need anything else?"

"Nope, I'm fine."

As Jackson walked back to Jimmy's office, he imagined the ribbing Logan would give him for stopping to help someone and getting robbed. Jeez, he wouldn't be living this down anytime soon; his brothers teased him constantly about his Good Samaritan tendencies.

Sitting at the scarred desk that looked as old as his friend, Jackson thought back to the fateful day he'd gotten the call from Jimmy about the death of his parents, younger siblings, and everyone else in the pack. A wave of sorrow washed over him; the memory fresh even though they'd been gone for several years. *Damn, I still miss them.*

Jackson's father, Striker, was the Alpha of the Fox River Pack and was his nemesis most of the time. His relationship with his father wasn't good, but the closeness with his mother and twelve siblings made up for his father's constant fault-finding. On that fateful day in May, the day he and his brothers were due home from college for summer vacation, disaster struck. Jackson and his brothers, Logan, Cody, Colton, Carson, Dakota and Zane, had detoured to Las Vegas to unwind from their year of college before heading home.

While they were gambling and enjoying the sights, the Silver Point Pack attacked the rest of their family on a moonless night and massacred every member of the sleeping Fox River Pack they could find. But they failed to kill the seven oldest sons of the Alpha. Enraged, the Silver Point Alpha sent a team of enforcers to wipe them out.

Jackson's feelings of guilt rose, remembering all the fun he and his brothers enjoyed while everyone they knew and loved lay dying. Luckily, Jimmy Blackwood, a lone wolf, caught word of the massacre and called Jackson in Vegas to tell him what happened. And if that news wasn't bad enough, he also learned Silver Point Pack was hunting him and his brothers. Jackson remembered the numb feeling that overcame him before asking

Jimmy why Silver Point would do this. Jimmy told him that the word was Silver Point wanted the Fox River Pack's land—but he didn't know why.

The days after that call passed in a fog. Jackson was now Alpha of the surviving six members of the Fox River pack and they relied on him. To keep his brothers safe, he changed the name of the pack to Blackwood, moving them to a new location.

Jackson knew the gods had smiled on him when he'd first met Jimmy and his wife, Mystia, who was a witch. They hit it off, became friends, and Jackson visited them regularly on his way to and from college. After the massacre, Jimmy and Mystia offered Jackson and his brothers a place to hide on their ten-thousand-acre property.

He could feel the tears form in his eyes but he would not cry. He'd shed too many tears already over something he couldn't change. Trying to forget the massacre was useless; his wolf constantly reminded him of the need for vengeance against those who had harmed his family and pack. Jackson refused to act on that need because revenge wouldn't help anyone. As he saw it, it might only end up causing the deaths of those who had survived the massacre. He took a deep breath, hoping to calm his emotions, and then placed a call home.

A breathless voice said, "Hi Jimmy, did you hear anything? We're just about to leave to find him."

Jackson recognized the voice of his brother Cody, and replied, "Hey, it's me. I'm safe."

"Are you all right? Where've you been? You scared us half to death. Everybody's been so worried and I've been bugging Jimmy to see if he knew or heard anything. Just a minute, I need to tell the guys."

Jackson heard the muffled voice of Cody speaking to the other pack members before coming back on the line and demanding, "What the fuck happened?"

"Listen, I'll tell you everything—will you pick me up at Jimmy's? My car was stolen and I need a lift home."

"I'll be right there."

"Okay. Cody? Be careful."

Just as Jackson hung up, Jimmy came into the office and sat down on the beat-up old chair in the corner which matched the rest of the décor in the dingy and worn room. After looking Jackson over, he asked, "Want to tell me about it?"

Jackson sighed. He gazed at his friend's short grey hair that looked as if Jimmy's hands had run through it many times today—*probably because he was worried about me.* His shirt matched two, light blue, piercing eyes set in a weather-beaten face lined with years of tough living. Jimmy was an old wolf and reminded Jackson of a grizzled range cowboy he'd seen in some Western movie.

"Not much to tell. I stopped to help a couple of dudes at the side of the road, they knocked me over the head, stole my money, clothes, and car. Came to and hitched a ride here. That's about it." He didn't mention finding his fated mate□the walking, talking, sex god□because he knew what Jimmy would say and he'd already made up his mind it wasn't going to happen. Jimmy and Mystia had been together almost forever and would nag him until he claimed his mate. Jackson sat still and returned Jimmy's stare, because if he didn't, Jimmy would know something was up. So, he kept quiet and waited for a response.

“Is that all that happened?” Jimmy asked, hoping Jackson would change his mind and reveal more, even though it was a long shot.

“How’s Mystia? Is she coming home soon?” Jackson asked, changing the subject, knowing Jimmy could never resist talking about his wife who acted as a mother figure to the Blackwood Pack. The surviving members of the massacre owed their lives to Mystia for putting a protection spell on all of them. That kept the Silver Point Pack from finding and killing the rest of them who’d been members of the now defunct Fox River Pack. Thank the gods no one knew of his friendship with Jimmy and Mystia before everything had gone to hell in a handbasket.

“She’ll be back tomorrow,” answered Jimmy, “and she’ll be wantin’ to see you about what happened.”

Jackson groaned silently. He knew what that meant. There’d be no way he could keep a secret that big from Mystia. He’d just have to convince her it was for the best, that his mate not be claimed. He heard a door slam, then, his brother, Cody calling out, “Yo, Jackson, where are you?”

“In here,” Jackson yelled as he got up from the desk. “Thanks Jimmy, I’ll see you tomorrow.” As he got to the door, Cody’s arms wrapped around him, lifting him off his feet. “Jeez, Jackson, don’t you ever do that to us again. We’ve been going out of our minds with worry.” Cody whacked Jackson on the back of his head as he put him down and then headed to their old green truck.

“Ow! What was that for?” asked Jackson, following Cody. “Aw, never mind. Let’s just go home. I need a shower.” Jackson climbed into the passenger side, leaning his head back against the headrest, closing his eyes.

He was already asleep when Cody slid in behind the wheel and turned the truck around, heading for the mountain behind Jimmy's. He glanced over at Jackson, saw the tension in his sleeping body and, even though he was eager to know what happened, was reluctant to disturb him. "Well," he mumbled, "soon we'll be home and he can tell all of us together. He's safe now and that's all that matters."

Chapter 4

Cody switched off the engine and shook Jackson gently. "Hey bro, wake up. We're home." Jackson slowly opened his eyes and blearily looked around. He saw his twin, Logan and the rest of the pack members surrounding the truck. He gave Logan a smile as he stepped out of the truck and was instantly embraced in his huge arms. Jackson could feel Logan's concern for him so he patted his broad back and murmured, "Everything is okay."

"Listen, I need a shower first and then something to eat. I promise I'll tell you all everything after that. Can Dakota make me a steak? I haven't eaten in over a day."

"Sure," Logan said, reluctant to let go of Jackson. "Are you sure everything is all right?"

"Yeah, it's cool, man."

Jackson headed to his bedroom and fatigue set in. He stripped on the way to the shower, dropping the borrowed sweatpants in the hamper. Turning on the hot water, his mind wandered back to his mate causing his dick to harden. *Shit, my wolf is unhappy that I didn't claim Steel. I have to talk to Mystia tomorrow to see what can be done.* So far, he had his wolf under control but for how long, he didn't know.

Thumping his cock, he reminded himself to control his thoughts around his brothers. If they smelled his arousal, they would wonder why, especially since they didn't know he'd found his mate. He knew if he told them, Zane, the youngest, would panic, thinking Jackson was going to leave, and the rest of the pack would also get nervous about any changes. *No, I'm going to keep that part of the story buried.*

He'd just gotten everything in order, which is why he'd been on the road. Most important was his visit to the lawyer to sign the papers releasing all the money his Grandparents had put in a trust for him.

He now had enough funds to take care of everyone which meant one less worry about the well-being of the pack. He wondered if Silver Point Pack would ever give up trying to locate them, but he snorted at the thought since he and his brothers still had rights to the Fox River land. If he could only figure out what was so important about the land that made it worth killing for.

"Hey, food's ready," called Cody, through the bathroom door.

"I'll be out in a minute." Jackson stepped out of the shower and grabbed a towel to dry off. He picked out a t-shirt and some pajama pants because that bed would be calling to him as soon as he ate and talked to everyone. *I'll make this short and sweet, focus on what I did with the lawyer and try to calm the pack down. Best to divert the attention away from me. Yup, a good plan.*

Jackson's mouth watered and his stomach growled as he entered the kitchen. Hell, it might just be his wolf growling; it'd been far too long since he'd eaten. He sat down at the earth-toned, granite-topped island, smiling at his brother.

"Thanks, Dakota. I'm so hungry I could eat the whole cow. Everything looks great." Cutting into his steak, he groaned with satisfaction—it was perfect, lightly cooked and still bloody, just the way his wolf loved it.

"So, what happened to you?" Logan asked impatiently, not willing to wait until Jackson had finished. "We expected you home last night and when you weren't here by morning, the whole pack was worried. Cody and I kept bugging Jimmy hoping he'd heard from you but when there was no word by late afternoon, we decided to search for you."

Jackson finished his dinner before answering Logan. He sat back before he spoke. "The good news is I saw the lawyer and was able to sign all the paperwork to release my trust fund along with yours. I opened a new bank account under a corporate name for my money and set it up so I can access the funds as we need to. I've set up a personal account for your money, Logan." Then he turned to the rest of his brothers. "We'll have to do the same for each of you when you reach the release date of your funds but for now, we won't have to worry about meeting our needs."

Cody growled, "Well, that doesn't explain why you showed up late and half naked."

"I was just getting to that. On the way home, I took the short cut through the orange grove. That's when I saw these two guys with their car parked on the side of the road with the hood up."

"Jeez, you didn't let your savior trait come out, did you?" Logan snarled. "Hells Bells, you know you always end up on the short end of the stick."

"Cool it, Logan. Yeah, I stopped to help, but got knocked out and robbed instead. When I woke up, somebody stopped and gave me a lift to Jimmy's." Jackson paused and looked at his brothers, before continuing on, "No matter what, I'll always try to help anyone who looks like they're in trouble. Now I'm going to bed because I'm exhausted. Everything else can wait for tomorrow."

He wearily pushed his chair back, stood up and turned to Dakota. "Just a heads up," he said, "Jimmy said Mystia will be back in the morning and they'll be visiting us. Let me know if we need to do any shopping before they arrive." Then mumbling, "See you all in the morning," Jackson shuffled off and headed for his big comfortable bed—it was calling his name.

Cody looked at his brothers. "He is not telling us something. Did any of you notice something different?"

Dakota, Carson, Zane, Colton, and Logan all looked at each other, shaking their heads. Zane spoke up, "What makes you think that? Was he acting strange when you picked him up? I'm just so damn happy he's home and in one piece."

Cody lowered his voice so Jackson wouldn't hear him. "There was a faint odor of an unknown wolf on Jackson—not on his skin, but I think he got those sweatpants from whoever gave him a ride and either that person was a wolf or those pants had been in close contact with one."

Panic crossed Zane's face as he raised his voice. "Oh, my gods! Silver Point? Do you think it was Silver Point?"

"Shhhh, lower your voice," Cody admonished. "No, it wasn't Silver Point. It's a scent I didn't recognize."

"So why didn't Jackson tell us he met a wolf? Why would he hide that from us?" asked Colton.

"I don't know, maybe it's nothing and Jackson didn't want to alarm us by saying he came across a wolf from another pack," Cody said, getting up to clear the dishes. "I know he's exhausted so maybe he didn't want to go into who the wolf and his pack are. Let's see what he says tomorrow, after he's rested."

~/~/~/~/~

Jackson climbed into bed, pulling up an endless loop of images of him and his mate in the throes of mind-bending sex. His cock rose to hardness bordering on painful, with pre-cum dripping onto his abs while he slowly stroked himself. Jackson already missed Steel and he knew unless he claimed his mate soon, his wolf would take over; shifting to hunt for him.

What a fucking disaster *that* would be—jeez, his only hope was if Mystia could cast a spell that would break the mating pull. He'd have to get her alone tomorrow for a private conversation so his brothers never found out he met his fated mate.

He needed to jack off or he wouldn't be sleeping tonight. His cock demanded its mate. His mind was flooded with visions of Steel on his knees, beautiful brown eyes filled with lust, looking up at him, his mouth filled with Jackson's cock. Stroking faster, he felt the tingling begin. Then his balls got rock-hard and drew up tight to his body. He finally exploded, squirting gobs of cum all over his hand and stomach. Slowly his breathing returned to normal. Grabbing his t-shirt, he wiped his cum off before throwing the soggy shirt into the hamper, then, turning over, he fell asleep, dreaming of his mate.

~/~/~/~/~

In the morning, Jackson, half asleep, reached out for Steel, but when he found only an empty space, he sighed and woke up fully. Sheesh, his dreams were so real, he could swear his mate was in bed with him. And, of course, his morning wood was like a guided, heat-seeking missile with only one target in mind—his mate's mouth. His goal today was to talk to Mystia alone, hoping she could make the need for his mate abate. Groaning, he got out of bed, headed to the shower, planning to rub one out.

The hot water relaxed Jackson's muscles, helping get rid of the soreness from yesterday. Of course, if he shifted, his body would heal faster but he was worried his wolf would race off to find its mate.

He was confused by his wolf's behavior since he was first-born and an Alpha, destined to submit to no one. So why was his wolf so ready to submit to Steel? Jackson was a timber wolf, the biggest wolf on earth; there were very few of his kind left, mostly up in Canada and Alaska, and he knew Steel wasn't a timber wolf. So, what kind of wolf was he to cause his wolf to turn belly up? *Hmmmm. A puzzle to solve.*

Quickly taking care of his needs, he turned off the water and stepped out. Toweling himself off, he heard Cody yell he was taking Jackson's clothes from the hamper to wash. "Okay." He pulled on a worn pair of blue jeans, a white t-shirt that hugged his chest and his scruffy shit-kicking boots before heading down to breakfast.

At the bottom of the stairs, Jackson stopped; it felt good to be home. *Yeah, at home with his bros.* They built this house after the massacre and made it a home. Looking into the den he saw the comfortable wide, dark brown, distressed leather couches on which he and his brothers had spent hours watching sports and movies on their big, flat-screen TV. The room had beautiful cream-colored walls, bold Southwestern Navajo rugs scattered throughout the large, airy space and plenty of wide club chairs, accented with pillows in every color of the rainbow. The overall feeling was warm and cozy.

Jackson's heart tightened as he remembered how close he'd come to losing his brothers. Getting his emotions under control, he headed for the kitchen. Dakota handed him his coffee. "Breakfast will be ready in about 20 minutes. Logan and Cody are on the front porch, if you want to join them."

Jackson took the mug, asking, "Do you need any help?"

"Nope, I'm good. And I'll be even better if you get out of my way," Dakota grinned.

Taking the hint, Jackson headed to the front porch. Opening the door, he was greeted by a cloudless, deep blue sky and the smell of the pine forest which he loved. They were so lucky Jimmy had offered this land to him. He sat down on one of the large, dark green, rocking chairs and greeted his brothers.

Logan gave Jackson a smirk. "Have a good night's sleep?" Jackson first looked at Logan, and then, at Cody, where finding the same smirk, he got a bad feeling in his gut. "I slept well, thanks for asking." He knew there was more his brothers wanted to ask but he'd learned in the past never to assume to know what someone wants to say.

Cody spoke this time. "That's good. Anything else you remember about what happened you want to share?"

The corners of Jackson's lips tilted up. It seems they were doing a good cop, bad cop routine. "No, not really. We'll have to talk about how to handle the theft of the car but I thought we'd wait until Jimmy gets here before making any decisions."

Logan spoke up, "Who gave you a lift to Jimmy's?"

"Just a guy who came along. Why?"

"Well, you came home smelling of wolf but you never mentioned meeting one. So, we were wondering how you picked up the scent," Logan said quietly. "Was it the man who picked you up or was it, maybe, a wolf he had contact with?"

Shit! Fuck! And double crap! Jackson knew anything he said less than the truth, Logan, being his twin, would know. But maybe he could get around it by just answering their questions and not volunteering additional information. Chancy, but he hoped it would work. "The man who gave me a lift was a wolf but I didn't recognize his scent; therefore, it's unlikely he's from around here. He certainly wasn't connected to Silver Point and that was my main concern. I didn't mention it because he drove off after he dropped me at Jimmy's and I doubt we'll see him again."

Cody asked, "Did he know you were a wolf?"

"No, I saw him surreptitiously sniff but he didn't come up with a scent. I think he thought I was human." Unfortunately, all this talk of his mate caused his cock to harden and Jackson knew within a short time his brothers would start to smell his arousal. *Best make a hasty retreat.* "I'm going in to see if I can help in any way to hurry breakfast along since I'm hungry. You guys coming?"

"We'll be there in a minute," said Logan, watching Jackson get up and head inside. After the door closed, Logan turned to face Cody. "I don't think he lied to us but I just have the feeling there's more to the story. I know Jackson and considering our situation, there's a reason he didn't bring up the fact he met a wolf. Did you bag the sweatpants?"

After Cody nodded, Logan then added, "Good, I want Mystia to sniff them to see if she can tell us anything about this wolf. I hate to go behind Jackson's back but I feel there's more to the story than Jackson's telling us. And that's exactly what worries me because Jackson has never kept anything from me."

“I know how it is,” agreed Cody. “Colton, Carson, and I are the same way. Triplets can’t keep secrets from one another. I don’t know why but it’s always been that way with the three of us. Let’s go in and have breakfast before Zane eats it all with the excuse, he’s a growing boy,” Cody said. He and Logan then broke into laughter.

Chapter 5

Steel's wolf was snarling and snapping as he drove away from Jimmy's after leaving Jackson behind. He just couldn't understand his wolf. *What am I missing here? Jackson is not my mate. My mate has to be a wolf*—he knew it because he'd been told not only by his mother who was an Oracle but by no less than three other Oracles. His mate would help save his species of wolves.

The importance of this was impressed upon him throughout his life. He stepped on the gas, eager to get home to do some research. He needed answers because he had a feeling of foreboding about what was going to happen to Jackson and that was driving his wolf crazy.

Finally arriving home, he stopped at the fifteen-foot-high gates, keyed in his passcode and then drove up the long driveway to his sprawling home, nestled among the trees on the knob of a small mountain. Although there were taller mountains to roam on his 200,000 acres of land, this spot spoke to his wolf spirit. He inhaled deeply as he got out of the truck, feeling his body reacting to the sights and smells around him.

Looking around, he wondered if Jackson would like this spot as much as he did. And that did it—his cock hardened in a second and his blood started to heat up. *What the fuck?* He drove the image of Jackson's firm body from his mind and thumped his cock several times to get it to go down.

Hmmm, what to do first? Decision made, he stripped out of his clothes and stood still for a second before he called on his wolf and shifted. Birds scattered as the noise of bones cracking and stretching filled the air.

When the sound faded away, Steel stood in his wolf form, shaking out his fur and scenting the air. Deer to the east, a small black bear and her cub ambling along the trail to the south and, yes there it was, a path that was free of any animal—Steel knew it wouldn't be a good day to engage in a sparring match. His wolf was too unsettled for that.

He struck out at a full run for the trail leading north to one of the tallest mountains on his land. His large paws made no sound on the thickly carpeted forest floor. Steel had gotten so many mixed signals from his wolf today he needed this time to figure out what was happening. He knew his wolf needed it also. While he was running, Steel examined his wolf's feelings regarding Jackson because it was much easier to understand his wolf when they were one, especially now, since he hadn't understood his wolf's reaction to a man who had no scent.

Taking in the smells and sounds of his forest, his mind searched and filtered through his wolf's feelings. Steel found possessiveness, yeah, he already knew his wolf wanted to claim Jackson. The next feeling was protectiveness; he saw this when his wolf wanted to find and kill the men who attacked Jackson.

Searching to see what else his wolf felt—*oh my gods—what the fuck, love?* His wolf loved Jackson because he knew Jackson was his mate. He nearly stumbled when that fact hit him. *No! No! No! Jackson was human and couldn't be my mate—or could he?* His wolf had never been wrong before. He turned around and raced back home. He had to do the research immediately because if Jackson was indeed meant for him by the Fates, then Steel needed to claim him fast.

Approaching his house, he fought his wolf to force a shift because his wolf was hell bent on finding his mate. Entering his home and ignoring his nakedness, Steel headed straight for his library. He impatiently yanked the door open and his wolf vision saw specks of dust dancing on the air currents of the huge, two-story, open room, lined with bookcases on both floors. His large desk sat in the middle of the room under a ceiling painted with stars and moons. He crossed over to his computer and entered the search terms he was looking for.

Waiting, he drummed his fingers on the desk, as Jackson's beautiful face flooded his mind. The quickness with which his cock hardened and the swiftness of the heating of his blood left him breathless. *Shit, my reactions are happening quicker and growing in strength.* His cock was now harder than he ever experienced in his long life and he stroked it vigorously, trying to relieve some of the pain.

The computer finished its search, displaying a list of documents and books to review. Quickly glancing at the screen, Steel printed it out and started his research. As the hours dragged on, he was no closer to finding the answers than he'd been in the beginning. So far, he'd found no evidence to support his wolf's claim the human was his mate.

Still, it could be true, since he still had over three-quarters of the list to review. Sitting among a pile of books, he rubbed his eyes to remove some of their tiredness. He'd been up more than 24 hours and needed sleep before starting fresh again in the morning. Before he did, though, he sent the picture of the tattoo on Jackson's chest to his mother asking her if she'd ever seen it before. He just had a gut feeling it was important and, hopefully, she would know what it meant. That knowledge would help narrow his search among the remaining documents and books.

Steel entered his bedroom, wanting to collapse on the bed but forced himself to the bathroom where he turned on the water, climbing into the shower. As the hot water streamed over his tired and dirty body, his mind again returned to Jackson. *Crap, I never got his last name. Well, at least I have an idea of where he lives. I wonder if anyone at the gas station...* And then before he completed the thought, his cock was up and proud, waving around as if it were trying to find Jackson's ass.

Moaning, touching his hardness, he knew it needed his attention immediately. As he wrapped his hand around it, he pictured Jackson on his knees, his full cock-sucking red lips wrapped around his cock as he thrust it down Jackson's throat. The picture immediately caused an orgasm and his roar resonated as he came, painting the glass walls with long endless ropes of his cream.

Falling to his knees while the water cascaded over him, he tried to catch his breath and was so weak he couldn't stand. Something was very wrong with him—this had never happened—and it was only getting worse. If he didn't solve this soon, he was going to start having spontaneous orgasms. His breathing settled down and he slowly got to his feet, turned off the water, and grabbed a towel. His hair was still damp when he stumbled into the bedroom, fell onto his bed and was asleep before he could draw the covers up.

Across the globe, Steel's mother, Oracle—whose name revealed what she was—looked at the picture Steel sent her. She walked toward her husband's mahogany-paneled study, calling out to him as she entered. "Maximus, the time has come."

"What time, Oracle?" Maximus asked absentmindedly, as he continued typing on the keyboard of his computer which sat atop his antique cherry desk. But when the happiness in his wife's voice finally filtered into his brain, he stopped, looked up at her and waited.

Oracle sat on his lap, wrapping her arms around Maximus' neck, kissing and licking him along his jaw. After giving him a long and sensuous kiss, she said, "Steel has found his mate, but he doesn't know it. We have to go and make sure he does not screw this up."

"What makes you think he'd screw it up?" Maximus asked.

"One, because he is thinking with his mind instead of his body, and two, his mate has a protection spell on him so even though Steel's body and wolf know the man is his mate, Steel can't smell him and therefore won't pursue him," Oracle explained.

"How do you know about the protection spell?"

"The Fates told me about it and last night Steel sent me a picture of a tattoo and asked me if I had ever seen it. The tattoo is a witch's symbol for a protection spell and this one is an anti-scent spell." She went on, "I will get our clothes organized and packed and please call to make sure our plane will be ready to go."

"Are you comfortable leaving our boy alone?" Maximus teased.

"For goodness sake, Maximus, Slate is an adult. I am sure he will be just fine." Oracle laughed at her husband's foolishness. She gave him one last kiss before she stood up to leave as he picked up the phone to call their pilot.

~/~/~/~/~

Steel opened one eye, then shut it and groaned as he turned over. He could tell it was near or after noon. He'd been too tired to close the blinds last night and the sun shining through his window was high in the sky. He loved this house. He'd told the architect to bring the sky inside as much as possible so he could always feel he was part of it.

From his second story bedroom, he was able to see the sky in all its shades of glory—from dark nighttime blue, adorned with star diamonds, to stormy rainstorm gray, to the deep blue shades of a cloudless day. Maybe he should learn to fly a plane. *Yes, that would be something I haven't done yet.* A smile creased his face, as he imagined what it would feel like, to be in a small, single-engine plane, high above the earth, feeling at one with the birds in the sky.

He jumped out of bed, eager to make breakfast and silence his grumbling stomach. Jeez, he was feeling good as he picked out his old, favorite, worn jeans and a green t-shirt. He walked barefoot down the steps, reaching the bottom just as his doorbell rang. Pausing, puzzled at the sound, he inhaled, trying to determine if he knew who might be at his front door.

It had to be someone who was close to him because they knew his security gate password. Suddenly he gasped. *Hot Damn! It was his parents! What? Why? How?* flitted through his mind, as he hurried to the front door.

"Mom, Dad," Steel yelled, yanking open the door. "When did you get here? Why are you here? Oh, my gods, is everyone all right?" He couldn't believe his eyes as his parents reached out to hug and kiss him. "Come in. Let me take your bags."

"Everyone is fine, sweetie," Oracle said, as she came through the door and set her purse down on the wood console table in the foyer. "How are you?"

Steel stopped and looked at his mother. *Something was up*. He just knew it by her tone. *Hmmm, what's going on?* "Actually, Mom, I feel great today. Why?" he asked, trying not to say anything until he could figure out what was happening. He glanced at his father hoping to get a clue about why they were here, but nope, his father's schooled face showed nothing. *Great!* Steel felt like a sitting duck, knowing something was going to happen to change his world but not a clue as to what it might be. *Well, two can play this game.* "Have you eaten yet? I was just about to grab a bite."

Oracle smiled. "That would be great. Why don't you let me make your favorite breakfast?"

Steel should've been surprised when his mother mentioned breakfast instead of lunch but she'd always been able to know things even if no words had been spoken. "That would be a real treat, Mom. I haven't had the pleasure of your cooking for far too long." Steel led the way to his state-of-the-art kitchen as his mother and father followed slowly, taking time to look around his home.

"This is a lovely home, son. The pictures you sent us don't do justice to the location and beauty of the area. How many acres do you own?" Maximus asked.

"200,000, Dad. It gives my wolf plenty of room to roam without running into anyone," Steel answered, as they reached the kitchen.

He sat down at the island next to his dad, watching his mother make his favorite breakfast of scrambled eggs and steak. And just like that, the image of Jackson sitting next to him eating breakfast resulted in a hard cock. *Crap!* Hoping to keep his parents from noticing his condition—*shit, how bad would that be*—he shifted in his seat, trying to erase the picture in his mind.

Casting around for a distraction, his glance fell on his mother. *Wait a minute.* Steel frowned. *This visit is just too coincidental; it has to have something to do with the picture I sent her last night. Does she know what that tattoo means? Does it have something to do with Jackson being my mate? But that would be contrary to what she's told me about my mate being a special wolf. But if Jackson is my mate, then Mom would have been wrong and that would've been a first.* Steel's eyes narrowed as he studied his mother hoping he'd be able to discover the purpose of her trip.

Unable to discern anything from her behavior, he turned and saw his father staring at him with an expression of hope before quickly reverting to a bland face. Steel was unnerved by his father's look. What puzzled him more, his wolf was calm and curled up without any of the aggression he had shown yesterday. *Enough!* All of this was making him wary and he wanted, no, he needed to know what was going on.

Just when he was about to demand some answers, his mother served breakfast. His stomach grumbled loudly at the smell of the steak and eggs, startling his parents. Mumbling an apology, he told them he hadn't eaten in a while. Even though he was more than curious about why his parents were visiting, he certainly didn't want to get into the story of why he hadn't eaten since meeting Jackson. Savoring his steak, he noticed his parents exchanging glances before they began to eat. He ignored it for the time being, focusing instead on enjoying the delicious breakfast his mother made for him.

Chapter 6

As the pack sat around the table after finishing the breakfast Dakota had cooked, Logan asked Jackson, "Are you going to file a police report for your stolen car?"

"I want to talk to Jimmy first. I'm not worried about Silver Point finding us through the police report but I'd rather use his address and phone number."

Logan nodded. "Good idea."

Jackson turned to Dakota. "Have you checked our food supply? Do we need anything in the short term? I want the shopping done once a month to limit our exposure. The less we're out and about, the less chances of running into anyone from Silver Point."

"We're set for a week or so, but I'll get a list together to give us a month's supply. It'll be trial and error for the first two or three months since I'm still trying to figure out how much I need to order for our little brother," Dakota said, smirking.

"Fuck you, Kota," yelled Zane, giving him the finger. "You know I'm a growing boy!" Dakota just laughed and threw a finger back.

Heading off to their chores, the brothers continued joking and teasing each other. Jackson smiled—it was a long time since that happened. He walked to his study, anxious to get the accounting set up so his brothers could access the corporate bank account. Sitting down at his desk, he booted up the laptop, but ended up staring out the large windows at the forest surrounding their pack house, a view he loved.

He was so lucky, he thought, to have gotten the first installment from his grandparents' trust before the massacre. It allowed him to build this home for his brothers and take care of their needs. Now that he'd received the rest of it, the financial pressure was off. He didn't think his Uncle, the Alpha of Silver Point Pack, knew about the substantial trusts for all his brothers, not to mention the trusts for their dead siblings.

But he'd deal with that another day, after he decided what to do about the actions of Silver Point. He'd thought about reporting it to the Universal Paranormal High Council but that would expose his pack to Silver Point and, right now, it was his word against theirs—not very comforting.

Jackson decided on the spur of the moment to do a Google search on Steel, hoping it would turn up something. He wasn't sure why he was so curious; Jackson wasn't going to claim him but he couldn't shake the urge to know something about his mate.

He leaned back in his chair, thinking maybe he should ask Jimmy if there was another wolf pack around here—although he hadn't run into any other wolf shifters while they lived here. Of course, they didn't go out much, trying to keep as low a profile as possible.

Glancing down at the screen, he was surprised nothing came up about Steel Valentin—not a thing. No address, no phone number, no mention of him anywhere on the web. *How could that be? Unless that wasn't his real name...* yet Jackson had smelled no deception from Steel. Great, he thought, another mystery to solve. No, *not* solve, as he remembered he'd decided not to claim his mate. He closed the search window, opened his accounting program and started working on that.

Logan was outside splitting logs when Jimmy and Mystia drove up. Setting down his axe, he ambled over to greet them before telling Jackson they'd arrived. Reaching out, Logan hugged Mystia, whispering in her ear, "I need to see you alone. It's about Jackson." She nodded her head slightly, indicating she understood.

Mystia turned to Jimmy, asking him to round up the rest of the boys so she could speak to all of them together. "Take your time," she told him, "I'm going to the kitchen to check on what food there is. Logan, you can come with me." Mystia took Logan by the hand and ushered him to the back of the house. As she pulled open the mudroom door, she turned to him and said, "Show me the sweatpants."

Logan's jaw dropped. *How did she know about the sweatpants?* Mystia pushed Logan's jaw closed with her finger and said, "Now be quick about it, we don't have much time and I need to see Jackson alone before I speak to all of you."

Logan nodded, quickly retrieving the sweatpants Cody had bagged in plastic. Tearing the bag open, he handed them to Mystia whose hands roamed over them while chanting in a language he didn't understand. After several minutes, she raised the sweatpants to her nose, closed her eyes, and inhaled deeply. Then she murmured, "Yes, yes, finally." Slowly lowering the sweatpants, her eyes opened, and a broad smile broke out on her face reaching from ear to ear.

"What's so special about these pants?" asked Logan. "Jackson told me they belonged to a wolf but didn't say who or what kind of wolf it was. He's hiding something but we can't figure it out," he added. "That's why I wanted to see if you could tell if this wolf is a threat to us—Jackson doesn't think he is. Do you know if it belongs to another wolf pack around here that could hurt us?" Logan asked, voicing his fears.

Mystia laid a hand on Logan's arm, immediately calming him and said, "No, this wolf means no harm to any of you but he has a role to play in saving all of you. That, however, is between Jackson and this wolf—who I expect we will be seeing. Now hush, *mon petit loulou*, everything will be fine and made clear soon, I promise you." Mystia, removed her hand from Logan's arm and left to talk to Jackson.

Jackson was shutting down his computer and didn't hear the door open. He was startled to hear Mystia's voice inside his study. Looking up, he saw a willowy, graceful woman dressed in a flowing black gown trailing on the ground. Long, white, silky hair caressed a beautiful face lined with a few wrinkles. He marveled at the aura surrounding her and as he zeroed in on her silver eyes, Jackson saw her love for him reflected back.

"Ah, just who I wanted to talk to," Jackson said, getting up to hug and kiss Mystia. "How was your trip? Learned any new spells or incantations you are planning to torment Jimmy with?"

Mystia smiled teasingly. "Be careful, I might use them on you," she said, holding Jackson close and giving him a sweet kiss on his cheek. "But I can save it for another day. Now, what did you want to talk to me about?"

Jackson guided Mystia over to a loveseat and then sank into a chair next to it. Now that she was here, he was tongue-tied as to how to start the conversation. He needed to break the mating pull because as the day wore on, he found himself in pain, not to mention the constant struggle against his wolf's desire to shift. Pausing while trying to figure out the best way to explain his predicament, Mystia solved the problem by asking, "Is it about your mate?"

Crikey, well, that was simple. "Yes, it is," said Jackson, relieved to have it out in the open. "The man who picked me up yesterday is my mate—my fated mate—but I can't claim him so I was hoping you'd have a spell that could remove or weaken the mating pull."

Mystia nodded but said nothing, so Jackson continued, "Ever since I scented him, my wolf has been going crazy and I'm fighting him constantly because he wants me to shift and go track him down. Only I can't do that," he confided to her.

"Why not?" she asked quietly.

Jackson looked at her with disbelief in his eyes. "You know why. I have my brothers to protect against Silver Point and I can't leave them."

"Why do you think you have to leave them?" Mystia asked.

"Because he's an Alpha, stronger than I am, my brothers would never accept a different Alpha for our pack," said Jackson, "especially after everything we've been through." He paused for a moment before he said, "But that's not the only reason. As his mate, I'd have to protect him from the danger he'd face from bonding with our pack. And while my wolf would be happy, it would kill my other half to know if anything happened to me, I'd have deserted my brothers in their time of need."

Jackson was getting agitated. "It's an impossible choice—I see no other way than to reject my mate," he said, looking at the floor to hide the tears forming in the corners of his eyes.

Mystia could see Jackson's face fill with longing and sadness over what he believed was the only right choice. "But what if you could have both your mate and your brothers protected so you wouldn't have to choose? Would you want your mate then? Or are you using the possible danger as an excuse to reject a mate you don't want?"

Jackson's head shot up. "What? No! I want my mate with my whole soul! He was chosen for me and I know he'll love me as I am; even though my father only saw weakness in me."

Mystia smiled gently at him. "*Mon petit loulou*, your father had his own problems, so please don't continue to carry them as your burden. Those problems died with him. He did love you even if he didn't understand who you were. Now, we must move on as your mate will be here shortly, so let's talk."

"You mean Steel will be here? I never told him where I lived. I told you I can't claim him! Oh, my gods, what am I going to tell my brothers?" Jackson asked, realizing his cock was once again hard.

Sensing Jackson's discomfort, Mystia said, "The longer you go without claiming your mate, the more pain you will experience, and no, I have no way of removing the mating pull. As you will learn, this mating was decided by the Fates for a very special purpose and they have made it very difficult for you or Steel to resist."

Mystia paused, allowing Jackson to think about what she'd told him before continuing, "I shall be removing your protection spell," she said, holding up her hand to forestall Jackson's objection, "because Steel must smell your scent as part of the claiming ceremony."

"Now wait just a minute," growled Jackson. "I'm not having sex with my mate in front of my brothers, or for that matter, in front of anyone else. No way, it's not going to happen! Wait! Are you telling me I have no choice whether or not I want to claim Steel? Because if I don't claim him, the Fates will be blackmailing me with pain until I cave?"

"Please, *mon petit loulou*, let me finish," Mystia said softly. "The mating ceremony is a private one between you and Steel. No one will be witnessing it. But your mate has to recognize your scent during the claiming and for that reason I must remove the protection spell. I promise you, though, that if you want me to cast it upon you again after you are mated, I will."

Mystia took Jackson's hand, assuring him, "You always have a choice in whether you claim someone, so remember that. Steel's parents will be with him and his mother, who is Oracle, will want to speak privately with you and your mate before you claim each other."

"Why does she want to talk to me?" Jackson asked.

"Let her tell you. Now let's join your brothers so I can explain what is about to happen and reassure them they are not in any danger."

Chapter 7

Pushing back from the kitchen island after he finished breakfast with his parents, Steel began to clear the dishes. "Why don't you guys go into the great room and I'll join you in a minute." He brought the dishes over to the stainless-steel sink and loaded them into the dishwasher. Then he put the rest of the food away and wiped off the counters and the island.

He knew he was delaying but couldn't figure out why. He had a feeling his whole life was about to change yet he didn't feel any apprehension—which was strange since, as a rule, he hated change. Knowing he wasn't going to get any answers standing where he was, he headed to the great room to hear what his parents had to say.

"Come, Steel, we have to talk," Oracle said, sitting down next to his father on the stark, black, modern sofa. Steel sat down across from his parents in his favorite well-worn black leather chair. He scrutinized them, wondering why they came to see him if it was about the tattoo. Why couldn't she email him with the information? It was now obvious his mother *did* know what it meant and how it would affect him. At last, he would have some answers. He sat silently, waiting for his mother to speak, but didn't have to wait long.

Oracle spoke in measured tones, watching Steel closely. "I received your email with the picture of the tattoo last night but before I tell you what it means, can you tell me how you obtained a picture of it?"

He resisted the urge to squirm which he had done as a child when his mother had caught him and his brother Slate causing trouble; no matter how they'd tried to hide their shenanigans, she always knew what they'd done. Thinking about what he would say, he hoped it would provide a clue to the mystery of his freaking hard-ons and the heating of his blood. *After all, that was what I was trying to find the answer to yesterday, right?*

Steel took a deep breath before starting his story, "Yesterday, uhmmm, was it yesterday, uhmmm, yep, yesterday, I was returning home from yet another meeting with a potential mate. He was a timber wolf but that didn't work out, so I headed home. When I was almost there I came across a naked man, hitchhiking on the shortcut I take."

He continued, "My body and wolf immediately reacted to him even while I was in the truck with the windows up. I thought chance had led me to my mate but when I rolled down my window, I discovered he was human. And that wasn't who you told me would be my mate.

"Anyway," Steel resumed, after pausing, "I gave him a ride to a gas station and when he got out, I snapped the picture of the tattoo he had on his chest right over his heart. I felt it was important to me but even with my research last night, I couldn't find anything. So, I sent it to you before I went to bed, hoping you might know what it meant."

"Why was the man naked?" asked Oracle.

"He told me he stopped to help someone, got knocked out, and they stole his clothes and car," replied Steel. "All he had was some old ripped pants he was holding in front of him."

"What was your body's reaction when you first saw him?" Oracle inquired.

"Mother! I don't discuss these things with you. Je-e-ez!!!" sputtered Steel as his face grew pink. While wolves were pretty open about sex, he never was, especially with his mother. *Did she really think I would be describing how hard my cock became just thinking about Jackson? Oh crap, not a good line of thought.* He burrowed down in his chair, trying to hide his erection.

His father chuckled as his mother said, "Oh, get over it. I don't need exact descriptions but surely you can tell me in general terms. Wait, I have a better way. When you saw this man… does this man have a name?"

"Jackson."

"Jackson who?"

Steel looked sheepishly at his mother, mumbling, "I forgot to get his last name."

His father roared with laughter and finally said, "There you go, Oracle, that should tell you everything you need to know about his reaction to the young man."

"Well, never mind," his mother pressed on, leaning forward, "we can find that out later. Now just tell me—in general terms—how you felt when you first saw Jackson."

Steel sighed. *Could I be any more embarrassed than talking to my Mom about the sexual reaction I had when I saw Jackson?* He tried to gather his thoughts so he could generalize what he was thinking that first moment. Steel's face was growing redder by the minute because just thinking about it caused his cock to twitch in his jeans and he knew his parents would soon smell his arousal if he didn't do something fast. "My temperature rose, my blood heated up, and I got an erection. Is that enough information for you?"

"Yes, and how did your wolf react?" Oracle quizzed on; she could barely hold back her elation.

"My wolf wanted to claim him immediately but I stopped him since Jackson was human. I figured he wasn't my mate. So, I couldn't allow my wolf to claim him since I'm in my *toirchigh* period. I did listen to you, Mom, even if you thought I didn't, when you warned me claiming someone other than my mate would have disastrous consequences. I understand my responsibilities and even though I also wanted what my wolf did, I controlled both of us."

Oracle smiled gently, glancing at her husband before speaking. "The reason you couldn't smell Jackson is because the tattoo is a protection spell cast by a witch. The spell masked his scent, and the fact that he's a shifter—the wolf who is going to be your mate. The reason your wolf felt a mating pull is he smelled Jackson's arousal which carries a faint scent of him and that is what led your wolf to demand his mate."

Steel was dumbfounded. He had his mate within his grasp and let him go. This would explain why his wolf was going crazy yesterday. But wait, maybe his mother was wrong—his wolf was curled up sleeping right now which was a blessed relief from constantly fighting him yesterday. But it just didn't follow; if Jackson *was* his mate, his wolf shouldn't be so laid back now.

"I think you're wrong about Jackson being my mate, Mother," he said, with a puzzled look. "Ever since I woke up today, my wolf is calm and relaxed. Even my reactions have gotten milder, which should be the opposite if Jackson were my mate."

His mother smiled. "Based on your knowledge, I understand you think I may be wrong, but your wolf is relaxed because he knew I was coming to sort everything out and get you and your mate together. Your physical reactions are driven by your wolf so if he is calm, your body reactions will be calm—well, to a degree, since I did catch the scent of your arousal several times today," Oracle said, with just a hint of a grin. His father, though, snorted with laughter as Steel glared at both of them.

"Stop doing that. Can't a guy have some privacy? Honestly, Dad, can't you get Mom under control—and yourself as well?" Steel pleaded, while the blood once again rushed to his cheeks as his father continued to laugh.

"Honey," his father said, "I think…"

But Oracle interrupted. "Oh hush, both of you. This is important, Steel. You're in your *toirchigh* period and only have a limited window of time to claim Jackson. Now, where does he live?"

Oh shit, Steel now realized he'd never found out exactly where Jackson lived because he was too busy thinking of fucking his ass. Well, now that he knew Jackson was his mate, he could find him and wouldn't have to face his father's laughter over his screw-up.

"I'm going to shower before I drive over to his place. How long are you two going to be staying?" he asked, hoping they would be leaving soon so he could get on with claiming his mate without his parents overseeing it. *Jeez, how weird would that be?*

His mother ignored the question and answered instead, "Great, we'll wait down here for you so we can go meet this young man who is to be your mate."

That did it. Steel was happy his parents came and that Oracle solved the mystery about Jackson but he was dammed if his parents were going to be hanging around while he fucked and claimed his mate. *No, No, No! No parents involved, thank you very much.* And just as

Steel was opening his mouth to protest, his mother stopped him, by saying, "Sweetie, you do realize when you met Jackson, he could smell you, knew you were a wolf, and also his mate? So, even if *you* couldn't tell he was your mate, why didn't *he* say something to you? You are fated mates. He felt the mating pull at full force—what's more, if he doesn't claim you soon, he will start to feel pain and his wolf will force a shift just so he can hunt for you."

Steel felt fear run though his body at the thought of his mate in pain; his wolf awoke and started pacing back and forth in his head demanding that they find their mate. The same as yesterday when he sensed his mate was in danger.

His protectiveness was consuming him, leaving him no choice but to find Jackson and claim him. When he thought about the rest of what his mother said, and that his mate had rejected him, a pain settled in his heart. He rubbed his chest, trying to ease the discomfort. Then suddenly, he jumped up and headed for the door, knowing he had to find his mate today.

It puzzled him that Jackson, knowing who Steel was, rejected him but he would find him and convince him this was a blessed mating decreed by the Fates and was not to be denied. Just as he reached the door, he felt his father's hand on his shoulder, holding him in place. Steel turned and snarled at him, warning him to let go.

Maximus' Alpha voice commanded. "Stop, Steel, listen to your mother—she has more you must know before you claim your mate."

Steel fought the demand of his Alpha but eventually backed down. He looked at his father, shaking his head, "You don't understand. I must go to him. He's in trouble. I sensed it yesterday and my wolf knows it. I don't know what danger he's in but I know he is and that's good enough for me. Please don't stop me."

Oracle came up, stroking Steel's arm, soothing him so he could listen to what else she had to say. "Steel, you know you and your brother are the chosen ones to carry on our species. We are the last of the Dire Wolves to roam the earth and after many appeals to the Fates they agreed we should not perish. And in keeping that promise, they picked another threatened species to become your mate—the Timber Wolf. Our species are alike, and because time has not been kind to either, we are both on the brink of extinction."

Oracle continued solemnly. "Your mate is special and the Fates looked a long time to find a wolf who had the ability to bear pups. So, it is important that you claim him when you are in your *toirchigh* period because during the act of claiming, you will impregnate your mate with the seed of a Dire Wolf."

"I know all this, Mother," said an exasperated Steel, "but you haven't explained what else I have to know before I claim him."

"Your mate does not know he can bear pups. He is the Alpha of his pack and before you claim him, he has to know what will happen—all of it. And you will need me there to help answer your mate's questions. Trust me, once he understands everything, your father and I will leave before you claim him." Oracle then broke into a wide smile as she saw the tension fade from her son's face.

Chapter 8

After changing his clothes so he looked more respectable, Steel felt ready to claim his mate. Settling his parents in the back seat of his black Range Rover, he started the car and headed for the gas station where he'd dropped Jackson off. He hoped someone there could tell him where Jackson lived—if he could convince them to tell him. No, he *would* convince them; his mate needed him now. *Wow! My mate! Mine! The man I will love forever, the man I will have a family with, and the man I will protect forever because he is the other half of my heart.*

Steel stepped on the gas, ignoring the speed limit—his wolf was snarling and pacing, telling him their mate was in pain. This time he concurred with his wolf because Jackson's pain was tangible; he figured it must be because even though he hadn't scented him yet, he now knew for certain Jackson was his mate.

Shit! He was so distracted and upset yesterday he hadn't trusted his instincts. Jackson had been within his grasp. *Why wasn't I more forceful in demanding to take Jackson directly to his home yesterday? Why didn't I ask for Jackson's phone number, or get his last name? Shit! Shit! Shit!* Deciding it didn't help to dwell on that line of thinking, he focused on his driving so he and his parents would arrive safely at Jimmy's.

Jackson sat in his favorite club chair, listening to the concerns of his brothers as they threw questions at Mystia. He was still trying to deal with the hurt and disappointment he'd seen on Logan's face when she announced he'd met his fated mate.

He knew how it would affect Logan; they were twins, well, fraternal twins, not that it mattered because they told each other everything. It was Logan who comforted Jackson after the tense episodes with his father. And Jackson protected his brother from the bullies who attacked him because he was small. Jackson snorted—not that his brother was small anymore, no, that's for sure—Logan was six inches taller and much wider than Jackson now.

But size never mattered between them because they'd always been so close and Jackson worried his decision might ruin that. Yup, he certainly needed to sit down with Logan and hash out any negative feelings. Jackson's mind tuned back to the conversation, and realized he'd been asked a question. *Huh? What did I miss?* "Say again?" he mumbled, coming out of his reverie.

Zane's eyes narrowed, looking at Jackson. "I asked what was going to happen to our pack if you are claimed. How do we fit into your new life?" Then, gesturing to all of his brothers, "If you leave our home here, do we have to leave too?"

"I know everyone's concerned about what this'll mean but the claiming is not a done deal. Mystia told me I have a choice, and before I claim Steel, we'll be discussing those issues first. I didn't tell any of you about meeting my mate because I knew everyone would be upset, seeing this is the first time in the last few years we've had a moment to catch our breath," Jackson said. "I want to take this one step at a time."

During the silence that followed, he looked at his brothers and was overcome with great affection. When he'd regained control of his emotions he continued, "According to Mystia, Steel will be arriving shortly.

After I have a chance to talk with him about my responsibilities and hear what he has to say, then, and only then, will I make a decision as to the claiming."

As he finished speaking, a cacophony of excited voices rose up, all clamoring to be heard at once. Finally, Logan's rose above the others. "What do you mean you have a choice? Mystia said you'd be in pain if you didn't claim your mate soon. It looks like you don't really have a choice," he said, as the rest of the brothers nodded their heads in agreement.

Jackson wondered how the pain would stop if he didn't claim his mate, but figured there was an option Mystia knew about but wasn't going to share with him right now. He absentmindedly rubbed his chest, trying to relieve the pain that only seemed to grow worse all afternoon.

"Look," he said, becoming slightly angry. "All I know, is Mystia said I have a choice and I believe her. She also told me Steel's mother would explain more to me. So, let's wait to see what she has to say before anyone goes off the deep end. I swear, you'll all be kept safe, no matter what."

Logan looked hard at Jackson, sensing his change of mood. If he was reading it right, Jackson was in pain which would mean Mystia was accurate about that much concerning the mating. "Okay guys," he said, "I think it's time for a break. I don't think Jackson can tell us anymore until he has a chance to talk to Steel.

"In the meantime, as I understand it, we're going to have three more guests for dinner, so Dakota, I'll leave that up to you. Cody and Colton, please prepare two guest rooms for the Valentins in case they stay overnight. I want to talk to Jackson about some accounting matters concerning the pack so we'll be in his study."

Logan offered a hand to Jackson, steering him out of the den and into the study. Once inside, he shut the door as Jackson sat down at his desk. Logan leaned against the door, staring at Jackson but said nothing and waited. Jackson returned Logan's stare and admired his twin's good looks. Unlike the triplets, Jackson and Logan did not resemble each other except for dark brown hair. Logan was taller and more heavily muscled; his face sported a scruff and his deep-set, gold-green eyes gave him a sexy, brooding look. Just like all the brothers, Logan was an Alpha, but never used the power to challenge Jackson's decisions or actions.

His brother possessed fierce loyalty to him and would fight to the death if it meant saving Jackson. He knew how much he relied on Logan and that's what made him regret he'd kept this information from his twin. Jackson lowered his eyes, wondering how to start. He knew why Logan pulled him in here and it had nothing to do with accounting.

Jackson let out a deep sigh, looking up at his brother before saying, "Look, I know you're hurt Logan, I get that, but I didn't tell you about my mate because I made a decision, I thought was best for the pack. I'm the Alpha and that's what I have to do, even if it's at the expense of my own happiness." He paused for a few seconds to let it sink in. Logan remained quiet as Jackson continued.

"You know how much I worry about keeping all my brothers safe from Silver Point. They're a daily threat to us and if something happened to one of you on my watch—especially if I had put myself first—it would kill me. You know all this, Logan, so why are you upset by the decision I made to keep it secret? I know you well enough to know you'd have fought me on this, so it just seemed better to keep it under wraps and avoid all that shit."

Logan walked over and lowered himself into the padded wooden chair in front of Jackson's desk, trying to sort out why he felt so hurt. He knew his brother was right and would gladly give up his own life to save the pack. Logan had always teased Jackson about his "Good Samaritan" tendencies, but behind all the joking, Logan was damned proud of Jackson's kind and caring personality.

It was the one thing their father hated about Jackson and tried so hard to eradicate. "An Alpha can't behave that way as leader of a pack" still echoed in Logan's head, etched there by his father's relentless shouting at Jackson. He'd lost count of the times he'd consoled his brother during childhood as Jackson cried his heart out over his inability to please their father.

When Jackson entered his teen years, he spent most of his time hiding from their father to avoid the daily dressing-downs. But their mother saw what was happening and defied her

husband, sending Jackson to spend a summer with her parents. Logan wasn't allowed to go with his twin and it was a wretched time for him, so much so, he always feared it would happen again.

He took steps to avoid it by going to the same college, sharing a dorm room and as many classes as he could with his twin. When Mystia told them about Jackson's mate, Logan's heart sank thinking they'd be parted. Yeah, he was hurt but more because he feared losing his brother again, rather than Jackson's decision not to tell him about Steel.

Logan cleared his throat and said, "I do understand why you decided not to tell me about meeting your mate; that you were putting the good of the pack first, but maybe I would have agreed with your decision not to claim your mate."

Jackson, shocked, blinked several times at the statement and then asked, "Why?"

Logan's cheeks turned pink as he sheepishly looked at Jackson, muttering, "I don't want you to go. That was my first thought when I heard you had a mate. I'm really sorry. I know it's selfish and something you don't deserve because you've always put me and the rest of the pack first."

Jackson took a deep breath before saying, "Logan, no matter what happens we'll always be brothers and I'll always have your back. I am the Alpha of this pack and I'm not giving that up regardless of who my mate is. I made that decision today when Mystia and I talked. How Steel will fit into the pack—or even if he'll fit at all—is yet to be determined. I'm not going anywhere."

Jackson's face grew serious. "My pack is in danger and it's my duty to protect and defend it. Maybe when Steel finds out there's a kill order out for all of us, he won't want to be claimed. That's one of the reasons I wasn't going to mate with him—because it would put him in danger." Jackson paused and then added, "Jeez, what a fucking mess!"

"But you have to claim him because until you do, Mystia said it would get more and more painful for you until it was done. Don't tell me you're not in pain! I can see it. Your shoulders are tense, your face grimaces every couple of minutes, and you keep rubbing your chest. She said you'd be in pain until you mate so what happens if you don't mate?" Logan asked.

"According to Mystia, I have a choice, so I presume if either of us decides not to claim the other, my pain will disappear. Look, that doesn't matter right now but what does matter is your help. Logan, I need your support going forward and our brothers will look at how you react to whatever happens. I promise you I will not leave you and the pack," Jackson said emphatically.

"Thanks bro, I appreciate it, and I'll be there for you," Logan said, rising from the chair.

Jackson came around the desk and hugged his brother. "I know you will be. Now, let's go meet my mate."

~/~/~/~/~

Steel pulled into Jimmy's, parked, and turning to his parents, said, "I'm going to see if someone knows where Jackson lives."

His parents nodded and Steel got out. Striding over to a scrawny young man in a cowboy hat pumping gas, he asked where he could find the owner. The man gave him a searching look before saying, "He ain't here right now."

"When will he be back?" asked Steel.

"He said he might be gone until tomorrow. I'm in charge. What can I help you with?" the man asked.

Steel could feel his own frustration showing so he paused, and took a deep breath in an effort to get it under control. He was wondering how to ask the man if he knew Jackson but didn't want it to appear as if he was stalking him. "Do you know a man called Jackson? I dropped him off here the other day but he forgot to give me back some sweatpants I loaned him. I thought I'd stop by at his house and pick them up."

Suddenly, the man broke into a smile. "Oh, so you're the one they told me about. Hi, I'm Bobby. Jimmy said if a man fitting your description came in asking for Jackson, I was to give you an envelope his wife left here for you." Then he wiped his hands off on his already dirty jeans and headed into the building.

Steel followed, hoping he was close to finding out where Jackson lived. But then, a dark thought crossed his mind. What if Jackson had left a "Dear John" letter for him—crap, that was a real possibility since Jackson knew Steel was his mate and had already rejected him once. Hell, Steel thought, there's no way he was letting Jackson go. He didn't care what he had to do, he would claim his mate because the alternative wasn't something he wanted to consider.

As he opened the letter, Steel took a deep breath, trying to ignore his frantically beating heart. When he got to the end, he exhaled, closed his eyes, and thanked the Fates who'd arranged this, for there, in the letter, were directions to Jackson's home. Letting out a loud whoop, he ran back to the Range Rover, jumped in, gunned it, and tore out of Jimmy's ignoring his mother's pleas to slow down.

Chapter 9

Jackson corralled his brothers and led the way to the front porch where they joined Mystia and Jimmy. *Why do Steel's mother want to talk to me about my mating with her son? Huh, if that even happens.* He wasn't going to agree to any mating unless Steel knew the whole story about the Fox River Pack and Silver Point Pack—and the danger Steel faced as his mate.

He picked up the sound of a vehicle driving towards them and his wolf started pacing, eager to see his mate; the thought caused a shiver to run down his spine. He was nervous about how Steel would react once he could scent him. He turned to Mystia, reminding her she hadn't removed his protection spell.

"I will, but let's wait until you talk with Steel's mother," Mystia replied. It wasn't the response Jackson expected but before he could ask her why, Steel drove up and parked in front of the porch. Jackson felt his wolf panting, eager to claim his mate.

Steel looked at the group gathered on the porch waiting to greet him and his parents. Jackson was standing in front of six men—three looked alike, the others were of varying heights and ages. He could see the family resemblance between Jackson and the six men and wondered who they were.

He slowly got out of the car, inhaled deeply, but again could not scent his mate—the protection spell must still be in place—but the scent of another wolf was in the air—that of an old wolf standing next to a witch.

He glanced at his mother but she showed no concern. However, his wolf fought back a growl, upset at a strange wolf near Jackson. *Who's that wolf standing next to my mate?* He opened the door, helping his mother out, then, taking her hand, led her over to his mate as his father followed.

Jackson stood on the front porch with the other Blackwood Pack members watching them get out of the Range Rover. He figured the man and woman were Steel's parents and as he eyed them, he could see where Steel's good looks came from.

The woman was stunningly beautiful and though she appeared to be old, her body was tight, her face unlined, and the only indication of her age was the long silver hair falling in layers around her face, highlighting sculptured cheekbones and soft lips. Her ice-green eyes were like lasers that could latch onto prey with pinpoint accuracy. She walked with uncommon grace in her loose and floaty light-green dress.

The man with her was beyond handsome; his salt and pepper hair was long on the top and short around the sides. His face sported a small, very short beard matching his hair color, while beautiful deep blue eyes, a straight patrician nose and high cheekbones set off his wide lips. He was taller than the woman but shorter than Steel, and Jackson could see his muscles rippling beneath a pale grey sweater he wore under his open blue sports coat.

Jackson shivered as Steel and the couple approached him and his brothers. He didn't know who Steel's mother was but a powerful force radiated from her, encompassing all within her sight.

"Mother, Father, this is Jackson," Steel said, looking Jackson over from head to toe. *Yup, I'm one lucky fucker to get a mate this gorgeous. Our babies will be beautiful.* He envisioned seeing both of them surrounded by a family of pups scampering around their feet. Then back to reality—finishing the introductions, "Jackson, this is Oracle and Maximus Valentin, my parents."

Jackson stepped forward, "Welcome, Mr. and Mrs. Valentin, to the Blackwood Pack. These are my brothers—Logan, Cody, Colton, Carson, Dakota, Zane and our surrogate parents, Jimmy and Mystia Blackwood." Reaching out to shake Maximus Valentin's hand, he felt the strength the man possessed.

"Call me Maximus."

Steel's mother nodded to each of Jackson's brothers, then stepped forward to grasp Mystia's hand, pulling her into a hug and whispering in her ear, "This has been a long time in the making, hasn't it? I am so grateful you and your husband watched over and protected Jackson."

Stepping back, Mystia dipped her head in deference to the Oracle, saying, "Yes, but it was meant to be. It is a great honor to meet you."

Once again, as it did on the first day he met Steel, the scent of oranges, cloves, and bourbon reached Jackson's nose, causing his blood to respond, rushing to the part of him that wanted his mate. Fuck, his mate was hot and so beautiful he couldn't think of anything else except to claim him now.

Somewhere in the haze of his desire, he heard Mystia calling him. He shook his head, trying to clear it, slowly realizing she was trying to get him to take Steel's mother to his study for 'the talk'. Hell, that was the last thing he wanted to do when his mate was so close and willing to be claimed. Then he felt Logan's hand on his back pushing him toward the house, and he abruptly came back to the present, allowing his twin to guide him.

Steel entered his mate's home and could immediately feel warmth and love reflected in the way the house was decorated. Following Jackson into a big room filled with comfortable chairs and couches—all dotted with colorful pillows—Steel immediately felt at home.

He claimed a chair while his father sat down on a couch and Jackson's brothers scattered around the room. Steel wasn't sure what was going to happen next but he was eager to have the meet-and-greet move ahead quickly so he could get to the fuck-and-bite part of the evening.

Jackson turned to Steel's mother, pointing to a doorway leading to a hall. "We can talk in my study where it's private, if that's okay." He was curious about what he would hear but he was more eager to speak with Steel alone so he could warn him of the trouble facing him if Jackson claimed him. Yet, manners dictated he delay that urge and speak to Mrs. Valentin first as Mystia asked him to do.

Mrs. Valentin walked through the doorway and down the hall until she reached Jackson's study. He was nonplussed as to how she knew which door his study lay behind, but said nothing. He followed her into the room, motioning toward the loveseat while he sat down in a chair kitty-corner from her.

Jackson began. "Mrs. Valentin, I'm at a disadvantage because while Mystia told me you needed to speak with me, I have no idea about what, although I think your son and husband know since they didn't seem surprised when I invited you to my study."

"Please, call me Oracle," she said warmly.

"Are you an Oracle?" he asked.

"Yes, I am, and I am also Steel's mother so first let me speak as a mother. Have you been told anything about Steel by Mystia?" Oracle asked.

"No, she only told me you needed to speak to me first," Jackson replied.

"Steel is one of the last four Dire wolves on earth; the other three are his brother and his parents."

Jackson gasped, a look of incredulity crossing his face.

"So, you know what a Dire Wolf is?"

"Yes, but they don't exist anymore—they've been extinct for hundreds of years," Jackson exclaimed.

"Well, that's a myth circulated for centuries in order to save the last of the Dire Wolves. After my sons were born, we left our home and moved to Scandinavia to protect them. It allowed us to be isolated should any wolf packs attempt to seize the Dire Treasure. My sons grew to be fine young men, were educated at top universities, traveled the world, and eventually managed the family businesses.

"After many years, Steel felt the need to take a mate which happens when Dire Wolves begin their *toirchigh* period. So, he moved here to search for one. I'm delighted he finally found you. You are a very special wolf."

Jackson was puzzled. "What does this have to do with my mating with Steel—if I do? And why isn't Steel telling me this instead of you? Am I missing something?" Jackson asked, and suddenly a thought occurred to him. "Certainly, we are not a threat, are we? Because I assure you, I wouldn't harm Steel or his family. You must know that."

"Of course, I do," Oracle said.

"Wait a minute," said Jackson. "What do you mean I'm a special wolf? I'm just a timber wolf and we may become extinct but that doesn't make me special—just endangered."

"I think we have come to that part of our discussion that should help clear things up," Steel's mother said, "and I am now going to speak to you as the 'Oracle'—do you understand?"

Jackson nodded, waiting expectantly for her next words. He knew whatever she said was going to have earthshattering consequences for him.

"Long ago," the Oracle began, "the Fates decided the Dire Wolves had squandered their lives by constant fighting—trying to seize and take control of the Dire Wolf treasure. This was long before your time. Every five years, the Fates awarded the guardianship of the treasure to the Alpha of a Dire Wolf Pack who demonstrated his ability to take care of shifter wolves in need, regardless of their species. It was a highly coveted honor and the Fates felt it would motivate all Dire Wolf Alphas to be good and kind to all so they might be chosen next."

Oracle paused, her eyes misting up before she continued. "However, that did not happen because one Dire Wolf Alpha decided to fight and defeat smaller Dire Wolf packs to improve his chances of getting the honor. And so, it went. War soon wiped out pack after pack until only one Dire Wolf Alpha and his pack remained to fight the Dire Wolf Alpha guarding the treasure.

"Finally, a great battle raged throughout the night, and when the Alpha of the treasure realized his pack was losing, as a last desperate measure he entrusted the treasure and his son to a witch, hoping she could hide them until better times might come."

The room became silent and Jackson tried making sense of it all. Then he asked, "Your husband is the son that was taken and protected?"

"Yes, he is. And Mystia was the witch who took him to her home, protecting him the same way she has protected you," smiled Oracle. "As he grew up, Maximus studied and learned about the purpose of the treasure and honored his deceased father by setting up a number of businesses whose sole purpose was to educate, employ, and help shifter wolves of all kinds. The Fates rewarded him with a mate, me, who could help him with the Fates' decisions. Maximus has the gentle and kind soul of his father and has greatly benefited, as do the wolves he helps, by my power. Our sons now run the daily affairs of these companies while my husband oversees things."

"But I don't see how this affects me," Jackson said, still puzzled. "If I do mate with Steel, I would never interfere with his work."

"I am getting to your role in this tale," Oracle continued. "The Dire Wolf pack that attacked and killed the Alpha of the treasure, soon realized both the treasure and the Alpha's son were missing and a great hunt began for them. Greed and jealousy consumed their minds as they fought each other trying to find the treasure. Eventually, all died and we became the last Dire Wolves on earth."

Oracle paused, lifting an eyebrow to see if Jackson had a question and, with none forthcoming, she continued. "At first, I was relieved my sons would be safe and I was content to spend the rest of my days providing love, support, and help with the family businesses. I kept in touch with Mystia and she made a comment once that made me realized my sons were paying the price for the greed and jealousy of others.

"So, I prayed to the Fates and begged them not to wipe out the Dire Wolf. It took many years, but they finally agreed to provide mates for my sons so they could experience the joys of parenthood and preserve the guardianship of the treasure. They also decided to help another species in danger of extinction and that is why you were selected as Steel's mate."

Jackson was flabbergasted, his mind raced in a thousand directions all at once. But his primary thought was *Why me? I can't bear him pups. The Fates got this all wrong. Steel's mate has to be a female* and as those thoughts sunk in, a profound sense of sadness washed over him. *How could the Fates be so cruel as to dangle the perfect mate before me only to have him be snatched back because I don't have the proper equipment?* Oracle could see the sorrow on Jackson's face, then said softly, "Jackson, the Fates did not get it wrong; all will become clear soon, I promise you. First, tell me about your parents, please."

That request startled Jackson but he responded, "My father was the Alpha of the Fox River Pack, mated to my mother, and together they had 13 children. What else do you want to know?"

"What type of wolf was your mother?"

"She was an Omega"

"I assume you were the oldest because you are the Alpha of the Blackwood Pack, is that correct?"

"Yes. Logan and I are fraternal twins but I'm the first born."

"Did you enjoy a good relationship with your parents?"

Jackson paused, thinking about whether he wanted to reveal his father's treatment of him, afraid he would appear weak but then decided the Oracle knew it anyway so he opted for complete honesty. "I had a stormy relationship with my father who always felt that I was too soft and incapable of making hard decisions. But my relationship with my mother was the best; it carried me through all the trying times with my father."

Oracle nodded and then said, "Steel met you after you had been robbed—what happened?"

Jackson's cheeks turned light pink as he thought back to his stupidity in stopping to help the men.

"Don't be embarrassed," said Oracle. "Helping others is never a dumb thing to do."

Jackson looked down, then raised his head and smile. "That's what my mother said all the time but my father saw it as a defect in me. I can't explain it but I always needed to help anyone I could and I guess it wasn't a good move that day. After knocking me out, they stole my money, clothes, and car. Steel picked me up and took me to Jimmy's. That's how we met."

"Jackson, that desire to help people—the caring gene—came from your mother. But that's not the only thing you got from her. You are a hybrid, a very rare hybrid, a cross between an Alpha and an Omega with traits and abilities from both. From your father,

your Alpha leadership qualities are readily apparent in how you took control after your parents and other members of the Fox River pack died.

"You made hard decisions at a chaotic time and got your brothers to safety. Look at what you have accomplished—your brothers are safe in a new home and protected from their enemies. Your father could not have done any better and I know he is proud of you."

"Thank you for that," said Jackson, "it means a lot to me. But if, as you say, I have traits of both my Alpha father and my Omega mother, how does that make me the right mate for Steel?"

Chapter 10

Oracle hesitated and then, looking Jackson in the eye, said, "You, as an Alpha/Omega hybrid, have the ability to bear children. That is why the Fates have chosen you to be Steel's mate."

Jackson was flummoxed! *What, I can have children? No, that can't be! She is wrong, oh so very wrong!* Then a hopeful thought entered his mind—a picture of his own pups, frolicking around his feet with Steel's dark straight hair and melted chocolate brown eyes. And then it hit all at once—the need, the desire and the absolute rightness of his mating with Steel. *My own family!* Something he never imagined he'd ever have—at least not since he realized he preferred men. Why didn't his mother tell him? She knew he always wanted kids.

"Why didn't my mother or father tell me this?" he asked. "They must have known."

"No, Jackson, neither your mother nor father knew you would be able to bear children. This would only surface after you found your mate."

Jackson's mind was spinning. This was unbelievable! He wanted it to be true—much to his own surprise—but it just couldn't be; he'd never heard of this happening before. Dammit! He was an Alpha and they didn't bow to any wolves.

But then he remembered his wolf bowing in submission to Steel's wolf and his wolf had never done that before. So, did he trust his wolf in this matter? Humph, well, his wolf didn't seem inclined to object to the news they could get pregnant. No, his wolf was busily cleaning himself as if he were getting ready for a date. *Great, well, then it is up to me to figure this out.*

Jackson sat there, trying to get his thoughts in order. First, did he believe this to be true? His heart and wolf were telling him yes—his mind might need more convincing. Second, why him—and if he was special, could the rest of his brothers also have children? *Whoa, that won't go over well with some of my brothers.*

Third, does Steel know this and, if so, what does he think? Does he even want kids? Jackson knew he couldn't bring a child into this world unless both parents could love it, no matter what the child turned out to be. The damage his father tried to inflict on him was *not* going to happen to any child of his. Fourth…

"Jackson, I am sure you have questions I can answer so please ask them. I can hear the wheels turning a mile a minute over there," Oracle said with a kind, gentle smile.

Oracle startled him out of his deep thoughts but he realized if she had some answers to his questions, it would help him sort this out faster. "You said I was a hybrid, are my brothers also hybrids? All of them or just some of them and, if some, which ones?"

"Only your story is being written right now. Each of your brothers will have to wait to see what the Fates have in store for them. I can't give you any other answer than that."

"Does Steel know about my ability to have children?"

"Yes, he does."

"Does he want them?"

"I think it best if you ask him that question."

"Mystia said I had a choice as to whether I wanted to mate with Steel. I have scented him and, as I understand it, if I don't claim him, then I will be in intense pain. So, if I choose not to mate, how do I get rid of the pain?"

Oracle bowed her head; tears filled her eyes and, as one slowly made its way down her cheek, she paused for a minute before answering, "Steel will die so you will be free of the pain."

"What??? NO FUCKING WAY!!!" Jackson roared, quickly standing as he looked around to see who would threaten his mate. His wolf stopped grooming and was now standing with his hackles up, growling and snarling. Jackson's heart was pounding so fast, he thought it would explode!

An intense pain of sorrow swept through his body and he wailed "Nonononooo" as tears ran down his face. He could never sentence Steel to death by refusing to mate with him—he would sooner die than cause his mate harm. As he watched his tears fall to the floor, he realized his choice was made. And just like that, his mind cleared, his wolf stood down and Jackson knew he would claim Steel—the sooner, the better.

He sat down; calmed now by what he knew he was going to do but he'd have to disclose the danger his pack was in and, by association, Steel.

"I do want to claim Steel as my mate," he said strongly, "and I'm really very happy with the gift the Fates have given me. I love children and have always wanted them but never felt that dream would come true. To find out it can happen is truly amazing. My brothers will be surprised but happy also."

Then, in a more serious tone, he said, "I must tell you, though, about the danger my pack faces. That's the reason I never said a word to Steel when I first met him. I could not and would not put him in danger if I could prevent it."

Oracle gazed at Jackson, her eyes still moist with tears. "I'm aware of the danger your pack is in; however, I have not told Steel. But he has sensed it and has told me so. Talk to him about it, let him make his own decision as he has let you make yours," she said, reaching out for Jackson's hand. "But I can assure you on behalf of my husband and myself—and I believe Steel as well—that the Blackwood Pack will enjoy our full protection from now on. Do you have any more questions or would you like me to send Steel in?"

Jackson stood, still holding Oracle's hand, and drew her up. As she rose, Oracle pulled him into her arms, hugged him, and whispered in his ear, "Welcome to the family."

Momentarily taken aback, he returned the hug, with a fervent, "Thank you."

Jackson stepped back. "Would you give me a few minutes first before you send Steel in?"

"Of course," she smiled.

Oracle left the room and Jackson moved over to his desk, sitting down heavily. *Oh, my gods!* His mind was in complete disarray. *A mate who is a Dire Wolf...unfuckingbeleivable! The extinct is alive again! What a mind blower! That alone is mind-boggling, but no—it's even crazier because a Dire Wolf is my fated mate, picked by the Fates to be exactly who I need.* He had to do some research about Dire Wolves so he'd be able to help and protect his mate.

Those thoughts led Jackson to his other discovery this afternoon—children! *I can have children!!! How can I be so accepting of this bomb dropped in my lap?* Even as he questioned Oracle, he knew she was telling him the truth about his ability to have pups.

He was the oldest and taking care of his siblings had been his responsibility as he grew up—it was the chore he loved the most. Many times, he was more their father than brother, especially when pack problems took their father away from home for many days and nights. And he loved that feeling!

When he learned his younger siblings had been killed, he grieved deeply for days because it felt like he'd lost his own children. And he supposed they were, in a way. And now the Fates found a way for him to be a father—this time a real father—not the surrogate he'd previously been with his siblings. A million more questions swirled in his mind interrupted by a knock at his study door.

"Come in," Jackson called, standing and waiting to greet the man who would be his mate. Steel opened the door, entered, and shut it behind him. Jackson ogled his mate, eyes darkening with lust as they roamed over Steel's body, landing on the erection that was filling his jeans. He could hear his wolf's howl echoing his need for the first touch, the feel of his mate's hand against his naked skin. He stood still, as his mate examined him, hoping he would please Steel. But Steel's response was unexpected. "Why?" he asked.

Oh shit, Jackson knew immediately his mate was upset by his initial rejection of their mating. He didn't need any other clues except the hurt he saw in Steel's eyes. Jackson cleared his throat, as he thought about how to explain why he'd done it without causing any more damage. "I'm very sorry I hurt you but I felt it was the only way to protect you from the danger our pack faces."

Jackson held up his hand to stop a response, before continuing, "Several years back the rest of my family was massacred by the Silver Point Pack whose Alpha is my uncle. I had no idea there was bad blood between the packs because my father, the Alpha of the Fox River Pack, kept a lot of those issues from me. Anyway, they massacred the Fox River Pack one night while everyone was sleeping. They thought they'd killed all of them but then discovered the seven oldest sons of the Alpha were missing and sent a team of enforcers to kill the rest—namely me and my brothers."

Steel looked stunned as Jackson continued. "Knowing we have a death sentence hanging over our heads, I wouldn't subject my mate to the same fate. I figured you'd never know we were mates because of my protection spell. So, I was fulfilling my need to protect you by not alerting you; it was the only way I could think of in the heat of the moment. I would never hurt you intentionally, please believe me."

As Steel listened to Jackson's story, different emotions consumed his body—sadness at his mate's loss, anger at the cowardly attack and finally, stronger than any other emotion—and one his wolf was in total agreement with—his fierce desire to protect Jackson forever. Steel and his wolf made a promise to each other: they would seek out and destroy any threat to Jackson for the rest of time and would never stop until their mate was safe.

He now understood why his wolf loved Jackson—here was a mate who would sacrifice his own happiness to make sure Steel was safe. He felt like getting down on his knees and thanking the Fates for sending him the other half of his heart. Steel made a vow, right then and there, never to disappoint the Fates; he would care for his mate and show them he treasured the gift they gave him.

Jackson saw the different emotions crossing Steel's face before seeing his mate's wolf make an appearance—claws extended, incisor teeth dropped, and hair growing on Steel's hands and arms. As he fought the shift, Steel vibrated with intensity and, just when Jackson thought Steel would lose the battle, his wolf retreated. Steel's eyes narrowed, studying Jackson with blatant desire

"I understand—and thanks for acting as a mate would. It must have nearly killed you to make that choice. But that's moot now. My mother tells me you intend to claim me—as I will you—so I will stand proudly by your side to fight and protect you and those you love. That is my right as a mate."

Steel stepped toward Jackson, compelled now to touch him, and saw Jackson take a deep breath before closing his eyes. His reaction to Steel's scent was obvious by the big bulge in his crotch and when his mate opened his eyes, Steel saw Jackson's wolf shining through them. He had to touch his mate—now! Steel grasped Jackson by his arms, pulling him tight to his body, their hard cocks rubbing against each other. Steel swallowed a moan as his mate's body merged with his, lowering his face to Jackson, now needing to taste him more than anything else. Fisting one hand into Jackson's soft hair, Steel lowered his lips until they were just a hair's breadth away from Jackson's, whispering, "I need to taste you."

Jackson felt his body tremble as Steel whispered against his lips and instantly, all anxiety about their mating fell away as he rose up on his toes and pressed his lips against Steel's. Warm, soft, yet firm lips moved against his as he pressed hard in his need to claim Steel. Jackson parted his lips, his tongue peeking out to take a taste of Steel and then, connecting with Steel's mouth, savored the flavor of his mate, a moan rising from his chest.

Steel drove his tongue in, memorizing every part of Jackson's mouth, growling as the flavor of his mate spread throughout him until it was in his soul—indelibly etched there forever.

Suddenly, Jackson sucked Steel's tongue in and out of his mouth, demonstrating what he wanted Steel to do to his ass. Steel could feel his cock leaking pre-cum and he knew if he continued, he'd be claiming his mate on the floor. And that wouldn't do at all. He also didn't want it to happen with everyone here, so he reluctantly pulled himself away from Jackson's mouth and, looking into the glazed, lust filled eyes of his mate, murmured, "Let's take this to my home where we'll be alone."

Jackson felt the sudden loss of heat as Steel pulled away. He pulled Steel back toward him so their bodies could touch again and where he could continue to lose himself in Steel's mouth. When that didn't happen, Jackson growled with frustration and tried to pull harder. Steel resisted and instead pulled him toward the door.

As he regained awareness of where they were and what he wanted to do in his study, Jackson's face turned pink. *Damn, I was going to fuck my mate right next door to where my brothers and Steel's parents are. Well, that was an erection killer.* Jackson glanced at Steel, embarrassed at his wanton behavior and said quietly, "My bedroom is upstairs if you'd like to claim me there."

Steel looked at his mate's face and chuckled softly, "Let's take this some place more private. I have a home not too far away and we can be alone. If you have the space, my parents will stay here and make sure no harm comes to your brothers."

Jackson nodded and Steel took his hand, leading him out of the room and down the hall to the den. As they entered the room, there was silence and all eyes were on them. "Jackson and I will be going to my home for a while."

Jackson looked at his brothers' faces and saw worry.

Logan spoke up, "Jackson, is that all right with you?"

Jackson answered, "Yes, I'm fine and everything is okay. While I'm gone, would you show Oracle and Maximus to the guestroom? And Dakota please see that they have something to eat. When I get back, we'll have a pack meeting." After his brothers nodded their assent, Jackson headed for the front door.

Mystia got up and walked over to him. "I need to remove the spell in order for Steel to claim you. Do you have a problem with me doing that?"

Softly Jackson said, "No, go ahead."

She raised her hands, held them over Jackson's chest and chanted. Jackson saw her lips move but even with his wolf's hearing he couldn't make out her words. Mystia stepped back and smiled at Jackson. "It is done."

Jackson knew the protection spell had been lifted when he heard Steel inhale deeply and felt his lips descend behind his ear, nuzzling and licking while mumbling how much he loved Jackson's scent.

Embarrassed by the PDA, Jackson pulled Steel firmly through the front door and shut it behind them. "We'll have to use your car since I haven't replaced mine yet," Jackson said.

And with the reminder of the harm that had befallen his mate in the orange grove, Steel's wolf snarled, eager to track down the assholes who had hurt him.

Chapter 11

Driving down the road, Steel turned on the radio and "Little Bit of You" filled the air. He glanced at Jackson who was staring out his window. Saying nothing, Steel softly sang along with the song as he focused on getting to his house as fast as possible.

Jackson stared sightlessly at the scenery, his mind in turmoil as the scent of Steel swirled around him. He tried to control his response but his cock refused to cooperate—it was wet and hard, filling him with lust, causing him to breathe erratically as if he just completed a marathon. His wolf was excited; he'd rolled over, huffing in anticipation at the idea of Steel claiming him.

Trying to gain some composure, Jackson asked the question foremost in his mind. "Do you want children?" Shit. He sounded belligerent. "I'm sorry, I didn't mean to sound so aggressive. It's still so new. I'm having a hard time wrapping my mind around the claiming, my life, and just everything."

Steel looked briefly at Jackson, and seeing the tension coursing through his mate's body, tried to figure out exactly what he was asking. After going over several possibilities, he decided to go with his gut response. "Well, if you're asking me if I like children, yes I do. Being gay, I never felt it could be a reality for me. When I discovered the Fates would give me a male mate who would be able to bear my children—well, I don't think I came down from the high I was on for months," Steel replied, with a broad smile and a chuckle.

"The fact you've accepted having children and want to claim me is unfuckingbelievable! So, in answer to your question, yes, I want to have children very much and I want to have them with you. But more than children, Jackson, I want *you*—the other half of my heart, my reason for living, and who shares my soul. If there were a choice of having you or children, I'd choose you, now and forever. My blood grows hot and boils with need every time I'm near you."

Jackson stared at Steel, stunned at the ferocity of his answer. That's what he needed to hear; the tension flowed out of his body. Steel reassured him he wasn't mating with Jackson just to produce Dire Wolves. That would have been hard to handle and though he knew the Fates didn't make mistakes about fated mates, this paring was unique because Jackson was an Alpha/Omega hybrid□something he'd never thought possible.

Shit, that brought up another thought which disappeared as soon as Jackson felt Steel's hand on his thigh. He placed his hand over it, linking his fingers through Steel's, shifting in his seat to face him… his lust intensifying. Looking intently at Steel's face, he saw emotions reflecting his own.

And if that wasn't fucking hot! His mind pictured him touching and kissing Steel's naked body as they discovered each other. Sucking in his breath, he realized he needed to get a grip on himself or else he'd be demanding Steel take him right now instead of waiting for a bed.

When he reached his fifteen-foot-high gates, Steel punched in his security code causing the gates to open slowly. Driving for another ten minutes, Steel finally stopped in front of his home, turned off the engine and faced Jackson. “Are you ready to go in? Or do you have any other questions before we do this?”

Jackson tore his gaze away from Steel, and turned his head to look at the timber and glass modern house in front of them. *Holy cow!* It filled his view, yet that was just part of it; more was nestled into the woods. It must be close to 10,000 square feet, and for the first time he became uneasy when he realized Steel was worth more than his and his brothers’ entire inheritance combined. He suddenly felt he was lacking in the eyes of his mate.

In all of Jackson’s daydreams about a mate, thoughts of his being the “poor relation” never entered his head. Mainly because it was always a long shot to find your fated mate. After all, the Fates didn’t hand out a ‘where to find your fated mate’ card to every wolf, so it was truly amazing when it happened. Fuck, he didn’t want this problem as he was already facing another—Steel was the bigger, stronger wolf which would be a problem for his brothers. They definitely needed to have a conversation about these two matters and he was sure there’d be more.

As Jackson studied the surroundings, Steel could feel his mate’s anxiety and guessed what it was about. Instead of addressing it, he said, “Let’s go in and then decide what comes next.”

Jackson took a deep breath, trying to ignore the roiling in his stomach caused by his thoughts. He reached within himself to find the strength Oracle spoke of, remembering how he survived his family's massacre and took care of his brothers. His wolf was pushing him to get on with claiming his mate.

He looked at Steel and replied, "Okay. Let's go in."

Steel released the breath he was holding and removed his hand from Jackson's thigh. "Stay there," he said. Then he jumped out of the Range Rover and circled it to open Jackson's door. When his mate got out, Steel put his hand on Jackson's back just above his luscious bubble butt. The heat of his mate's body penetrated his hand, rose up through his arm and coursed through him. Steel moaned, feeling the same need to fuck and claim as Jackson did.

As they made their way to the front door, Steel's cock was dripping copious amounts of pre-cum; his body heating up, his blood near boiling. He hoped Jackson didn't need to talk too long because he wasn't sure he'd be able to keep himself from pulling him to the floor and his mate deserved better than that.

After Steel unlocked the front door, he stepped aside to let Jackson enter. Keeping his eyes on the sexy sway of Jackson's ass, he followed his mate inside. *Hot Damn!* His fingers itched to touch it, rub it, and grab it with both hands. Men with bubble butts—high, round, and firm—always attracted him but his mate had the finest of all.

Jackson looked into the great room, taking in the huge fireplace, floor to ceiling windows, white walls, and pale wooden floors. Large, black, modern leather sofas and chairs were scattered throughout the room and he came to the conclusion it needed more color and a touch of coziness.

It was gorgeous, though it told him nothing of the man behind him. It reminded him of a hotel lobby. *Logan could do so much with this room, to give it an inviting aura. Wait, am I thinking I'll be living here? What about my brothers?* He needed to be near them to protect them. Jackson sighed, adding that problem to the discussion list.

Steel watched Jackson survey the great room. *Shit, he doesn't like it. His place is nicer… hell, I like his better. Crap.* He hoped Jackson moved in with him. *Or not? Yeah, that would be something to discuss but right now I really need to claim my mate.* Finding him, then losing him, and finally reconnecting had all been too much. Steel knew his wolf already loved Jackson and he was sure he wasn't far behind. Enough of these thoughts—his wolf was telling him it was time to claim his mate.

Jackson's wolf assumed a submissive position encouraging Steel's wolf to claim him and it seemed to be working as Jackson heard his mate's quick intake of air. Turning to Steel and reaching out for his hand, Jackson's eyes focused on the very large protrusion in his mate's jeans.

Jackson gulped. *Holy Shit!* He could feel his butt cheeks clench, picturing that rod in his ass. He'd been fucked many times; in fact, he regarded himself as a bottom. He loved to have someone take charge in the bedroom; it gave him respite from his heavy responsibilities as the oldest. But he didn't think he'd ever had a cock that large in him before and yet, he wanted *that* particular cock in him right now! He dragged his eyes away from

Steel's groin, looking up to see lust and need swirling through his mate's eyes.

"Where's the bedroom?" Jackson rasped.

Steel was instantly onboard with his mate's plan, grabbing his hand and pulling him along. When they reached the staircase, Steel could wait no longer. He lifted Jackson into his arms, taking the steps two at a time. He could feel his body preparing for the claiming of his mate. Steel knew he had to control himself so he wouldn't come too fast—he wanted to give Jackson the attention he deserved. Taking deep breaths, he forced his body to slow down; otherwise it would be over before it started.

Holy Fuck! Jackson was overcome by his romantic mate and he wrapped his arms around his neck. Climbing the stairs, Jackson heard Steel's quick breaths and wondered if he was too heavy for him to carry. Even though he wasn't as tall as Steel, he wasn't a lightweight, either. Just as he was going to suggest Steel put him down, his mate shoved open a door, beyond which was the biggest kick-ass bed Jackson had ever seen. Steel pushed the door shut with his butt, striding over to the bed and setting Jackson down.

Holy cow! Jackson staggered, reaching out to steady himself but was beaten to it when Steel put his arms around his waist, holding him close to his enormous chest. Jackson inhaled deeply of his mate, wallowing in the scent and the security he hadn't felt in a long time. At that moment, he knew it had been futile to think of not claiming his mate...Steel was the other half of his soul... and already deeply embedded in his heart.

Making sure Jackson was steady on his feet, Steel stepped back to ogle his mate, starting at his face and slowly lowering his eyes until he reached Jackson's bulge. His mate was ready. Steel stepped forward, placing his hand over that large bump, and firmly palmed it, inducing a series of low moans from Jackson. *Fucking-be-damned!* If that wasn't the most arousing sound Steel had ever heard.

Lifting his other hand to his mate's head, he drew Jackson's lips to his. Once they were touching, his tongue slowly ghosted over them, wanting to memorize their feel so he'd know them even in the dark. Jackson's moans turned to whimpers as Steel's tongue gently pressed between his lips and, as they parted, Steel could feel the heat contained within.

Pushing in further with his tongue, he found Jackson's searching for his. As the two tongues started the slow, teasing dance of twisting together, Steel embraced Jackson tightly so their cocks could rub together. Grinding against Jackson's jeans only served to feed Steel's need to see his mate naked.

As they stood there bound at mouth and hip, Steel felt his body changing, getting ready for the *toirchigh* of Jackson. He didn't want this first time to be brief; he wanted to drive his mate out of his mind with passion and lust before coming. He slowly stepped back to remove Jackson's clothes but this elicited a series of protesting whimpers from Jackson whose hands reached to pull Steel close again.

"*Mo chroí*, soon, but first I'm going to undress you," crooned Steel, grasping Jackson's t-shirt and pulling it up over his head. Steel paused, wanting to study what he uncovered so far. *Damn!!* He loved his mate's nipples, pierced with small bars! Steel's hot gaze swept over Jackson's hairless chest and down to the treasure trail leading to what he coveted. He slowly caressed his mate's muscles while leaning in to lick and suck the metal adorned nipples. Lowering his fingers, Steel slowly unbuckled his mate's belt, drawing it apart so he could unsnap the jeans. During his exploration, Jackson gave a steady stream of moans and whimpers while pleading, "Please Steel," over and over. Steel pulled down Jackson's jeans an inch at a time while kissing and licking every naked part he could find on his mate's body.

Jackson grabbed Steel's biceps, trying to pull him closer, but without success. Steel was in charge. Jackson never had this much attention shown to him before and he loved it. He felt so cherished and desired; one need now drove him—to get Steel's cock in him.

He lowered his arms to Steel's waist where he found what he was looking for. Fumbling, Jackson tried to undo and pull-down Steel's jeans in an effort to reach his objective. But Steel grabbed his hands and held them, saying, "No, you first." Jackson nearly came in his pants at the hotness of it all.

His mate's hard and leaking cock sprung free as Steel finally pulled the jeans past it, his mouth watering for a taste of Jackson. Kneeling, Steel gazed at the cock as it twitched in the cool air surrounding it, and then zeroed in on the juicy, leaking tip begging for his mouth. He froze for a second at a deep growl from Jackson, a growl urging him to move.

Refusing to be rushed, Steel continued to pull Jackson's jeans down an inch at a time, all the while memorizing every part of his mate's body he was exposing. When the jeans reached Jackson's boots, Steel tapped his mate's right leg signaling his intention. Jackson leaned down, placing a hand on Steel's shoulder to steady himself before lifting his right leg, then his left as his boots were slipped off along with his jeans.

Steel gazed up the length of his mate's naked body—seeing muscles rippled with tension as Jackson tried to control himself—until his gaze met his lover's eyes, swirling with passion. He knew Jackson was ready for the next part of the claiming. "Spread your legs!" Steel commanded.

Chapter 12

Jackson faced him, his legs spread, eyes blown wide with lust. Steel needed to touch Jackson's cock but held back. Instead, he caressed Jackson's left leg while his tongue followed, licking and softly biting up to his groin but stopping short of the promised land. Then he did the same on the other leg and Steel could feel Jackson's body shake with the overwhelming sensations he was arousing.

Forcing Jackson's legs further apart, he reached up and took one of his mate's balls into his mouth, softly sucking and licking it. As the taste of his mate penetrated his tongue Steel moaned deeply then, wanting more, he repeated it with the other ball.

Looking up to check the progress of his mate's passion Steel saw Jackson descending deeper into the throes of desire. As he removed his mouth from Jackson's ball sack and licked his way up his mate's shaft, Jackson's ragged breathing increased. Steel's tongue was licking and gently biting repeatedly beneath the dome of Jackson's cockhead, seeking out its most sensitive parts. He knew his lover was close to erupting; he could taste Jackson's drips of cum. *Holy Fuck!* It was a perfect mixture of salty-sweetness and made his own cock so hard he thought his zipper would bust.

Steel could hold off no longer swallowing Jackson's cock to the root and burying his nose where his mate's most intense scent could be found. He felt Jackson gripping his head, trying to get him to move. Slowly, he slid back, licking and nipping the length of Jackson's rod with his teeth until the tip reached his lips. Pausing for a second, he then sucked hard, letting Jackson's cock slide deep into his throat.

Sucking and swallowing his mate's rod repeatedly, Steel felt Jackson's balls draw tight to his body signaling his mate was on the verge of shooting and, while he really wanted to swallow Jackson's cum, there were other things he wanted to do first. Drawing back, Jackson's cock slipped from his mouth coated with spit. *Perfect!*

Steel stood, stepping back from Jackson whose eyes were half closed from the lustful sensations coursing through his body. "Stroke yourself, now!" commanded Steel. Jackson's eyes opened wide as he looked at Steel, and seeing his heat reflected in Steel's face, he reached down, wrapping his fingers around his heavy cock. Slowly pumping it, Jackson's mind cleared momentarily and as his eyes drilled Steel's, he declared, "You, sir, are overdressed."

Did he just call me 'sir'? That word filled Steel's mind with exciting images, and *yup, it was official,* he'd met the man of his dreams. "Well, I'll have to remedy that," Steel grated out, slowly pulling off his shirt and letting Jackson see his body for the first time. *Oh yeah, there it was, the flaring of Jackson's nostrils, the deepening color of his eyes, and the sudden unsteadiness of Jackson's hand on his cock. I love it!*

"Like what you see?"

"I don't know if I can answer that yet," murmured Jackson.

"Really? What do you need? Can I help you in any way?" rasped Steel, palming the bulge in his pants.

That fucker is playing me! Jackson swallowed hard, at his limit now, dying to see Steel completely naked.

"I need you naked now!" Jackson snarled, his patience gone.

Steel gave himself a few more rubs before lifting his hands to his jeans. Unsnapping them, he slowly lowered them until the moist, dripping tip of his cock was exposed. He paused, giving Jackson time to wallow in the sight before he dropped them further. Jackson's loud moan reverberated through Steel, causing his balls to tighten. *Hot Fucking Damn!*

Steel pushed his jeans all the way, kicking them off along with his boots. His engorged cock pointed straight at Jackson, pulsing, needing to be buried in him now. But he still wanted his mate to reach his peak and he could tell he wasn't there yet.

Steel reached down, wrapping his fingers around his cock, tugging at it slowly. Jackson's eyes caressed his body with so much heat he thought he might self-combust. Steel slowly walked to Jackson, never letting up on stroking his cock, until they were touching cock tip to cock tip. Jackson gulped as he felt a fiery heat leap between them. Brushing Jackson's hand away from his cock, Steel declared, "Mine!" encasing the two cocks together in his large hand.

Stroking them, he pulled Jackson's head to him for another taste of his mouth. Jackson opened his lips, sucking in Steel's tongue, and dueling with it as Steel sought to reach every nook and cranny of his mate's mouth. Jackson's body was shaking with passion now and finally, letting go of their cocks, Steel backed Jackson to the edge of the mattress, gently sitting him down. "Lie down in the middle, *mo chroí,*" growled Steel, his wolf now very close to the surface.

Jackson rolled to the middle, his hand once more gripping his cock, the need to stroke it too great to ignore. Steel grabbed some lube from his nightstand and followed Jackson onto the bed. He straddled him, lining up his cock with Jackson's, then bending to kiss his nipples. Jackson seized the opportunity to grasp both cocks, rubbing them together to get the friction he desperately needed.

Steel's tongue moved to Jackson's ear, licking behind it before moving down to his mate's jaw, loving the feel of Jackson's scruff scraping his tongue. He knocked Jackson's hand away from their cocks, growling, "MINE!" as he continued to lick Jackson's chest. On his downward descent toward his mate's cock, Steel stopped at Jackson's pierced nipples, sucking and licking until both were puffed up. Then he continued licking, sucking, and nipping down his mate's rock-hard abs until he heard Jackson demand, "Now, Steel!"

Picking up the lube, he liberally coated his cock and fingers. Then, tossing the bottle aside, he lowered his mouth to Jackson's cock, his hand reaching for that puckered hole that would soon be filled by him. Pushing one finger in, Steel felt Jackson tense up. He stopped, looking up, murmuring, "Relax, *mo chroí*." And when he felt Jackson ease up, Steel lowered his mouth, continuing to lave Jackson's cock while, at the same time, pushing his finger further into him.

Jackson moaned when Steel's finger entered him fully, loving the feeling of having his mate inside him even though it wasn't what he really wanted. Steel continued to stretch Jackson open, finally able to insert three fingers, scissoring them back and forth while feeling for the magic button.

"FUCK!" Jackson screamed, arching off the bed. Despite having his mate's cock in his mouth, Steel smiled at the confirmation that he had found Jackson's prostate. Letting Jackson's cock slip from his mouth, Steel rose up on his knees, grabbed Jackson's legs and bent them up. Jackson held them against his chest as he begged, "Steel now, please, fuck, I need you now. Fuck! Please..."

Steel looked down at Jackson whose head was tossing from side to side, moaning and whimpering at his need not being met. *Well, that was about to change.* He grabbed his cock, lined it up with that puckered rose and shoved it in half way with his powerful hips, pausing for Jackson to adjust.

Looking up at the gorgeous man above him Jackson thanked the Fates for giving him this gift but right now he needed Steel to give him... "More, dammit"...he could wait no longer.

Steel heeded the demand, feeding the rest of his cock into Jackson and when his balls finally reached Jackson's ass, he stopped, waiting for a word from his mate.

Jackson could feel the cock twitching inside him, setting off tingles of pleasure throughout his groin. He was in heaven—no cock ever felt so good.

Steel felt his cock encased in the tight, soft heat of his mate's ass and it took every ounce of strength to hold still and wait for Jackson who finally yelled, "MOVE, DAMMIT!" And Steel, eager to make his mate happy, started a slow tortuous dance for both of them as he leisurely pumped his cock in and out of Jackson.

Letting his legs fall onto Steel's shoulders, Jackson grabbed his own cock, stroking it in time to the thrusts of the cock in his ass. Steel shifted his position, looking to reach that special spot inside and, as he found it, a scream was torn from Jackson, his hips jerking in response to the pleasure coursing through his body. But

Jackson needed more, and snarled, "Faster! Harder! I need more!! Now!!!"

Steel ratcheted up his thrusts, his hips becoming a blur of motion pounding into Jackson. He could feel his body heating up and his blood boiling as his fangs dropped in readiness for the claiming bite. Jackson saw Steel's wolf appear in his eyes and when he saw Steel's fangs, Jackson's dropped also. He knew—somehow—they would be biting each other simultaneously and he bared his neck.

Steel leaned down to Jackson's neck, all the while keeping up the incessant pounding of his ass, and turned his head to give Jackson a clear path for his bite. Steel bit down hard through Jackson's skin and muscles, sucking in and tasting his mate's blood while feeling Jackson's bite at the same time, causing their cocks to erupt in unison.

Oh, my gods! Jackson instantly felt a fiery heat course through his body as his blood boiled in his veins. He retracted his fangs, trying to cope with the sudden pain of it all. While in his state of painful suspension, he could feel Steel's wolf inside him, merging with his own. Finally, Steel's wolf left his body and Jackson's pain retreated.

Exhausted, he wasn't aware of anything at first but then, slowly, he felt Steel caress his body while murmuring words of love and comfort. Steel was still buried deep in him and Jackson could feel the ache he would have, at least for tonight, but it would be a reminder he now belonged to Steel—and he loved it.

Jackson raised his arms to circle Steel's neck, pulling him in to reach his lips before moving to his jaw with tiny, light kisses and wallowing in the afterglow of sex that could only be described as otherworldly.

Steel slowly withdrew and small whimpers left Jackson's lips at the loss of him. Then rolling Jackson to his side, Steel spooned against that beautiful bubble butt, drawing his mate close to him. Resting his head on Steel's bicep, Jackson could hear the quick beating of his own heart as his breathing slowly grew quiet.

Steel nuzzled Jackson's hair, and then asked, "Are you okay? No pain anywhere?"

"Mmmm… I'm fine," Jackson murmured, closing eyes as sleep finally claimed him.

Steel lay there, holding his mate while listening to the faint snores coming from him. He looked for his wolf, finding him curled up, asleep and at peace for the first time in a long time. He still couldn't believe he found the mate the Fates gifted him and that he was now holding him in his arms after claiming him. And he knew that his *toirchigh* period would now subside since the man lying in his arms was pregnant with his pup.

He wondered if Jackson would be as happy as he when he learned Steel's seed had taken. He hoped so, because he'd waited a long time for this to happen and he was so over the moon about it, he wanted to go for a run to the highest mountain and howl so the whole forest would know there was a new Dire Wolf pup on the way.

He smiled as he imagined his parents' happiness at the news and that thought led to another—Jackson had no parents left to be happy for him. *Fuck Silver Point Pack!* He needed to turn his attention to *that* soon because he knew they were a threat to his mate and pup.

Jackson became restless as he felt Steel's anger and began mewling tiny sounds of distress. Bashing himself for causing his mate's unrest, Steel schooled his thoughts while whispering loving words in his mate's ear, finally soothing Jackson back into a peaceful sleep.

Steel’s eyes closed, his breathing slowed, and he joined his mate in slumber.

Chapter 13

Jackson hovered in the space between sleep and wakefulness before finally giving in and opening his eyes. The delicious scent of his mate triggered his memories of his mother and siblings celebrating the Long Night Moon Festival. He and his brothers had ignored the holiday since losing their family, but now it seemed like a good time to start again, especially if pups were in the future.

He could tell his mate was still sleeping by his slow, even breathing and he remained still waiting for Steel to wake up. He felt his mate's morning wood nestled in the crack of his ass and—*holy shit…that was one big cock*—which led his thoughts to last night's claiming.

Wow! Mmmm… his mate was a fantastic lover, driving Jackson out of his mind with lust and desire, giving him the very best orgasm of his entire life. *Oh yeah…* he couldn't wait to see what the next round of lovemaking with his sex god would be and he was especially eager to suck Steel's cock.

Last night Steel had kept the focus all on him and while Jackson didn't expect such an unselfish lover, he loved feeling he was the most important person in Steel's life. He let the feeling seep into his soul. He knew no one ever made him feel so special and sent a silent prayer of thanks up to the Fates.

Steel, listening to Jackson's thoughts, knew his mate thought he was asleep but he loved this new gift of mind linking that came with claiming a fated mate, so he lay still, listening. But somehow his mate realized he was no longer asleep because suddenly Jackson turned over, grabbed Steel's cock and gave it a few tugs.

"Good morning, lover," Jackson crooned in a voice reaching down to Steel's balls. On hearing a gasp leave Steel's mouth, Jackson scooted down, taking his mate's cock into his mouth, sucking it deep. Running his tongue around it, he searched for the thick blue vein, laving it up and down until he heard Steel moaning. Letting his mate's cock pop softly from his mouth, Jackson looked up at Steel's eyes which were almost black with need. He pushed Steel onto his back, settling between his mate's legs and lowered his head, letting Steel's cock slide back into his mouth.

Steel couldn't remember ever waking up in such a delightful way as with those full, cock-sucking, red lips encasing his morning wood. *Fucking Damn!* He needed to move—the sensations pulsing through his groin demanded it but Jackson held his hips down, forcing a new level of frustration for Steel. Moans interspersed with whimpers were among the

torrent of sounds now falling from Steel's lips as he was driven to a new high with Jackson's head-giving skills.

His mate's hands were all over him—tweaking his nipples, massaging his balls and then, a wet fingertip pressed into his opening. *Oh, my gods!!!* Steel felt the tingling in his groin growing and his balls tightening when Jackson's finger broke through the ring of muscles, pressing down on that magic button, Steel arched off the bed, roaring as his cum spurted down Jackson's throat. Collapsing back onto the bed, Steel closed his eyes, floating back to earth.

Jackson cleaned Steel's cock with his tongue, savoring each little bit of cum he found and then crawled up, laying his head on Steel's chest where he could hear his heartbeat still pounding from Jackson's efforts. Curling his fingers into Steel's thick chest hair, Jackson closed his eyes—smiling and enjoying the first morning of mated bliss before drifting back to sleep again.

~/~/~/~/~

The touch of Steel's hand caressing his back accompanied by a chuckle awakened Jackson.

"What's so funny?" he asked.

"Your stomach has been growling for the last ten minutes so, as your mate, I'm going to make you some breakfast, pronto," replied Steel. "Can't have your bros saying I'm not taking care of you."

"Well, food is good, but you still haven't fulfilled all your duties as a mate because there's something else you've not taken care of this morning," said Jackson, slyly.

Laughing, Steel stroked Jackson's dick. "No, I haven't, but I want wet sex so get up and let's hit the shower."

Jackson walked into the en-suite bathroom, starring at the shower—a massive array of body jets, multiple rain shower heads and—*holy fuck*—steam. It seems his mate didn't do anything half way. "I can't believe you have steam. Shit, I have to try that out," exclaimed Jackson, hurrying over to the shower. "Oh, my gods, this shower is bigger than my whole bathroom at home." He pulled Steel in, eager to try everything at once.

Steel turned on all the rain shower heads and grabbing the body wash, he pulled Jackson's back against his chest, nestling his cock between Jackson's cheeks. Then he began soaping up the chest muscles of his dream man. Slowly, ever so slowly, in never ending circles Steel's hands went over each part of Jackson's body, washing away the sweat of their mating.

Leaning against Steel for support—because otherwise he was sure he'd fall—Jackson felt his mate's soft caressing hands driving him mad with lust even though his cock hadn't been touched. Needing friction, he reached down to grip his cock, stroking it with a tight fist. Steel knocked his hand away, growling, "Mine!" and wrapped his soapy fingers around Jackson's cock, using it as a leash to pull him over to the shower's back wall. "Spread your legs and place your hands on the wall. Do not move," Steel commanded.

Hot Damn! Steel is going dominant on me. My favorite kind of lover! He moaned as Steel started pumping Jackson's cock with just the right amount of pressure and the friction he so desperately needed. When he felt Steel's, other hand grabs his balls, Jackson squeaked, rising up on his toes, feeling the fleeting pain morph into pleasure. His balls and cock were finally getting the attention he dreamed of. His rising need caused his body to heat and blood to boil.

"Oh please, I need… now…please," wailed Jackson, his body shaking. He was perched at the edge of the cliff, needed only a little push to fall over and he wasn't getting it. Jackson howled, his body now so hot, he no longer had coherent thought. A finger sliding into his hole propelled Jackson over the edge. Long, copious strings of cum painted the shower wall as he screamed wildly.

His orgasm finished, Jackson collapsed into Steel's strong arms, exhausted, yet so filled with joy that he'd have this man forever.

~/~/~/~

Jackson awoke alone in the bedroom where Steel carried him after their shower. He missed the warmth of his mate but then the smell of coffee sneaked up his nose. Looking around, he spied a steaming mug on the nightstand with a note leaning against it. Jackson read it as he sipped his coffee. "*Mo chroí, I'm in the kitchen making you breakfast. Please join me, I miss you. Love, Steel.*"

Jackson held the note to his heart, his love for his mate overflowing. *His Steel... who was kind, thoughtful, considerate, and selfless all rolled up in the most delicious body he had ever seen.* Jumping out of bed, eager to see his mate, he spied the sweatpants and t-shirt Steel left for him. *Yeah, I hit the jackpot as far as mates go.*

Dressing quickly, Jackson followed his nose, navigating through the house, zeroing in on Steel's scent. After descending the stairs, he froze at the scene in front of him. Steel was dancing and singing to Rascal Flatts. Jackson laughed to himself so as not to disturb the performer; Steel was holding up a big spoon, using it as a microphone, and singing into it about being on a highway. Hips swaying, body twisting, head tossing, Steel was poetry in motion. Suddenly he saw Jackson and stopped, a faint pink blush appearing on his face. Smiling at his mate, he asked, "Ready for breakfast?" and turned off the music.

Laughing, Jackson replied, "Sure, but don't I get to see the rest of the concert first?"

Steel was mesmerized by the beautiful sound of Jackson's laughter. "Maybe later, but first I think food is in order for both of us."

Smirking at the sound of his stomach growling, Jackson said, "Now that I think of it, that's a very good idea."

Then, sniffing, he added, "Smells great, what did you make?"

"Pancakes, scrambled eggs, steak, bacon, sausages, toast, and fresh squeezed orange juice. Do you want anything else? Did I leave anything out?"

"Do you plan to feed an army?" Jackson joked, sitting at the island counter.

"Shut up and eat," Steel grinned. "I might have gone a little overboard but I wasn't sure how hungry you'd be this morning."

Surprise showed on Jackson's face. "You know, come to think of it, I really am starving. I have to give you full marks for knowing what I need before I even do." Then, leaning over, he gave Steel a kiss; his tongue gently licking and thrusting into Steel's mouth, then pulling back with Steel's bottom lip between his teeth before he let go.

Steel watched Jackson dig into the food, relishing the thought he was providing for his mate and child. As he began to eat, he thought about how long he waited for his mate, sometimes becoming depressed because it was taking so long, but never giving up.

Now he was sitting with Jackson, eating breakfast and feeling good with the quietness, companionship, and the thought it would be that way for the rest of their very long lives. It still seemed unreal that after searching for over a hundred years, he'd finally found his mate at the side of a road and he smiled at his luck.

Jackson kept glancing at his mate; he would never tire of him. He admired Steel's throat, itching to lick that Adam's apple, bobbing as he swallowed his juice. Then Steel smiled and Jackson inhaled sharply at the sheer beauty of his face. *I'm one lucky dude*, and he could feel his body getting hot.

Jackson jumped out of his thoughts as Steel stood to put the leftovers away. "Are you finished?"

"Sure," Jackson confirmed. Getting up, he quickly gathered the breakfast dishes, and took them over to the sink for a rinsing and then put them in the dishwasher. "This is a beautiful kitchen. Dakota would love cooking here."

"He's one of your brothers, right?" When Jackson nodded, Steel continued, "I take it he likes to cook?"

"He was studying to be a chef before our family was murdered. His training was put on hold when we went into hiding. He's taken some on-line cooking courses, so hopefully that will make up for the loss somewhat," answered Jackson, sadness washing over his face.

Steel's heart hurt, realizing his mate was reliving the trauma of what happened to his family. He vowed it would be his mission in life to avenge the lives stolen from the Blackwood brothers. Steel moved over to Jackson and, hands on his hips, leaned in to give him a soft, gentle kiss, murmuring, "Maybe I can help him get back to cooking school. Let's talk about what can be done.

Jackson nodded, "I also have some questions about our mating." Steel entwined his fingers with his mate's, leading Jackson to a black leather sofa in the great room. Jackson surveyed the room more thoroughly than before, noticing the mountain framed by the floor-to-ceiling windows, the giant fireplace into which a log, big enough to celebrate the Long Night Moon Festival would fit, and plenty of deep, comfortable furniture scattered around—just the right size for wolves. But he again noticed no books or photos, without which, the room exuded a cold and impersonal feeling.

When Jackson finished scanning the room, Steel asked, "What do you think? Do you like it?" and before Jackson could answer, he nervously added, "You can change anything you want," and sat down next to his mate.

"I think the house is gorgeous, Steel, but before we go there, I want to ask about our mating."

"Sure, shoot."

Jackson grinned, "I already did," leaning into Steel's side, turning his head to bury his nose in his mate's neck while inhaling the rich, deep scent he found there.

Steel laughed. "I remember." Running his fingers through Jackson's long hair he added, "Smartass."

Turning his face to look at his mate, Jackson began. "Seriously, right? Last night, as we claimed each other, at one point I could have sworn I felt your wolf in me—mating with my wolf. Now, I know that can't happen, so what did happen?"

Steel thought for a minute and said, "You're right. My wolf wasn't in you even though it felt like it. My wolf's spirit entered you to become one with your wolf. In a sense they were mating, but only spiritually. It only happens with a Fated Mate during their *toirchigh* period," Steel explained.

Jackson looked puzzled. "What is the *toirchigh* period? I've never heard of that."

"Certain paranormals have a specific time during which they are able to impregnate their mate. It's only during this *toirchigh* period that it's possible," explained Steel. "*Toirchigh* means 'to make pregnant'. Once the mate is pregnant, then the *toirchigh* period ends until the next cycle."

Jackson thought about what Steel said and when he put the pieces together, he came to only one conclusion. "Are you still in your *toirchigh* period?"

"No, I'm not."

"Are you telling me I'm pregnant?" asked Jackson in a voice so soft that Steel needed to rely on the hearing skills of his wolf to know that his mate even spoke.

He couldn't tell how Jackson felt because he didn't want to use their mind link again until his mate knew about it. He took a deep breath before replying. "Yes, you are," he said quietly.

Chapter 14

Jackson froze. He was pregnant. He, no, *they* were going to have a pup. A pup! His own baby to care for, nurture, and raise with unconditional love—from both parents! *Oh, my gods!* Jackson leaped into Steel's lap, holding his mate's face between his hands, looking Steel in the eye, saying, "I love you," and following with a kiss that quickly morphed into tongue dueling as Steel gasped at Jackson's declaration.

Pulling back, Steel looked into Jackson's beautiful blue eyes, rubbed his thumb along his mate's puffy lips, uttering, "I love you, Jackson, now and forever and that won't even be enough time, *mo chroí.* You are my heart, my soul, my everything."

As tears of joy ran down Jackson's face, he leaned forward to snuggle in his mate's arms, finding the security and love he'd sought his whole life. Listening to Steel's strong, steady heartbeat, peace came over him, settling his soul and centering his universe.

Jackson took a deep ragged breath, trying to stem his tears as Steel soothingly rubbed his back. He was loathed to leave his mate's arms but wanted to continue their conversation; if he stayed where he was, they would be having a different conversation with body parts. Reluctantly drawing out of Steel's arms and lap, he moved to sit next to him.

Steel loved Jackson's reaction to the news he was pregnant as he did his affirmation of love. Yet he was surprised at how quickly Jackson had accepted the 'you-can-get-pregnant' news, so he asked, "*Mo chroí,* I'm delighted at how easily you accepted that you could have a baby. Did you know it before my mother told you?"

Looking down, pausing to gather his thoughts, Jackson brought Steel's hand to his lips, kissing it before he moved it to rest over his heart. Then he spoke, "As I grew up, my father spent hours lecturing me on the duties and responsibilities of being an Alpha and, while I did my best, I always felt I was lacking somehow." Steel started to object but before he could speak Jackson said, "No, shush," holding a finger over Steel's mouth.

"What I mean is, parts of being the Alpha were very hard, such as sending men out to fight because I knew in my soul if one died on my orders, it would affect me far greater than it should. So, I tended to over-think decisions, always trying to find a peaceful solution so no one would have to pay with their life.

"My father hated that part of me and tried to crush it with insults and putdowns which only resulted in me retreating into myself. My mother finally sent me away to spend a summer with her parents. They taught me how to handle my father's verbal assaults and when I came back, I never allowed his words to hurt me again."

"But you *are* a good Alpha," asserted Steel, not wanting his mate to denigrate himself. "Look at how you took control after the massacre."

"Yes, I took control of my brothers and made sure they were safe. But I couldn't bring myself to order the revenge my family deserved. I would sooner cut off my right arm than put one of my brothers in harm's way," replied Jackson sadly. "That's exactly what my father hated about me. So, my family still doesn't have the justice they deserve, and my mother and siblings have the right to it—maybe more than my father—because they were innocents in all this mess."

Jackson paused before going on. “This part of me was the reason I rejected claiming you at first. I knew if—no, make that when—the Silver Point enforcers found us, I would have to stand with my brothers to defend them and that meant I wasn’t putting you first, as a mate should. It was an untenable position and either choice would devastate me if harm came to anyone.”

“What changed your mind?” asked Steel.

“Mystia,” said Jackson. “She talked me down off the edge, so to speak, and made me see my mate would stand with me and my brothers and it wasn’t an ‘either/or’ choice.”

“Your brothers are my brothers now,” growled Steel, upset his mate was still threatened. “They will be protected with all the resources of my family.”

Jackson’s eyes began to fill with tears as he listened to Steel’s vow. Looking at his mate with watery eyes, he said, “That means more to me than you’ll ever know. Thank you.”

“Hey babe,” Steel crooned, taking Jackson’s hand, lifting it to his mouth and licking off some fallen tears. “Know I will do anything and everything for you just so I can see your smile.”

Jackson, leaning in for a kiss, said, “Remember when you found me at the side of the road?”

“How can I forget?”

“Well, what caused me to help those men is the trait my father ridiculed me for, every time I helped someone in trouble. He said I was weak and it was conduct unbecoming an Alpha. But what he didn’t understand is it’s a part of me that comes so naturally—I mean, to me it’s like breathing. I literally *have* to help someone who’s in trouble.

"All this contradiction inside of me caused me to spend my childhood and teen years in a constant state of feeling I was two people. When your mother explained that I was an Alpha/Omega hybrid, everything fell into place. My whole life just clicked and I knew why I could lead my brothers and yet care about those who needed help."

Jackson stopped for a moment before continuing, "That's when I understood why I was reluctant to seek revenge for my family's death. And it explained why I loved taking care of my siblings when I was growing up. When I learned I could get pregnant, it was as if I'd known it all along. I don't know how else to explain it."

Steel was inordinately proud of his mate at that moment as he thought about all Jackson had to overcome in his life. He was amazed and humbled at his mate's strength, pledging to himself he would make Jackson's life easier from this moment on. That thought led him to say, "What can I do to help your brothers? I have a great deal of resources at my disposal."

"I don't know at this moment," said Jackson. "We still have the Silver Point enforcers hunting us and I know my brothers won't feel comfortable until I eliminate that threat. I'm unsure how to proceed." Then he added, "But now with a baby on the way, this becomes the main priority. I just wish I knew why they want the Fox River Pack's land."

"You're not alone, babe," Steel said "I understand why you don't want to fight them and I agree. I've been thinking about what I can do to stop them and make their Alpha call off the kill order but I need to talk to my father and my brother first." Then almost as an afterthought he asked, "Did you make a complaint to the Universal Paranormal High Council yet?"

“No,” Jackson said, “Because right now it’s our word against theirs since none of us was there during the massacre, so there aren’t any eyewitnesses. The other issue about making a complaint is it would expose us to Silver Point.” Jackson sighed, thinking once again of the insurmountable odds of finding a peaceful solution while still getting justice for his family.

And then something Steel said clicked in his mind and he exclaimed, “You have a brother? Oh fuck, of course you do, your mother told me but I guess I was distracted. Shit, what a crappy mate I’m turning out to be. Is your brother older or younger? Where does he live? Will I meet him? Hot-diggity-damn. I have another brother.”

By the end of Jackson’s outburst, Steel was laughing so hard, he was holding his stomach. Jackson swatted at him. “Stop it. Tell me about your brother,” he demanded, even though he, too, had a hard time holding back his laughter.

Still chuckling, Steel answered, “My brother, Slate, is younger by about two years. We basically grew up together but when I moved here, he decided to stay with our parents. Even though I miss him, I’m glad he did cause it took a lot of worry off me. He works in the family business and he’s one smart dude, though if you tell him I said that, I’ll tickle you mercilessly until you agree to anything I want.”

Steel then leaned over, giving Jackson a taste of his threat. Jackson grabbed at his mate’s hands to stop him from reaching his very ticklish sides, but he failed and threw himself against Steel pushing him down on the sofa.

Steel looked up into his mate’s eyes which were dancing with merriment, sucking in his breath at the absolute beauty he saw. Pulling Jackson's head down, Steel's lips gently grazed the soft, pliable lips of his mate, licking and gently biting Jackson's lower lip until he finally opened his mouth, allowing Steel in. He groaned as his tongue tasted his mate. Deepening the kiss, Steel's hand snaked into Jackson's soft hair, pulling him closer until Steel could no longer tell where his mouth ended and Jackson's began.

Jackson responded immediately, by tongue dueling for dominance over Steel's, finally succeeding when he entered his mate's mouth, where he explored its contours and wallowed in the taste.

Feeling his mate's hard cock up against his groin, Steel started to grind his body against his mate's. Jackson could wait no longer; he needed to feel his mate's naked cock against his. He reached down to unsnap Steel's jeans and then heard music. Ignoring it he struggled to pull apart the jeans—difficult since he was lying on top of them. Rolling over to his side, he was finally able to wrench them open, finding the object of his desire—Steel's cock.

What the fuck? Steel was pushing him away. Confused he pulled back to look at his mate, wondering what was wrong when Steel's words finally penetrated his head. "Babe, your phone is ringing. I think it might be your brothers. Don't you want to answer it?"

Jackson shook his head, trying to clear away the lust consuming his body. He blinked several times before he answered, "Yeah, I should probably do that." He slowly sat up on the sofa, trying to locate his phone. Spying it on the floor, he picked it up, answering the call. "Hi, what's up?" *Not my cock anymore*, he pouted to himself.

"Jackson?" asked Logan, "Are you all right?"

"Hi bro, yeah, I'm fine. Is everything okay there?"

"Yeah, everything's good. We're wondering when you'll be back." Logan hated how he sounded so needy. *Shit, I'm an Alpha, suck it up.*

Jackson heard the slight panic in Logan's voice, knowing he needed to get home soon to quiet the waters roiling with the uncertainty as to what his mating would mean to his brothers. "Just a minute," said Jackson, as he turned to Steel. "Logan wants a timeline as to when we'll be coming back."

"How about five tonight?"

Jackson nodded and said, "We'll be back around five. Is Mystia still there? How're Steel's parents?"

Logan breathed an internal sigh of relief. "They're fine. Mystia's here but Jimmy went back to the gas station. See you then. Bye"

Steel studied the tension in Jackson's body. "Is everything okay at home?"

"Yeah, but I know my brothers are unnerved by our mating. And that doesn't even take into account my pregnancy," said Jackson, a shadow crossing his face as he thought about the Alpha status of his mate. He just knew he couldn't ask his brothers to follow Steel just because they were mated. It was too soon and his brothers still were wary of other wolves which is why they'd been irritated when Jackson hadn't mentioned a wolf gave him a ride to Jimmy's.

Steel thought he had an inkling of what was bothering his mate, but he also knew Jackson didn't want to bring it up because it might hurt his feelings. He decided to make his position clear and then see what Jackson had to say. "*Mo chroí*, come over here and sit with me. I have some more things I want to tell you."

Jackson walked over, sitting as close as he could to his mate, feeling the need to touch Steel. Burying his nose in Steel's neck, Jackson took deep breaths of the unique scent which could calm him in seconds and, after his tensions had eased, he looked up with a weak smile and asked, "Now, what are you going to tell me? All good, I hope?

Chapter 15

Hoping to ease what he thought was Jackson's biggest worry, Steel said, "Babe, I don't expect to become Alpha of the Blackwood Pack. You're the Alpha and I think you have, and are doing a damn fine job."

Jackson interrupted, "What are you talking about? You're just as good as I am, probably better." He wasn't going to let anyone question his mate's abilities, including Steel himself.

Steel hugged Jackson a little tighter, smiling at how protective his mate was—he loved that. He knew the Fates picked the right person to be his mate; very strong but able to counterbalance his pure Alpha tendencies with the empathy he was missing. *Jackson will make a perfect parent for our family of Dire pups.* "Babe, I think my time will be best spent dealing with the Silver Point pack issue and the kill order hanging over you, your brothers, and our pup. It may even include Jimmy if they find out he helped you."

Steel continued, "While I'm not too worried about Jimmy—because Mystia will protect him—there's always the possibility he can be caught in a surprise ambush. As for your brothers, the mating and pregnancy is a lot for them to handle right now. Let them get to know me first and then we'll see how it goes, but know this, I'm not eager to take on the Alpha role."

He paused for a second before adding, "But also understand this, *mo chroí*, at no time will I allow you to place yourself and our pup in danger. So, while I expect you to talk to me first about whatever actions you want to take, I will not interfere with your role of Alpha in front of your brothers. Your safety comes first and I'm asking you to respect my position on that matter."

Jackson's body tingled with the possessive growl coming from his mate that resonated deep within his soul. Not only was Steel protective, he clearly knew what would make Jackson happy and handle his worry about his brothers. *What a fantastic mate I have!* He didn't know how, but somehow Steel sussed out Jackson's little niggling worry when he found out he was an Alpha/Omega hybrid: *Would Steel view him as a lesser Alpha—or as not one at all?*

Steel reassured him that he not only respected the Alpha part of Jackson, he also viewed it as equal to his. Still, there was one issue Jackson wanted clarified. "How can I talk to you first about what I want to do if we're in a pack meeting? Do you want me to excuse us both so we can talk in private? That could be awkward."

"Yes, it would. We'll use our mind link—which all fated Dire mates have—for privacy," responded Steel.

"But we don't have one," grumbled Jackson. "I haven't been able to hear your thoughts at all since we mated."

"We do have one," Steel assured him. "I know because I heard your thoughts this morning when you first woke up. Because it appeared you couldn't hear mine, I closed my link since I didn't want you to think I was taking advantage of you. Let's try now. I've opened my mind link, see if you can hear my thoughts," prompted Steel.

Jackson focused inwardly, trying to hear Steel but failed to make a connection. "Maybe I can't do it because I'm not a Dire Wolf," complained Jackson. He scrunched up his face, as if it would help, trying again to hear Steel talk to him. Nope, he had… wait, yes, there Steel was! Jackson whooped, sending a message back to his mate.

"I love you too," purred Steel, lifting Jackson's face and kissing his eyes, nose, jaw, and ear before ending on Jackson's lips. Steel then pulled back, loving the dazed look Jackson gave him. "Any more questions, babe?"

"Yup, one more. Will you fuck me?" asked Jackson, grinning.

It was four o'clock when Jackson and Steel headed back to the Blackwood Pack house. As they drove down the driveway through the trees, Steel could see the tension in his mate.

Jackson, still awed by the setting, faced Steel and asked, "I know your house is gigantic but how much land do you have to run on?"

"Two hundred thousand acres," replied Steel. Then, taking a quick look at his mate, he said, "Of course part of that includes several mountains so it's not all flat land."

Jackson whistled. "Why so much land?"

"I moved here to find my fated mate and if it happened, I knew we'd be having pups. I wanted enough land to give them plenty of running room and also ensure our privacy," explained Steel. "And there's plenty of game for the pups to learn their hunting skills."

Jackson put his hand on his belly where his pup was growing, smiling at the wonder of it all. Sometimes it seemed he was dreaming—he'd never been so happy in his entire life and, especially after the massacre, he never thought it possible. He pictured his pups scampering through the forest, his mate trying to corral them as they were drawn in different directions by every new scent and sound.

As they drove through the security gate, Jackson laughed at the silliness of his dreaming. He leaned over, kissing Steel on his cheek and put his hand over his mate's crotch, he squeezed the bulge gently. "I love you, mate of mine and can't wait until our pups are running all over this land."

Jackson's laugh made Steel's heart skip a beat at its glorious sound. He wanted more of it but the picture his mate planted in his head while squeezing the source of the pups… well, Steel was ready to pull over and ravish him again. *Shit, I need to get control of my thoughts*; his cock was growing uncomfortably hard in his jeans. Looking over at Jackson, he saw the deviltry in his mate's eyes; Jackson knew exactly the effect he was having on Steel's groin.

Steel growled, "You better stop it or you'll find yourself bent over the hood while I take care of what you caused."

Jackson's eyes widened as the image of Steel's threat flashed in his mind and lust blew through him like a wildfire. *Damn! I want that!* He squeezed Steel's cock harder, trying to make his mate carry out his threat.

Steel groaned as his body heat went up and a fierce need to take his mate enveloped him. Spying a copse of trees that would provide cover from passing motorists, he pulled into them. Grabbing the hand that was tormenting his cock, Steel lifted it to his lips, licking the fingers before sucking two into his mouth. Lavishing them with spit first, he then ordered Jackson to get out, bend over the side of the hood and get himself ready.

Watching his mate comply, he then savored the hottest thing he'd ever seen. He slowly got out of the Ranger Rover, walked to his mate and watched Jackson's fingers working to open that beautiful pink rose for

Steel's cock. Keeping his eyes on his mate, he unzipped his jeans and slowly taking his hard, dripping cock out, stroking it while waiting for Jackson to say he was ready. Steel hoped he didn't have to wait too long—he was in danger of coming just viewing the erotic scene playing out before him.

Jackson couldn't believe he wanted to be fucked outside, realizing with a start he was a bit of an exhibitionist. *Who would have guessed? Not me.* Bending over with one hand on the hood, he worked his fingers in and out, widening his hole for his mate's thick, long cock. Steel got out of the car, and stood behind him, watching as he worked to open himself. *Oh, my gods!* This was the sexiest thing Jackson ever experienced, causing him to drop his head as feelings of passion took hold in his groin.

His rigid cock was now slapping against his stomach as his body jerked in response to the thrusts of his fingers. Glancing behind him, he saw Steel stroking his eager cock with his eyes fixated on Jackson's ass. His knees shaking, Jackson knew it was time. "I'm ready," he rasped, unable to say anything else as his need was now at the boiling point.

With a powerful thrust Steel's cock entered Jackson, finally surrounded by sweet, wet, heat. Moaning at the sensation—sure he would never get enough of Jackson's fantastic ass—Steel stopped when his cock was finally balls deep, needing to savor the moment.

"Move dammit!" yelled his mate. Steel grabbed Jackson's hips, pounding his mate's ass as Jackson braced himself against the hood. Harder and harder, Steel pumped, determined to make Jackson come first. A steady stream of curses and moans poured from

Jackson's mouth, ratcheting up the need in both of them.

And then, just when Steel thought he'd have to lend his mate a hand, he felt his cock being squeezed as Jackson roared, shooting his cum into the wheel well and onto the tire where it dribbled to the ground. Seconds later, Steel joined him, coating his mate's insides with his seed. He wrapped his arms around Jackson to keep him from collapsing, holding him tight to his body. Then he whispered sweet words of love into his mate's ear.

Jackson slowly descended back to earth, his body quieted from the intense sensations that had engulfed it. When he finally heard Steel's words of love, Jackson turned his head, seeking out his mate's lips, kissing them with all the love he had for Steel. Suddenly he heard Steel's voice in his head, asking if he was all right. Smiling against his mate's lips, he answered through the mind link. *This is so cool!* He felt like a member of a secret club like the one he and his brothers had when they were children. Steel laughed, asking, "Secret club? Really?"

"Of course, it was just the seven of us older kids and we had a secret clubhouse and everything. We passed coded messages at the dinner table and even developed a secret language so no one would know what we said," explained Jackson.

Steel stood up, gently pulling out of Jackson. He tucked his cock back in his jeans, watching Jackson carefully do the same, taking care to make sure no cum dripped on them. When Jackson saw Steel smirking at him, he frowned, "What?"

"Afraid your brothers will smell your cum?" Steel asked, smiling.

"No, not my brothers, but I certainly don't want your parents to smell it and then have to look them in the eye as we sit down to dinner," Jackson retorted, watching Steel blanch.

Steel took his mate's hand, leading him to the car door. "Do you feel better now? Are you ready to meet your brothers as a mated wolf?"

Jackson nodded, getting into the car. Leaning over to buckle his mate in, Steel kissed Jackson's jaw, licking down to his mating bite which he nipped gently. Jackson shivered from the after effects of the action and a smiling Steel rounded the car, got in and started the engine. Linking his hand with Jackson's, he pulled onto the road and headed for his parents and new brothers.

Jackson was amazed again that Steel knew what he needed even when he didn't. That hard pounding fuck settled his nerves and gave him the peace he needed before facing his brothers. A whirlwind of thoughts swirled through his mind as he tried to figure out how to tell his brothers the impossible had happened: he was pregnant.

Part of his uneasiness came from the uncertainty of how his brothers would now view him… *will they think I'm not Alpha enough to lead the Blackwood Pack? Will they view me as an oddity with no right to be around them?* He really didn't think so, but one never knew how someone would react when faced with something out of the norm.

And I am so far out of the norm, it's not even funny. Unconsciously, Jackson's hand cradled his belly in a protective manner; he hoped his brothers would welcome his pup with the joy he and his mate felt.

Steel heard his mate's thoughts though he was sure Jackson wasn't aware of it. But they confirmed he was right about what was bothering his mate and that's why he'd decided to stop and give Jackson something else to focus on. It worked because Jackson, while still concerned about his brothers' reactions, was now much calmer.

He just hoped they'd accept what he was and even show joy at the coming addition to the family. Gods help them if they rejected Jackson or viewed him as less than the wonderful Alpha he was. If that happened, Steel knew he wouldn't hurt any of them but it didn't mean he'd ever forgive them.

Jumping a little bit, Jackson realized Steel was turning onto the road leading home. *Shit, it was going to get real, very fast.* He hoped Mystia would still be there to help him answer his brothers' questions about what it meant to the pack. Driving up, Jackson could see his brothers, Mystia, and Steel's parents on the front porch waiting to greet them.

Chapter 16

Stopping in front of the porch, Steel turned off the engine. He looked at his mate, who was nervously biting his lip. Reaching over and grasping Jackson's hand, he brought it up to his mouth, kissing it softly. "Remember, I'm here by your side and my parents and Mystia will help by answering any questions and smoothing the way with your brothers. It'll be all right."

"I know," Jackson said, "let's just get this over with so we can move on."

"Stay there," commanded Steel, leaning over to give Jackson a kiss on his cheek. Leaving the car and walking around to his mate's side, he opened Jackson's door, and helped him out. Heading for the house, Steel saw several brothers looking at them with narrowed eyes, not at all happy with what they saw. He wrapped his arm around Jackson's waist to support and comfort him.

Logan bounded down the steps, smiling, holding out his arms to hug Jackson. Steel could feel his mate's relief at the warm welcome he was getting from his twin and, as he caught his mother's eye, he knew she'd already told Logan about Jackson. So at least he had one ally and Steel could only hope the other brothers were as open to the news as Logan seemed to be.

His twin's unexpected welcome surprised Jackson and as Logan held him tight, he heard him whisper, "Oracle told me everything. I'm so happy for you and the pup-to-be. You can count on my support with our brothers." Tears filling his eyes, Jackson murmured, "Thanks, Logan. You always have my back and your support means more than you'll ever know." Slowly pulling apart, the twins gazed at each other with love in their eyes.

Logan turned to Steel. "Welcome to the family!" Steel reached out to shake his hand but Logan used it to pull him into a hug, whispering into his new brother-in-law's ear, "Congratulations on the mating and the baby but if you ever hurt my brother, there will be no place on this earth you'll be able to hide."

Steel smiled, whispering back, "Duly noted." When they separated, Steel's arm went back around Jackson, leading him up the steps with Logan following.

Stepping onto the porch, Mystia engulfed Jackson in her arms, squeezing him close to her, "Congratulations on your mating, *mon petit loulou.* How are you feeling?"

Jackson felt himself blushing but smiling shyly at Mystia, he said, "I feel great but a bit tired."

Oracle clucked a "tsk" sound before saying, "Why don't we get everybody inside—I think Dakota has dinner ready."

Jackson laughed as Zane, hearing her comment, rushed past him and made a beeline to the dining room. "According to Zane, he's a 'growing' boy who needs lots of food. Best if we all stand out of his way in situations like this," he cautioned. As the rest of the brothers filed in, Steel's mother and father approached the new mates. Oracle spoke first. "Congratulations to both of you on your mating. I am so happy you found each other. May your life be joyful and blessed with children, as they provide the purpose for everything in life." She reached out to Steel, hugging him close, kissing his cheek.

Then turning to Jackson, she said, "You are a very special person—not only because the Fates bestowed a gift on you but because you are able to put love in my son's heart, a sparkle in his eyes, and a purpose to his life. I promise you this, I will be whatever or wherever you need me to be and more important, the protector of you and your mate, your children, and your brothers. Welcome to our family." By this time, Jackson was in tears. He pulled Oracle to him, hugging her tightly and in a broken voice said, "Thank you so much for everything."

Oracle stepped back and Maximus gave Steel a one-armed hug along with several thumps on his back, "Congratulations son, I'm proud of you." Then, extending his hand to shake Jackson's, Maximus said warmly, "Welcome to the family, son. If you ever need anything, just ask. It would be a privilege to help another Alpha."

Jackson was an emotional mess; his breath hitched, trying to stop his tears. *Crap, I've never been this emotional before—is it the pregnancy or all the words of support that are helping to erase some of my fears?*

Steel gathered him in his arms, drenching Jackson in his scent, and he could feel his mate relax and calm down. When the tears stopped, Steel licked off the remaining wetness on Jackson's face before bending down to give his mate a gentle kiss. Then, he asked, "Are you okay now?"

Embarrassed at his show of emotion, Jackson ducked his head into Steel's neck, mumbling, "I'm fine. Let's go in now—if that's all right with you."

Steel took Jackson's chin between his forefinger and thumb, pushing it up so he could look at his mate's face. Jackson didn't know what Steel was searching for but he must have found it because he replied, "Sure, let's go feed our baby."

Everyone was already seated and Steel noticed the dining room possessed the same warm and cozy feeling as the den. The soft cream walls, wide-planked dark-colored pine floor, colorful rag rugs, and bright red dining room chairs were warm and inviting. Two empty chairs at the head of the long wooden table beckoned to him and his mate.

Zane called out, "Come on, if I don't eat soon, I'll begin to shrink." Looking at Jackson, he saw his brother's death stare. "Sorry everyone, just happy Jackson's back," muttered Zane, embarrassed for being called for his lack of manners.

Steel and Jackson sat down. Dakota had outdone himself; the table was laden with enough food to feed twice the number of people there. After surveying all the delicacies, Jackson turned to his brother. "Thank you, Dakota, the food looks absolutely delicious. Dig in everyone!"

Steel kept a careful eye on the food Jackson was placing on his dish, making sure his mate was eating enough after a very emotionally tumultuous day. He was pleased his mate was not skimping on what he ate. Steel knew as the pregnancy progressed it would take a toll on his mate's body and he wanted to make sure Jackson had all the sustenance necessary for the task ahead—giving birth to a Dire Wolf was not going to be easy.

Talk was scarce at the table but Steel couldn't tell if that was normal or if everyone was feeling the tension emanating from his mate. Either way, best to get this part of the evening over so his mate could finally find the answers he was seeking about his brothers' feelings.

Jackson felt Steel's hand on his thigh as a sign of support. He was nervous about the upcoming pack meeting even though he knew Logan would support him, but the others… well, he just didn't know.

Dammit, he *should* know his brothers better but his Alpha responsibilities had been focused on their survival for so long he'd let that slip. He knew his brothers were still dealing with the tragedy but they'd all come a long way since those dark and fear-filled days. He ticked his brothers' names off in his head, cataloging their possible reactions when dealing with something new.

Cody was the oldest triplet. He was level-headed and thought things out before making any decisions. He'd be okay with Jackson's mating and pregnancy. Colton was the next born and most reserved but was also the most caring about the well-being of the family, which made sense since he was studying to be a nurse.

Carson was the youngest triplet who took the most risks, always trying to outdo Cody and Colton—Zane was like that, too. Carson had a good heart but usually bragged about his Alpha abilities instead of keeping some of them concealed as any experienced Alpha leader would do.

No sense in telling your enemies everything about you—it just makes you easier to defeat. Hmmm. Jackson suddenly realized what his father tried to teach him had sunk in more than he'd thought. Jackson felt if Cody and Colton were okay with everything, then Carson would fall into line.

After the triplets, Dakota was the next. Steady and quiet, he always loved spending time in the kitchen with their Mom, cooking and baking up a storm. No wonder he'd chosen culinary school. And by the taste of the food he'd whipped up tonight, he'd have made a damn fine chef. Jackson hoped Steel could figure a way for his brothers to resume their education. How would Dakota feel about Jackson's situation? Not a clue. And what about Zane?

Zane was the youngest and usually acted like it. He was the unknown in Jackson's band of brothers. He would be the protester. He knew in Zane's book, an Alpha could only be an Alpha and nothing else. If Jackson thought Carson was a little too Alpha, well, it was a definite understatement when it came to Zane who believed too much Alpha still wasn't enough. He was pretty sure the first objection would come from Zane.

Steel heard the running commentary in his mate's head which prepared him for the pack meeting with at least some background on the brothers' personalities. His role would be strictly as support, never to appear as exerting power over his mate and, by extension, over the pack.

But that didn't mean he'd tolerate any disrespect of his mate. *Nope, I draw the line there.* He hoped Jackson would invite Mystia and his parents to the pack meeting—as they'd be able to answer questions he or Jackson couldn't.

Jackson was so deep into his thoughts, he was startled to realize everyone had finished dinner, waiting for him to announce what was next. *Damn, I need to get my head in the game because right now I'm looking like a clueless asshole.* "Carson and Zane, clear the dishes. Cody and Colton, put away the leftover food. I need to talk to Logan for a few minutes and when everything's finished, the pack meeting will begin in the den, say in about fifteen minutes."

Steel pulled his mate's chair back and Jackson stood up. Looking at Mystia, Oracle, and Maximus, he said, "I would appreciate it if the three of you attend the pack meeting; I might need the benefit of your knowledge."

After they agreed he left them and led Steel and Logan to his study. Jackson sat down at his desk and Steel pulled up a chair, sitting next to him. Logan took a seat across the desk, examining Jackson's face. "You look happy, bro, maybe even glowing."

Jackson lit up with the brightest smile Logan ever saw on his brother's face. *Fuck, if that's how it feels to be mated, then sign me up*. Logan continued, "I take it you want to tell me about some decisions you and Steel made about the pack."

"Yes," said Jackson, "I intend to remain Alpha of the Blackwood Pack for the immediate future. I hope I can count on your support." He saw Logan nodding his agreement, so he continued, "You know about me being an Alpha/Omega hybrid but I didn't get a chance to ask your thoughts on it."

Logan remembered how twin lances of envy and jealousy pierced his heart when Oracle told him his twin could have children. He wanted that—to have a baby with his fated mate, a family of his own, something he never contemplated as a possibility since he'd realized he was gay. Now he had hope, even though Oracle couldn't tell him if he possessed the same ability. What the Fates planned for him would only be revealed when he found his fated mate.

Logan snapped back to reality, replying with a broad smile, "Honestly bro, I think the pup is the greatest thing ever to happen to this family. I can't wait to greet our newest member—and I think he'll give us all hope life will get better."

Jackson could feel the truthfulness of Logan's feelings. "Thanks, I really appreciate your support. At dinner, I was trying to figure out how our brothers would react and Carson and Zane concern me the most. What do you think?"

"Yup, those two will be the most problematic. Our other brothers will be okay with it and probably think it's cool—I mean, think about it, Jackson, it's simply amazing this can happen."

Pausing for a few seconds, Logan continued, "Look, I know all of us suffered with guilt at surviving the massacre when our parents and siblings weren't as lucky. So, with this news about your ability to bring new life into our world, I like to think the Fates saved all of us for a reason. As difficult as it was to have gone through the pain, I think we'll survive because the Fates have a special purpose for us and we'll all find happiness."

"You've said what I've been thinking," smiled Jackson. "As I said before, I'll continue to be the Alpha of the Blackwood Pack. Steel's priority is to find a solution to the Silver Point Pack issue, preferably without any fighting. So, I'll need a room next to my study set up as an office for him." Looking at his mate he asked, "What do you need in it? If you tell Logan, he can arrange to get any computer and office equipment you want."

"Thanks, babe," Steel said and turning to Logan, asked, "let's meet some time tomorrow to discuss the office and what I need, okay?"

"Sure, mid-morning all right?"

"If you don't mind, how about early afternoon, since I need to speak with my father in the morning," countered Steel.

"That's fine," said Logan.

"Anything else can wait until tomorrow," said Jackson. "It's time to start the pack meeting."

Steel stood, moving his chair back, offering a hand to his mate. After Jackson rose, Steel drew him close to his side, nuzzling his nose in Jackson's hair, soaking up his scent. Guiding Jackson from the room with his hand resting just above his mate's perfect bubble butt, Steel began to think of what he would do with his mate that night. *Shit, no good, hard cock.* As he discreetly tried to rearrange his dick to make his erection less obvious, he heard Jackson snicker.

Jackson leaned in to Steel's ear, whispering, "That's what you get when you think dirty thoughts about me." Steel's eyes widened, realizing he was broadcasting his thoughts to his mate. Jackson leered at Steel, adding, "Wait until you see what *I'm* going to do to you tonight," and winked lasciviously.

"You are *so* going to pay for that, cock tease," growled Steel as they entered the den. Jackson felt a shiver go down his spine, ending up in his groin. "Bring it on big boy," he purred to his mate, putting his hand on Steel's chest, pinching his nipple hard. A low snarl came from his mate's throat. Jackson smiled. *Tonight should be interesting.*

Chapter 17

Guiding Jackson over to the big leather club chair by the fireplace—and after Jackson sat down—Steel moved to the mantle, propping his arm on it. He wanted to be close but not so close as to detract from Jackson's authority. He looked around the room, seeing Mystia and his parents sitting together on one of the distressed leather couches while Jackson's brothers had scattered themselves around the room, with the exception of the triplets, who sat together. Logan sat on the left side of Jackson as if guarding his flank. Steel smiled inwardly, glad to see that Jackson's brother intended to give moral support and maybe more, if necessary. Steel hoped it wouldn't come to that.

Jackson began to speak. "I want to ask some questions to find out what everyone knows. Oracle, did you tell my brothers the history of the Dire Wolves?"

"Yes, and I also filled them in on the Valentin family history."

"Okay, does anyone have any questions about that?" Jackson asked, looking at each of his brothers, receiving no reply. "Good," he said. "Now the next item is, I intend to stay as the Alpha of the Blackwood Pack. Steel will be a full member as will his parents and brother. He's been assigned to resolve the issue with the Silver Point Pack so we can get back to living again. As he gets into it, I expect he'll want to speak with each of us to get any information that'll help him achieve his goal. Any questions?"

"Why isn't Steel going to be our Alpha?" asked Zane. "After all, isn't he the strongest wolf in your mating?"

Just as Jackson was about to answer, Steel asked, "Do you mind if I answer this, mate?" And when Jackson waved his hand for Steel to proceed, he continued, "It takes more than sheer strength to lead a pack, Zane, and while it's true I'm bigger and physically stronger than Jackson, he is far superior to me in the mental toughness needed to make hard decisions for the benefit of the pack and not for himself."

The room grew quiet as Steel continued. "Your brother initially refused to mate with me because he felt his first loyalty was to the Blackwood Pack. Since your future concerning the Silver Point Pack is an unknown, Jackson didn't want to have divided loyalties in any potential fight. Ask yourself—would you be able to sacrifice your happiness for the good of the pack? Jackson was willing to. When a pack finds an Alpha who'll sacrifice himself so others will have a better chance to live, it better keep him. That's why I feel no need to become Alpha of this pack."

Jackson's heart was overflowing with the love he felt for his mate at that moment. Then he heard Zane asked him, "So why did you mate with Steel?" Zane had zeroed in on the main point of this pack meeting and Jackson knew the next few minutes would be fraught with difficulties as he tried to explain to his brothers what he was.

"Before I get into that, does anyone else have something to say?" Jackson looked around at his brothers. With only silence answering him, Jackson took a deep breath and started, "It turns out I'm a hybrid—an Alpha/Omega hybrid and I have the attributes of both. I learned about it when I found my fated mate."

Cody spoke up, “Exactly what do you mean ‘the attributes of both,’ Jackson? I know the Alpha part but what part of Omega do you have?”

Carson interrupted, “You’re not a full Alpha?”

“Let him finish,” demanded Colton. “What are you trying to tell us?”

Jackson knew this was the pivotal moment and would decide if he stayed as Alpha or not. What surprised him was how much he wanted it, especially after fighting with his father about it.

“My Omega part allows me to get pregnant and give birth to pups,” he said with a steady voice.

Dead silence ensued. Jackson looked at his brothers’ faces and saw an array of emotions ranging from shock to disgust. In response to the brothers’ reactions, Steel moved closer to him, as if to shield him from the negative emotions. Then the room exploded as a cacophony of voices shouted at him.

“What the fuck…”

“You’re an abomination!”

“Are you pregnant now?”

“Will I have the same ability?”

“You can’t lead us anymore.”

Jackson heard his mate snarl and growl at Carson and Zane, obviously disliking their comments. Jackson held up his hands and as the brothers fell silent, Jackson answered, “Colton, in response to your question, yes, I’m pregnant now. Dakota, I don’t know if you’ll have the same ability—I did ask, but no one knew the answer. Carson, if you want to challenge me for the Alpha position, then submit a formal request. Until I receive it, I'm the Alpha and will continue to lead this Pack."

Then he turned to Zane. "Shame on you for thinking you know more than the Fates who decided this is who I should be. I am no more an abomination then you are. The Fates did this, it wasn't my choice; I didn't wake up yesterday and decide I'd be an Alpha/Omega hybrid. This is the hand that was dealt to me by the Fates, and I'm not, nor will I ever be, ashamed of who I am."

Zane's jaw dropped, listening to the rebuke his beloved brother, his Alpha, gave him. Suddenly, he knew he had to get out of there—this was all too much. Leaping from his chair, he turned and ran to the front door. Opening it, he shifted before running into the forest, his shredded clothes scattered on the ground. Jackson sighed.

He'd known this would be hardest on his youngest brother who had still not come to terms with the death of his parents and the kill-on-sight order hanging over their heads. Any change in an already fragile existence, not to mention the size of this one, stretched Zane beyond what his newly-acquired coping skills could handle. Steel spoke up, "Do you want me to go after him just to make sure he's safe?" Jackson shook his head. "Logan, go after Zane and make sure he's safe. Don't try to make him come back—wait until he wants to."

"Will do."

Before Logan left, Cody turned to him and asked, "You haven't said anything about Jackson. What are your thoughts?"

Logan stood, looking at Jackson, then turning to his brothers, "I think it is the coolest thing I've ever heard. As I see it, Jackson's still what he's always been to me but now he is just a little bit more. So, yeah, I'm okay with the fact that I'm going to be an uncle." Logan paused for other questions but hearing none, he left to find Zane.

Jackson remained still as quiet settled in the room. Dakota spoke first, "Congratulations Jackson and Steel, both on the mating and the pregnancy. I have no problem with anything you said tonight but I still have questions about how this all came about."

Oracle, who was silent during the discussions, began to speak. "Dakota, maybe I can answer some of your questions if that is all right with Jackson."

"That's fine," said Jackson. "Go ahead, Dakota, and ask. What do you want to know first?"

"Not now, if that's okay. I want to think about this first but I mean it, bro, I support you wholeheartedly."

"Thanks Dakota, whenever you're ready, talk to Oracle."

The triplets were looking at each other and Steel could see they were communicating among themselves silently. He only hoped the final results would be positive for his mate. Steel knew Zane's reaction hurt his mate deeply and he marveled at Jackson's calm demeanor when faced with hateful words. He was on the verge of shifting when Zane shouted those foul words, but years of practicing control stood him in good stead.

Zane's actions, however, were tempered by Dakota's words of support and for that reason alone, Steel vowed to find a way to help Dakota finish his schooling. Now Steel was waiting for the final three to voice their feelings.

After imperceptible nods from his brothers, Cody spoke. "Congratulations on your mating Jackson. We're happy for you, bro—you deserve it. We reaffirm our allegiance to you as our Alpha. Regarding the elephant in the room—yeah, you have our support there too. To say we weren't blown away would be an understatement. I didn't even know it was possible. I thought only Omega wolves could get pregnant, so this is fucking unreal."

Steel let out his breath; just Zane left to decide how he felt after calming down. Shit, the end of this meeting couldn't come fast enough. He needed to take his mate to bed and kiss him senseless. Jackson smiled at the triplets. "Thanks guys, that means a lot." Then he stood, signaling the end of the meeting. He walked over to Mystia. "Are you going to head back to Jimmy?"

"Yes, he's missing me," Mystia said.

As she rose to embrace Jackson, he whispered in her ear, "I have more questions about this pregnancy but they can wait until later. Thanks for being here for me." Mystia smiled and Jackson asked Cody, "Can you give Mystia a ride down to Jimmy's?"

"Sure, no problem, bro."

Steel was at his side as Jackson turned to Oracle and Maximus. "Thanks for being here. Colton, please make sure that Steel's parents have everything they need." Steel then took his hand and said, "Good night, everyone, I need some alone time with my mate," and at that, the room erupted with rowdy laughter and cat calls.

His paws dug down, disturbing the forest floor, tossing pine needles and dead leaves aside. He couldn't help it. He had to escape, so he ran. Finally, he stopped. Now the anger was gone but Zane was still upset. Fucking hell, he was so screwed up in his head. *Jackson—having a baby? No way.* His father made it clear what an Alpha did and having babies wasn't one of the jobs. He couldn't wrap his head around it. For the first time ever, he was glad his father was dead so he wouldn't be embarrassed by his firstborn son being a freak. But just thinking about Jackson that way made him feel he was betraying him.

And that thought drove Zane crazy because Jackson meant the world to him. He'd picked up the pieces of their lives and by sheer strength of will, forged a new one for all of them. He wasn't sure how Jackson had done it because, Zane was mostly out of it; too busy grieving for his parents and siblings. He'd just gotten to a place where it didn't feel he was drowning—*yep, my head is now firmly above water*—when this news threatened his new-found peace. Could he blame Jackson? No, not really, his brother was right—the Fates made Jackson this way.

This meant his outcry about the Fates making a mistake was wrong and, what was worse, he knew it when he called his brother an abomination. *Shit, Shit, Shit, how could I hurt Jackson that way?* Zane owed his brother his support even if for no other reason than what Jackson had done for him since the massacre. Zane lifted his nose, sniffed the air, snorting as only a wolf could; it seemed Jackson was still protecting him even if he didn't deserve it for being such a brat.

Zane watched as a beautiful white wolf sauntered into the clearing, stopping before him. He knew it was Logan and his brother wasn't angry; he just looked at Zane and then licked his face. A sudden shimmer and Logan, appearing in his human form, asked Zane, "Do you want to talk about it?" Zane thought for a moment, nodded and another shimmer appeared as Zane shifted back. He flopped down on the moss-covered forest floor, staring through the trees at the darkening sky. Logan lay down next to him, mirroring Zane's actions and waited.

"Logan, I'm sorry I said that about Jackson. I guess I opened my mouth before I thought it through. I know I hurt him and will apologize," he said. "I know it's not a choice—the Fates decided it. It just caught me unaware and I hate change," he said, closing his eyes. "I never used to until Mom and Dad were killed. Now I try to make every day just like the one before. And when Jackson said he could get pregnant, I knew I'd never be able to find security in the sameness again. So, I got angry at him and wanted to hurt him. Does that make me fucked up or what?"

Logan filtered Zane's confessions through his mind and sought to find the right words to help his brother. "You know, Oracle told me about this before Jackson came back from his mating and at first, like you, I was shocked. But then I felt envy and jealousy. How lucky Jackson was to have a pup of his very own. Something none of us even thought possible unless our fated mate turned out to be a male Omega. And you know how rare those are."

Logan let those words sink in and continued, "But now that obstacle has been removed from Jackson. So yes, at first my feelings were negative. But then I got to thinking, it's not the only strange thing. For instance, the seven of us are gay, we're all Alphas, we're all white wolves. And only the white wolves in our pack survived. Strange, right? So, after talking with Oracle, I think we're each meant for some special purpose here on earth and I can't wait to find out what mine is."

“Do you think that’s why the Fates saved us?” asked Zane.

“Yes,” replied Logan.

Zane was quiet for a while, then asked, “What happened at the meeting after I left?”

“I don’t really know. Jackson sent me to keep an eye on you right after you shifted and ran into the forest.”

“So typical,” Zane smirked. “Always the big brother.”

“You got that right, bro and don’t you forget it. Ready to head back?”

“Yeah, and… Logan, thanks.”

Chapter 18

Leading Steel to his bedroom, well, now actually their bedroom, Jackson was satisfied with the results of the meeting even though Zane ran off. He hoped in the end his brother would sort his issues out and be happy for Jackson, but it was up to him.

His cock twitched with excitement as visions of what he'd do to his mate swirled in his mind. Walking over to the bed, he knew what Steel envisioned, causing his mate's erection on the way to the pack meeting—but he wanted to turn the tables and set Steel's body on fire before he fucked Jackson. Steel shut and locked the door; Jackson's evening was now entering the fun stage.

As he stood by the bed looking at Steel who was leaning against the door, his eyes traveled the length of his mate's gorgeous body—his broad shoulders, burly chest and arms, trim waist, and thighs bulging with muscles. Then his eyes landed on Steel's groin. There was the treasure he sought, his mate's long, thick, and by-now-dripping cock. Jackson's mouth watered for a taste of his mate again. He wanted to be on his knees, sucking that cock, savoring the flavor and texture as he took it down his throat.

Steel felt his cock rise as Jackson's eyes ogled his body, settling on the one part of him that lusted to be in his mate's ass. He knew his mate had plans tonight and Steel couldn't wait. When Jackson did nothing, Steel raised a hand to his jeans, but before he could unsnap them, Jackson issued his first command. "Stop. That belongs to me now. Remove your hand and put it back down at your side."

Oh shit, a bossy mate and wasn't that a turn on!

As Steel dropped his hand, his cock grew in length and hardness, responding to the tone Jackson used. He stood still, waiting to see what was coming next.

Jackson strolled over to his mate and, reaching out, began rubbing his fingers over Steel's jeans-covered cock, all the while staring at his mate while sucking his own bottom lip behind his upper teeth. He then winked at Steel.

That dirty fucker, he's deliberately teasing me.

Jackson could see the heat in his mate's eyes, widening and glowing in response to his orders. "Don't move," commanded Jackson when he saw Steel lift his hand. Jackson reached into his pants, pulling out his cock, giving it lazy strokes as he ordered Steel, "Now you can remove your shirt."

As the shirt landed on the floor, Jackson dropped his own jeans past his balls. Steel's nostrils flared instantly, taking in the strong scent of his mate. Jackson stood still, continuing to stroke his cock, releasing more of his scent into the air. He could see Steel's muscles beginning to twitch with the effort of remaining still. "So, let's see, what was it you wanted to do to me? Oh yes, you were going to bend me over the bed, rimming me but not allowing me to come. mmm. Remove your shoes, and take off your jeans."

Steel moved fast and soon stood naked. Jackson's eyes lingered on his mate's treasure trail leading to the most beautiful cock he'd ever seen. He moved closer to his mate, tracing his finger over Steel's chest, stopping to tweak his nipples before moving his finger up to Steel's neck, then to his chin and jaw and finally, after circling behind his ear, the finger stopped on Steel's lips.

Steel hoped his mate would insert the finger so he could suck it in and finally get the taste of his mate he was so desperately seeking. But no, Jackson wasn't going to give him that satisfaction; he removed his finger from Steel's lips causing him to let out a deep groan.

Instead, Jackson replaced his finger with his mouth, lightly kissing Steel's lips, catching the bottom one with his teeth, pulling on it before letting go. Next, he lavished a plethora of light kisses on Steel, circling his broad chest and muscled back before standing once again in front of his mate.

Steel could feel his knees shake from anticipation; he'd been moaning and whimpering for some time and really needed to fuck Jackson now. "Babe, please, I need to fuck you now...please, oh baby, now, please," Steel babbled. He was in danger of losing his mind as it clouded over with lust and need.

Jackson slowly stripped out of his clothes while Steel continued to beg and then, closing his eyes tried to gain control of his body, wondering what else his mate had planned. When he opened them, he saw Jackson kneeling in front of his cock. Steel nearly lost it when he felt Jackson's lips kiss his tip and, looking down, saw his mate's plump cock-sucking red lips slowly swallowing his manhood all the way to the root.

Oh, my gods, nobody had ever done that to him before and he didn't want to think how his mate learned to do it, he just wanted to enjoy the tightness of Jackson's throat. Steel's cock was now firmly compressed in his mate's throat causing tears to run down Jackson's face. Placing his hands in his mate's hair, he started to face-fuck Jackson who froze in place, letting Steel do the work.

Jackson loved the feeling of his mate's cock fucking his mouth and his tongue was put to good use, licking Steel's cock, driving his mate to grip Jackson's head tighter until he was machine gunning his hips into Jackson's mouth. Jackson kept one hand on Steel's balls to prevent them from tightening up too soon. His own cock was leaking all over the floor as Steel begged him to please let him come. Jackson released his mate's balls and as they began to tighten against Steel's body, Jackson fell back, removing his mouth from his mate's cock.

Steel roared in frustration; his release denied. He stood trembling—wondering if he should dare reach for his cock to finish.

Jackson stood, kissing his mate so Steel would have a taste of himself and then turned, bending over the bed. Smiling over his shoulder, he purred, "Is this how you want me?"

Steel looked at Jackson through half-crazed eyes; the fucker had made him so needy all he could think of was putting his iron rod in that winking hole, now so very exposed. As he narrowed his vision to the object of his desire, Steel moved towards Jackson's very open ass. Grabbing the lube from the nightstand and swiping some on his throbbing cock, he pushed in with one stroke, sinking into heaven as his balls touched his mate's. Steel growled with pleasure and, while waiting for Jackson to adjust to his cock's size, bent over his mate's back licking and nipping along the muscles he found there.

"Move, dammit," snarled Jackson.

Steel waited no longer, snapping his hips back and forth again and again—so hard he had to grip his mate's hips to help him remain standing. Jackson had primed him so well he soon felt a tingling in his groin signaling his approaching orgasm. Steel reached down, grabbing his mate's cock and, with a couple of strokes, Jackson came… screaming Steel's name.

Steel kept the action up on his mate's cock until Jackson had emptied his balls, giving several more snaps of his hips before coating the insides of his mate with his seed while bellowing Jackson's name—his cock continuing to throb and twitch.

As they both collapsed on the bed and their breathing slowly returned to normal, Steel whispered in Jackson's ear, "*Mo chroí,* I love you more than you will ever know. My home is wherever you are because my heart and soul are in you forever."

Then, as Steel slowly pulled out of his mate, Jackson murmured, "Ditto, love." After helping his mate up, Steel wrapped Jackson in his arms, and buried his nose in Jackson's neck, inhaling his mate's scent while gently kissing him. "I'll never get enough of you," he said, lifting his mate in his arms and carrying him to the bathroom. After setting Jackson on the counter, Steel filled the bathtub with steaming hot water, throwing in some bubble bath soap that was sitting on a shelf above the tub.

Once the tub was filled, Steel gathered Jackson up, lowering him into the bubbles and then joined him, arranging his mate between his legs with Jackson's back against his chest. He felt his mate's body slowly relax as the hot water removed the aches of their hard lovemaking. Steel gently caressed Jackson's body in slow circles, hoping to drive out the rest of the day's tensions.

The water cooled. Steel embraced Jackson in his arms, lifting him from the tub. Setting him on his feet, he slowly toweled both of them dry and then carried his mate to their bed, placing him in the center. Steel climbed in pulling Jackson, who was falling asleep, over to his side so he could spoon with him all night. Jackson snuggled his ass into his mate's groin, whimpering in his sleep. Steel pulled the covers over them and they drifted off.

~/~/~/~/~

Jackson woke surrounded by heat; Steel's arms and legs were wrapped around him. He remained still, relishing the feel and scent of his mate, thinking about all that happened in the last few days. For the first time since losing his family, he was filled with joy.

He thought about the sadness and longing he saw in Logan's face when they were in his office before the pack meeting and hoped his brother would soon find his fated mate. Jackson shivered when he thought how close he'd come to throwing all this happiness away.

He was still nervous about Silver Point Pack but not as much now that Steel had come into his life. Now at least, he had a powerful defender on his side. Jackson slid his palm down to his belly, cradling it, wondering how long it would take before he showed. He'd have to talk to Steel and maybe Mystia about it because there was so much he didn't know.

Steel feigned sleep while listening to Jackson's thoughts. He wanted to give his mate some time to reflect on what was happening to him and made a mental note to discuss Jackson's pregnancy with his mother so he'd have the answers. He couldn't wait until Jackson began to show and they'd feel the pup move inside his absolutely beautiful mate.

His feeling of possessiveness was all-consuming as was his need to protect not only his mate but the pup, too. Steel's body grew tense at the thought of the danger his mate was facing. Suddenly he felt Jackson push his ass against his groin, grinding.

"Hey babe, what's got you so uptight?" asked Jackson.

Steel buried his nose in his mate's neck, inhaling Jackson's unique scent that had the power to calm him. He reached down to hold his mate's cock, gently tugging it as he answered, "I was thinking of the danger facing you and our pup. I want to start on this problem today so your pregnancy can proceed without you worrying about our pup or your brothers. But that can wait," he smirked, "until I give you your morning blow job."

Rolling Jackson onto his back, Steel slid down, sucking his mate's cock to its root in one motion. Jackson bucked off the bed in response but his mate pushed his hips down, holding them in place so he couldn't move—which only drove Jackson's need higher and higher.

Steel heard the animal-like sounds coming from his mate's throat as he continued cock sucking while adding a light scraping of his teeth on the upstroke. His mate was trying hard to move his hips but couldn't gain traction, Jackson's head whipped from side to side while his fisted hands tore at the sheets. Finally, Jackson cried out. "Please, please…no more…more…babe I need… oohhhhh," his voice ending in a whimper.

Steel's left hand moved to Jackson's balls, massaging them gently, pushing his mate to the edge, dipping his tongue into Jackson's cock slit, scooping up his mate's essence. Waiting for the moment his mate reached the height of passion, Steel quickly inserted a finger into Jackson's puckered hole seeking the magic button and, when he pressed it, Jackson came apart with a screaming howl, shooting copious globs of cum down Steel's throat.

After several minutes of Jackson's panting, Steel gently licked his mate's cock clean, moving up to lie next to him. With his mate resting on his chest, Steel slowly carded his fingers through Jackson's soft brown hair. He could feel his mate's heart slowly return to normal and his breathing quiet down. When soft snores reached his ears, he closed his eyes and dozed off, loving the feeling of his mate in his arms.

Chapter 19

It was mid-morning before Jackson and Steel awoke and, after having a round of shower sex, they headed for the dining room, hoping to find some leftovers for breakfast. When Dakota heard them, he peeked in from the kitchen. "I have breakfast ready for you, so sit down and I'll bring it in."

Surprised, Jackson stared and said, "You don't have to wait on us, we can get it ourselves.'

"Shut up, bro. This is my mating gift, so stop the shit."

Jackson's face broke into a wide smile. "Okay, then. Thanks."

Dakota retreated to the kitchen as Steel took Jackson by the hand, leading him to the table. "That was nice of Dakota," said Steel in a very low voice.

"That's the way Dakota is. I really hope he can finish culinary school."

"I know sweetheart, and I promise I'll find a way for him to do so," murmured Steel, bringing Jackson's hand to his lips for a kiss.

Dakota came bustling in, loaded with scrambled eggs, bacon, sausages, toast, and hash browns. After setting the heavy tray down in front of them, he went back to the kitchen, bringing in orange juice and a cup of coffee for each. Turning to Steel, he said, "I know what Jackson likes for his breakfast, but I'm not sure if you like the same stuff, so if you want something else, let me know and I can whip it up in a minute."

Steel kept heaping his plate with the amazing food before him and, looking up at Dakota, said, "Thanks, but this is great. I'm willing to cook for Jackson but my food never turns out as good as this. You are a master of the kitchen."

Dakota's cheeks became rosy, soaking up the praise from his brother's mate. "Thanks," he mumbled, "just call if you need anything," and scurried back to the kitchen. Steel was puzzled that his compliment embarrassed Dakota.

Jackson, reading Steel's thoughts, explained, "It's because our father always put Dakota down for the time he spent with our mother in the kitchen. 'That was women's work'," Jackson growled, parroting his father. "I convinced my grandparents to release part of my trust fund early so I could pay for him to go to cooking school."

Steel smiled warmly at his mate, "You are the best brother. Did your father know?"

Jackson faltered for a second, then said softly, "Initially no. But then Zane accidently slipped up when we were home for the Long Night Moon Festival. My father went ballistic, saying so many hurtful things to Dakota that I packed up the car and took him with me to our grandparents for the rest of our vacation. We never spoke about it, but I know it still weighs heavily on his mind—the hostility he got from our father that night. Poor Zane. After seeing father's reaction, he couldn't apologize enough."

Learning about the careless remark from Zane that caused the problem for Dakota, Steel had second thoughts about forgiving Zane for the comment about his mate at yesterday's pack meeting. *Jackson is not an 'abomination' and Zane better correct his way of thinking fast or I'll do it for him. Zane is a brat, that is for sure.*

Suddenly, Steel heard Jackson talking, "Zane can be a brat but he really doesn't mean any harm. He's suffered the most from the massacre, but he's getting there. I'm sure he's sorry about what he said yesterday, so for me, babe, give him a chance."

Steel sighed, nodding. "You're too kind, but I love you all the more for it."

"Are you still going to meet your father this morning, well, late morning?" Jackson asked.

"No, I'll speak to him this afternoon."

As they finished eating, Logan arrived and joined them at the table, "Oracle and Maximus went to visit Mystia but should be back shortly. I cleared the room next to your office and put in a desk and chair but Steel needs to tell me what else he wants. Zane is eager to talk to you both and Jimmy heard about a Silver Point pack member a couple of towns away from us but doesn't know anything else. He said he'll nose around for more information."

Jackson thought for a moment. "Tell Zane I'll be in my office in ten minutes—he can meet with us then. Afterward, Steel can meet with you and I'll call Jimmy about Silver Point. Thanks for the update. How are our brothers this morning? Any fallout from yesterday's meeting?"

"No one said anything this morning so I think everything's cool," Logan smirked. "Well, as cool as it can be when you find out your Alpha is going to have a baby."

Jackson's cheeks turned pink. "Funny, funny. Let's start the day."

Logan watched Steel lean over and kiss Jackson. Then he gave him another one after they'd gotten up and, with his arm wrapped around his mate's waist, they sauntered out of the dining room. Logan felt alone again as he watched them go, wanting what his twin had for himself with every fiber of his being.

He could only hope it would happen soon. *Yeah, like that's going to happen—not with me hiding away here with only my brothers for company. If I'm ever going to have a chance at being as happy as Jackson, I need to get out and meet people. No way around it. Hmmm, but how? Need to think about it and come up with a plan.* He was still thinking about it as he left to find Zane.

~/~/~/~/~

Zane stood outside Jackson's office, nervously wiping his hands on his jeans. He was pretty sure Jackson would forgive him but he was not so sure about Steel. There were butterflies in his stomach because he knew Steel was in full protective mode towards his mate and was probably pissed off at him for hurting Jackson.

Shit, how stupid I am for not thinking before speaking. Isn't that what my mother always tried to teach me? Zane snorted to himself. *It seems I haven't learned that lesson yet. Well, here goes nothing.* Raising his hand, he knocked.

"Come in," called Jackson.

Zane entered. His brother and Steel were at Jackson's desk, looking at a computer screen. As he approached them, Jackson smiled. "Have a seat, Zane, I'll be with you in a sec." Pointing at the screen, he said to Steel, "These are the boundaries of the Fox River Pack land and over here are the Silver Point Pack lands. As you can see, they aren't adjoining but still relatively close." Jackson then asked Steel through their mind link if he was ready to hear what Zane had to say. Steel replied he was, so Jackson turned to Zane. "Logan told me this morning you wanted to see us."

Looking at Jackson and Steel, he saw nothing but calmness in their faces while waiting for him to speak. He looked down at his hands in his lap, thinking about all his brother had done for him since the day he was born and felt a new wave of shame washing over him. "I'm really sorry, Jackson. I acted like a jerk yesterday and I'm even sorrier I called you a name."

As he looked up at Jackson, he could feel tears welling up in his eyes but ignoring them, he went on, "I have no excuse for my actions and I'll accept any punishment you give me." Before Jackson could respond, Zane turned to Steel. "I'm very sorry I disrespected your mate like that and I promise I'll never do it again."

Jackson felt sympathy for his youngest brother and knew he regretted his actions but though he was proud of him for apologizing, he, as Alpha, couldn't allow Zane's conduct to go unpunished or his brother would never learn to control his anger.

"Thank you, Zane," he said. "I accept your apology and consider the matter closed. I know this pregnancy was a shock to you, as it was to me, but your behavior yesterday was out of line and a punishment will be given. As soon as I decide what it is, I'll let you know."

Steel squeezed Jackson's hand, then spoke. "Zane, I accept your apology this time, but make no mistake about my position. In the future, I will not tolerate any disrespect toward my mate or my child. I consider Jackson and our pup to be the greatest gifts from the Fates I could ever receive and I expect you to accept it in the spirit the Fates intended. Jackson is going to need all our support as he goes through this pregnancy and my goal is to make it as stress-free as possible, so I hope I can count on you."

Zane nodded. "Yes, I now feel that way, too. I'm sorry I didn't think before speaking yesterday but I'm really looking forward to being an uncle. I miss my younger siblings terribly and the Fates have seen fit to give me a nephew to love. So yes, count me in—whatever you need done for Jackson, I'll do."

"Thanks, I'll take you up on that some time," Steel said, smiling at Zane before leaning over to kiss Jackson. "I'll leave you both now and go find Logan so I can get my office set up."

Zane watched his brother's face, realizing he'd never seen him this happy. He now understood what Logan meant yesterday—about being envious of Jackson's mating. Then it hit Zane. *Shit, I'm also jealous of what Jackson has. Hell, I just have to trust Logan was right about someone special being out there waiting for me. The sooner the better.*

Jackson shifted his eyes from Steel to Zane as his mate left the room. "One more thing before you go, bro. In the next day or so, please tell Steel all you know about our father's dealings with Silver Point. Resolving our problem with that pack is top priority for all of us."

Zane stood up, nodding. "Sure thing, I've been thinking about what I know that could help Steel find a solution. I don't like living this way."

"None of us do," said Jackson, as Zane headed for the door.

~/~/~/~/~

Steel sat in his office a week later, looking at his father seated across from him. "Here's the background of the two packs involved in this dispute. Jackson's grandfather, Nathan, was the Alpha of the Fox River Pack. He had two sons, Josiah, the eldest, and Striker, Jackson's father. Josiah challenged Nathan and lost, so he left the Fox River Pack and formed the Silver Point Pack.

"After Nathan died, Striker assumed the title of Alpha of the Fox River Pack, met his fated mate and they had 13 children who include Jackson and his brothers. Meanwhile, Josiah, the Alpha of Silver Point Pack never met his fated mate but did mate with a woman so he'd have heirs. The Silver Point Pack had less territory than the Fox River Pack but there were no outward signs of trouble between the two."

Maximus pondered Steel's information. "Have we had any dealings with either pack?"

"I asked Slate to search our records but I haven't heard anything yet. Jackson and I feel the massacre had something to do with the Fox River Pack lands but just what, I haven't been able to figure out. I'm going to head out to look at the land Silver Point wants so badly. Like to join me?"

Maximus nodded, getting up. "First, let me tell your mother where we're going, then I'll meet you out front in a few."

Steel smirked. "Yup, I gotta do that with my mate, too."

~/~/~/~/~

Jackson looked up from his computer as Steel entered his office. "How's it going, babe? Anything you need?"

Steel walked over, and standing behind his mate, started massaging his neck. "Your muscles are tight. What have you been doing?"

"I'm trying to figure a way my brothers can resume their education, because sitting around waiting for death to come knocking at the door isn't doing them any good. They need to feel this nightmare will eventually end and I want them to focus on their future—which means continuing their classes," Jackson said, slumping back in his chair.

"Got it. Maybe I can help but let me think about it. It would help if I could find a solution to the Silver Point problem sooner than later. Regarding that, I just came in to tell you Dad and I are going to look at the Fox River Pack lands. I told him we thought the massacre occurred because Silver Point wanted the land so Dad's going to try to figure out why someone would kill for it. We'll be home before nightfall," Steel said, bending down and nibbling at his mate's ear.

Jackson turned toward him and Steel took the opportunity to kiss those full red lips he loved so much. Hearing Jackson moan, he deepened the kiss, his tongue seeking entry to his mate's mouth. As Jackson's lips parted, Steel thrust his tongue deep inside his mouth needing to explore every part of it before tongue-dueling with his mate. Steel's cock grew hard, desperate for his mate's touch, groaning at the pain of it being confined by his jeans.

Jackson was consumed by his mate's assault on his mouth. Reaching down, Steel palmed Jackson's dick through his jeans. *Oh, my gods*, he needed his mate to take him right now because all thoughts of work were out the window. Off in the distance he heard a door open and a very embarrassed voice say, "So sorry, I'll come back."

Steel pulled away and Jackson whimpered at the loss of his mate's mouth. He looked up with dazed eyes, slowly realizing Steel was talking to Maximus who had a twinkle in his eye. Jackson felt a full body flush hit him, starting at his toes and ending up at his now very red cheeks.

As Jackson tuned in to them, he realized Maximus wanted a map of the Fox River Pack land to take with them. "Sure, I can give you one," said Jackson, reaching to open a drawer. "Is there anything else?"

"No, see you out front, Steel," said Maximus.

Steel grinned down at Jackson. "See you later, babe," he said, leaning over to kiss his mate.

"Just a quick one this time or your father will be back wondering what's taking you so long," Jackson insisted.

Steel began to object but Jackson interrupted. "To make up for the short kiss, keep this thought in your head—tonight you can decide what we do," he said, pushing Steel toward the door.

"Hey, that's not fair. I'm going to be hard all day and what am I going to tell Dad if he asks about it?" whined Steel.

"Awww, don't worry, I think your father will know why you have a hard-on and if he doesn't, tell him your mate is torturing you," laughed Jackson.

Chapter 20

Driving to the Fox River Pack lands, Maximus noticed his son was grinning—and that was something new as Steel had always been a serious man. Maximus was curious if he was drawing the right conclusion about the reason for his son's change in demeanor. "Well son, how are you and Jackson getting along? Are you happy with your mate?" he inquired. "Jackson seems like a good person and he does look nice, but I think some of his brothers are even better looking."

Steel's jaw dropped, glaring at his father. "What the fuck is that supposed to mean? Jackson is the most beautiful person I've ever met. Are you trying to piss me off—because you're succeeding," snarled Steel. "He's perfect for me and is beyond good—kind, generous, charitable, loving, and fair-minded. He would give the shirt off his back if someone needed it."

Steel was getting worked up. "Look at how he handled Zane at the pack meeting. His response was measured and thoughtful, taking into account Zane's issues. What more can a pack want in a leader? Just the fact that he would sacrifice his own happiness for his pack tells you what kind of man he is. Why are you dissing my mate, Dad?"

Steel could hardly control his wolf during this tirade. He meant it when he told Jackson and Zane he wouldn't allow anyone to disrespect his mate and that included his parents.

Maximus placed his hand on Steel's forearm. "I meant no disrespect son. I was trying, in a rather foolish way, to see if your mate was responsible for the never-ending grin you wear these days. Do you love him already?"

"Yes, I do," said Steel, calming down. "So much it scares me sometimes when I think of him giving birth and all the complications that can occur. I don't know what I'd do if I lost him. He's my world, Dad," Steel murmured, as his mind went to a dark place.

"Steel, stop, right now. Nothing's going to happen—don't let fear rule your mind. Be strong for your mate and everything will work out in the end," Maximus said in a firm voice.

"Sorry. You're right," Steel said, unwilling to discuss his fears anymore and, changing the subject, announced, "Here's our turn. Do you see it on the map?"

"Yes, turn here," directed Maximus, "and then drive another two miles and we'll be at the edge of the pack lands."

After fifteen minutes of driving, Steel pulled off the dirt road into a clearing. Leaving the pickup truck, they looked around to get their bearings in relation to the map they held. Steel lifted his head and sniffed, murmuring, "We've got company—a wolf. He's close. Be careful. Jackson told me the land was deserted but… Let's move to the south of him so he won't catch our scent."

Maximus nodded, turning south, leading the way through the forest. While he was hiking, Steel looked around, trying to figure out what was so valuable about this land but, so far, he could see nothing more than old growth forest with plenty of wildlife. He knew from the map the Fox River land had a number of fields and it included a few foothills of the Western Mountains along the Fox River that the pack was named after. He waited to ask his father what he thought until they could find out more about the wolf who was trespassing.

Steel saw Maximus raise his right hand, signaling he was stopping and then his dad pointed at someone standing about seventy-five feet upwind from them. Steel looked at the wolf and let out a small gasp—there in front of them was the man from his last date before he'd found Jackson. "I know him, Dad," he whispered. Steel grabbed his father's arm, leading him some distance away before telling him who the wolf was.

"Why is he on this land?" asked Maximus.

"I don't know but I'm going to find out," replied Steel. "I'll lead this time, Dad."

Maximus grabbed Steel's arm. "Don't disclose the real reason we are here."

Nodding, Steel turned and hiked back to the wolf, making noise so they'd be heard. When they were within eyesight, the wolf turned to them with a guarded look on his face but then smiled when he saw Steel. "What a surprise," he said, "and a very pleasant one at that."

"Hi Khan, this *is* a surprise. I didn't expect to see anyone out here," Steel said, stopping in front of him.

"Oh, uhmm, I was looking for a place to build a house and someone told me about this land, so I came to check it out."

"Someone owns it?" asked Steel innocently. "I didn't realize that," he said as he turned to his father and said, "I guess my map reading skills are rusty. It seems we're trespassing."

"Oh, don't worry about that," Kahn reassured him, "the owner lives somewhere else, from what I understand."

"This sure is a beautiful area. How much land is for sale?"

Khan hesitated, "I-I-I don't know exactly."

"We better go now," Steel said, "since I want to get home before dark. See you around, Kahn."

"Bye," called Khan as Steel and Maximus turned to hike back to the pickup.

They didn't talk until they were in the truck, driving away. Then Steel shattered the silence. "What bullshit! Building a house! Land for Sale! All lies! But what I want to know is, who is this guy? What connection does he have to the Silver Point Pack?"

"Didn't you have lunch with him and talk about any of that?" asked Maximus.

"No, I knew once I met him, he wasn't my fated mate so I just wanted to eat and get out of there as fast as I could. Conversation was just small talk. All I know about him is he has no problem lying to my face," growled Steel.

"Do you think he's a member of the Silver Point Pack?"

"That's a fair assumption though I think we need more information to be absolutely sure." Turning to his father, Steel said, "I don't want to mention this to Jackson yet, Dad, until we find out for sure one way or the other. No sense worrying him."

"Are you sure about that? I have never found it a good idea to keep things from your mother."

"Nor have I, Dad," Steel chuckled. "Slate and I found that out when we were younger, trying to prevent Mom from discovering our exploits."

"Your mother would always tell me about your and Slate's effort to hide your adventures, but that's not what I meant, son. Jackson is your Alpha and you owe him full disclosure on anything that could affect the pack," warned Maximus.

"But he's pregnant and I won't have him upset over this. It might turn out to be nothing more than what Khan said he was doing," barked Steel, annoyed at his father's suggestion.

They both fell silent as Steel headed home. He didn't mean to snap at his father, but dammit, he was worried about what this extra stress might do to Jackson. His role was to ease his mate's life, not add to the problems he was dealing with on a daily basis.

But intuitively Steel knew his father had a valid point—he should tell his Alpha about the sighting of the man on Fox River Pack land. First, though, he wanted to do some research. Maybe his brother, Slate, would have some information for him that could put this issue to rest and get some justice for his mate.

~/~/~/~/~

Hoping for some news from his brother, Steel sat down at his computer, opening his email program. Sorting through the messages, he soon found what he was looking for and clicked on it.

"*Congratulations on your mating, dear brother of mine! I can't wait to meet your mate as Mom and Dad speak highly of him. Take a selfie of you two for me in the meantime. I found an application from the Silver Point Pack asking Dire Enterprises for funds to start a mining operation on land the Alpha Josiah claims he inherited after his brother, Striker, died. The funding has tentatively been approved, and will be released once they provide the required documents to complete the application. The main document needed is proof of title to the land. A warning, dear brother—the Silver Point pack has been notified of our tentative approval and the need for the proof of title, so guard your mate well. If this pack has done what your mate has claimed, then he is now in greater danger. Your brother, Slate. P.S. I have attached their application for you and Dad to review.*

Steel slumped back in his chair as stark terror struck his heart, followed by the rage of his wolf at the threat on his mate's life. This he absolutely needed to tell Jackson but first he must come up with a plan to neutralize this threat.

He sat there, going over different options, thinking about which his mate might accept. His mate would be angry to learn the reason for his family's death, but he also knew Jackson wouldn't take any measures against the Silver Point Pack that would require violence if it could be avoided.

Lost in thought, staring at the forest outside his windows, he didn't hear his father enter the office. So, when Maximus asked, "Have you heard from Slate?" Steel whirled around with surprise.

"Jeez, Dad, don't you knock anymore?"

"I did. What has you so deep in thought you didn't hear me?"

Steel threw a copy of his brother's email across the desk. "Read it and you'll understand." He waited until his father finished and then asked, "What do you think?"

Maximus studied his son. "Well, that explains why the massacre occurred. But what does Silver Point plan to mine?"

Steel handed his father the copy of the Silver Point Pack application, sitting back to wait for a response. He'd calmed down since first reading the email but was still agitated at Silver Point Pack's deceit.

Of course, Silver Point had no way of knowing his mate would be one of their prime targets. An involuntary shiver coursed down his back when he thought of his mate being in harm's way. Steel felt his restless wolf pacing back and forth, eager to hunt those who meant to hurt its mate.

Maximus sighed deeply, "This distresses me greatly, bringing back memories of the greed that consumed the Dire Wolf packs, fighting and killing for the treasure. I had hoped other wolves learned that an Alpha's greed only ends up harming the pack."

"It doesn't seem so," said Steel. "But what's really scary here is Silver Point almost got the money from us for their mining operation. You know it's not easy for wolves to produce titles to land so, as has happened in the past, our company might have waived this requirement. It's made me realize we might have to change some of our procedures to prevent this from happening again."

"I agree," said Maximus, "but I think that can wait. I'll tell Slate to put the Silver Point application on hold while you deal with the situation over here." Then he asked, "Are you going to tell Jackson about this?"

"Yes, I will, but first I want to come up with a game plan to recommend," said Steel.

"Good thinking. I assume that's what you were doing when I snuck up on you?" his father said, smiling.

"Yeah, I want Jackson to report the massacre to the Universal Paranormal High Council. I know my mate has told me it's his word against theirs but I think this needs to be made public. The High Council will investigate and it will take time, and during that period I'm hoping the Silver Point Alpha will call off his enforcers."

Steel paused for a moment in thought before continuing, "I also want to move the entire Blackwood Pack to my house. There's plenty of room and it's more isolated than where we are now. And finally, I want to hire a team of my own enforcers to patrol my land so my mate and his brothers are safe."

Maximus nodded, thinking about the measures Steel had proposed, decided to add one more. "I'm going to ask Slate to come here as additional backup. He's been after me to meet your mate, so it seems like a perfect time."

"Good idea," agreed Steel. 'Now let's go next door to see my mate and hear what he has to say about our plans." When they reached Jackson's office, Steel gave one knock before entering and once inside, walked over to his mate. "Hi babe, do you have time to talk? We have some information about the Silver Point Pack to share with you."

Jackson reached up, pulling Steel down for a kiss, murmuring against his mate's mouth, "I always have time for you, love." Then Jackson turned, acknowledging Maximus. "This must be serious if you're here. Is this about your visit to our pack lands?"

"Yes, in a way. I'll let Steel tell you."

"Babe, I asked Slate if our companies had any dealings with the Silver Point Pack and when I got back to my office this was waiting," Steel said. Handing the email to his mate, Steel watched closely while Jackson read it, seeing the exact moment red hot rage crossed his mate's face.

Chapter 21

"Are you telling me my family was killed because that asshole wanted our land for mining? That sonofabitch! He butchered men, women, and children—all because of greed? My mother and my younger brothers and sisters all slaughtered because he wanted the land? Sonofabitch!!! What's on our land that's worth killing for? Dammit, dammit, dammit!!!" yelled Jackson, anger burning into his heart as grief and frustration shook his body. He dropped his head into his hands, tears streaming down his face.

Steel gathered his mate in his arms, whispering words of love into Jackson's ear while rubbing his mate's back. He knew it was a lot for him to process—the senseless killing of his family and pack mates in the name of greed. Steel held Jackson until his tears stopped and his mate's breath only occasionally hitched.

Finally, Jackson sat up, embarrassed at falling apart in front of Maximus. Furtively wiping away tear streaks from his face, he turned toward his father-in-law, but Maximus wasn't there. Jackson looked questioningly at his mate. "Dad left the room because he felt you wouldn't want him to see you cry. He'll come back when you're ready to continue."

"I'm sorry about that," muttered Jackson.

"Babe, there's nothing to be sorry about. I was shocked when I read Slate's email, so I can only imagine how you felt when you finally found out. My wolf wants to hunt the Silver Point Pack down and make them pay for what they did to you," he said softly.

"I appreciate that, but I don't think that's the answer. First of all, I could never kill children and women as they did and, secondly, fighting would put my brothers in danger."

Steel nodded. "I knew that's how you'd feel, so I came up with a plan that doesn't include violence. Are you all right now? Can Dad come back in?" he asked.

"I'm okay, thanks, babe. Get your dad back in here and let's hear your proposal," Jackson said.

After hearing his son's voice calling him, Maximus walked in, smiling at Jackson. "Sorry for leaving but I needed to ask my wife a question."

"Okay, then let's continue," said Jackson, grateful for Maximus' sensitivity. He then looked at his mate, "Why does Silver Point want to mine on our land?"

"According to the application, the Fox River that runs through your land contains gold, and evidently quite a lot of it. It's in their application—here, have a look at it," said Steel, handing the paperwork to his mate.

"Gold? On our land? How would they know it was there?" asked Jackson.

"I'm not sure but they must have found it before the massacre took place. There's no proof but it's a reasonable assumption," replied Steel. "When I asked your brothers what they knew about the land, Zane told me your father had complained to his brother, Josiah, about their members trespassing on Fox River land."

"My uncle never took my father's complaints seriously, though," said Jackson, "because the two packs got along. We all knew the Silver Point members—they'd join us to celebrate the Long Night Moon Festival. Did Zane say more?"

“That’s all he knew,” Steel answered. “He didn’t think it was serious because he said your father and uncle were always bitching at each other.”

Jackson thought about it for a minute before saying, “On the surface, they seemed to get along but I always thought my uncle—who was the first-born—was pissed off that our father ended up as the Alpha of the Fox River Pack…though, I never heard that brought up.”

Then he asked Steel, “Okay, what’s the plan you want me to approve?”

“First, you need to file a formal complaint with the Universal Paranormal High Council and…”

“I know you’ve told me this before, but nothing has changed—it’s a case of ‘he-said, he-said.’ I have no proof Silver Point Pack is responsible, and if I file, my pack risks being exposed and discovered by their enforcers.”

“I’ve taken that into consideration,” said Steel, “and I still want the complaint filed because it might prompt Silver Point to do something that can be used against them. Next, I want everyone to move to my house. There’s enough room, it’s more remote, and I’ll hire a team of enforcers to provide security for you and your brothers.”

Jackson leaned back in his chair, thinking about Steel’s plan. “I have some questions before I can agree,” he said, pausing for a moment. “What do you hope the complaint about the massacre will do for us?”

“I think the Silver Point Alpha will pull back his enforcers because it won’t look good if the pack lodging the complaint is suddenly killed. But more importantly, I also hope it’ll buy us some time to build a case against Silver Point,” said Steel, waving off what he saw as the beginning of an objection from Jackson. "I know you think it's your word against theirs but when the word reaches the whole pack that a High Council investigation is taking place, I think some rats will want to jump off the sinking ship because the pressure will be too great."

"Okay," said Jackson, agreeing on that point, "but if the publicity will stop them in their tracks, why should we move to your home?"

"That's a back-up plan just in case some pack member starts feeling a little too much heat from the High Council's investigation. The house is plenty big enough and there's more than enough land for everyone to shift and take runs."

"Okay, let's say I agree with your reasoning—if your place is so remote and safe, why a team of enforcers?"

"That's my security blanket, babe. My wolf is very protective of you and our pup right now. So, with extra manpower, my wolf and I can relax more and I can give you the support you need during your pregnancy," growled Steel.

Jackson turned to Maximus, "Do you agree the Blackwood Pack should follow Steel's plan?"

"I do, and I am going to add one more item to his plan. I'll have Slate come here to help with security."

Jackson paused, thinking about Steel's plan and what it would mean to his brothers. He couldn't deny he was quite shaken about what Steel had told him tonight. And he knew now without a shadow of doubt, his uncle would never stop until he could eliminate the last living thread to that land.

Would it be better to move to Steel's house? It certainly was big enough but would my brothers feel comfortable there? They'd made a home here and everyone is settled in, even Zane, though that's still a work in progress. What will the move do to his brother's fragile equilibrium? Would Zane have a setback because of another change?

As Jackson sat mulling it over, he heard a knock on the door and Logan stuck his head in. "Oh sorry, didn't know you had a meeting. I'll come back later."

"No, come in Logan. Steel found out why Silver Point killed our family," said Jackson, handing his brother the email and application, then waited until Logan read them.

"Sonofabitch!"

"My reaction too."

"What are you going to do?"

Turning to his mate. "Babe, tell Logan what you propose for the Blackwood Pack."

Logan sat next to Maximus as Steel told him about the plan to handle the Silver Point Pack issue. Logan listened intently, contemplating all the points Steel made. *If it means more protection for his brothers, then hell yes,* but he knew the move would be unsettling, especially for Zane. *Is the tradeoff worth it?* Logan turned it around in his head several times before looking at Jackson. "Are you going to do it?"

Jackson nodded affirmatively. "Do you think it's a good idea?"

"Yes," Logan answered, "even with the drawbacks. I always thought we'd have to move at some point so this looks like a golden opportunity—to move to a ready-made house instead of building one like we had to do here."

Jackson's face softened with relief. "I'm glad you agree with my decision. Anytime I can give my brothers more protection it's a no-brainer, even though I know it'll be hard on some of them," he said. "Now, what did you want before I got you side-tracked?"

"Dakota needs supplies and he wondered who you wanted to send to get them."

"Have him prepare his list and Steel and I will go tomorrow morning after I stop at Jimmy's to tell Mystia what I've decided," replied Jackson. "Now that everything's settled, let's have dinner. I'm starving."

Waking up the next morning, Steel felt his cock encased in a hot wet mouth. Rolling onto his back, he lifted the covers, looking down at the most amazing sight that had appeared only in his dreams. Steel groaned at the wantonness of seeing Jackson's full red lips sucking his cock as if it were the best lollipop his mate ever savored. Licking, sucking, then a twist of his tip by his mate's hand while Jackson tongue-fucked his slit before deep-throating him. Steel moaned at the sensations, his fisted hands twisting the sheets.

His mate was deliberately teasing him with his unhurried actions. Steel lifted his hips to gain friction so he could come but his mate grabbed him, holding him down while continuing the maddeningly slow torture that Jackson obviously was an expert at. Frustrated, he was reduced to whimpering for relief, tossing his head from side-to-side. He was going to explode if Jackson kept this up. Finally, reduced to begging for release, Steel moaned, "Please...move dammit...more, please more."

Jackson glanced up at his mate, seeing his unfocused, lust-filled eyes, knowing it was time. Steel had been reduced to jelly—that was his intention. Jackson grabbed his mate's balls, gently rolling them in his hand while increasing his speed of sucking, taking Steel's cock deep into his throat repeatedly. Steel screamed and Jackson lifted his head so just Steel's cock tip was in his mouth, catching his mate's jism on his tongue and holding it in his mouth.

As Steel came back to earth, he pulled his mate up on his chest, gazing at Jackson's very swollen lips that were curved into a smile.

Jackson moved slowly up to his mate's lips, kissing them softly, waiting for Steel to open his mouth. When his mate complied, Jackson thrust his cum-covered tongue in, coating his mate's mouth with his own essence.

Holy Fuck! That was the sexiest thing anyone had ever done to Steel during a blow job. Swallowing his cum, Steel thrust his tongue into Jackson's mouth, sweeping through it to seek every bit of it he could find, loving the taste of it mixed with Jackson's unique flavor.

Slowly, Jackson pulled back, staring down at his mate, "I love you, babe," he crooned, his fingers carding Steel's long hair. He lowered his lips to Steel's neck, gently sucking, leaving a bruise behind.

"Did you just give me a hickey?" growled Steel.

Jackson had his nose buried in his mate's neck, inhaling deeply, knowing as long as he lived, he would never get enough of that intoxicating scent. "Yup," he mumbled, thrilled that his mate now wore his mark.

Steel smiled. He'd wear that hickey proudly, knowing his mate was telling all who saw it—*this man is mine!*

~/~/~/~/~

They finally made it to the dining room where everyone had begun to eat.

"Wow, look, they're only a little late for breakfast today," crowed Zane.

At the sound of laughter, Jackson's cheeks turned pink. Steel whispered in his mate's ear, "But it was so worth it, *mo chroí,* wasn't it?" giving Jackson's ear a quick lick.

Dakota spoke up, saving Jackson from further embarrassment, "There's more in the kitchen, so eat up."

After finishing his breakfast, Jackson poured another cup of coffee for Steel and himself before addressing his brothers. "Steel and I are heading out in a few minutes to pick up the supplies Dakota needs, so make sure if you want anything, it's on the list. And a heads-up, Dakota—Steel's brother Slate will be visiting us soon, so add him to the number of people you'll be feeding." Then he said, "When I get back, there'll be a short meeting about some decisions I've made."

Cody turned to Logan after Jackson and Steel left. "Fess up bro, what's Jackson going to tell us? I know you know, so spill it."

Logan took a sip of coffee, then slowly lowered his cup to the table, as he glanced at Cody. "What makes you think I know? And, even if I did, why would I go against our Alpha to tell you when he obviously wants to be the one." Logan shook his head. "I think you better get your work done by the time Jackson gets back instead of wasting your time badgering me about something that's never gonna happen. Now, if you'll excuse me, I got work to do," he growled, rising and leaving the room.

The remaining brothers looked at each other in astonishment at Logan's reaction to Cody and, when it seemed no one could explain it, they got up and left the room to do their chores.

Chapter 22

Steel parked by the gas pump after pulling into Jimmy's. He turned to Jackson, "Babe, why don't you go see Mystia, while I fill up. I'll join you after I'm done."

"Okay," Jackson said, getting out of the car. "Jimmy will put the gas on our account so don't worry about paying." Shutting the car door, he saw Jimmy approach him with his arms outstretched, ready to envelop him in one of his all-encompassing hugs.

"Good to see you. Mated life appears to agree with you," Jimmy said, thumping Jackson on his back several times. "Anything new?"

Jackson stepped back, warily glancing at Steel who was now frowning at seeing another wolf touch his mate. "Everything's good. I just stopped by to talk to Mystia. Is she here?"

"Sure, she's in the house."

Jackson walked around the building that served as the local convenience store and over to the steps leading to Jimmy and Mystia's home. He'd just put his foot on the first step, when the door swung open and Mystia appeared.

"Jackson, what brings you over here? I would have thought you were still buried in your mating bed. Are your brothers all right?"

Jackson hurried up the steps right into Mystia's arms, returning her hug with one of his own. "My brothers are fine, but I have news about the Silver Point Pack I want to share," said Jackson.

Mystia ushered Jackson into her living room, motioning him to sit down. As she sat facing him, she said, "Tell me, *mon petit loulou*, what is this news?"

Jackson told her what Steel had found out. He was grateful she didn't interrupt because it was hard enough just repeating the story. When he reached the end, she dropped her head and Jackson saw tears trickling down her cheeks, falling to the floor.

"*Mon petit loulou,* I'm so sorry. I know you must still feel the pain as if it had just happened." Then Mystia looked up at him. "What do you plan to do about it?"

Just as Jackson was about to answer, they heard a knock at the door. "Ah, that would be Steel," Jackson said.

"Come in," said Mystia quietly.

Steel walked in, sat down next to his mate, then grabbed his hand, giving it a light squeeze. "Hi babe," said Jackson. "I was just going to tell Mystia about your plan, but since you're here, why don't you go ahead."

Listening to Steel talk, Jackson wondered how Mystia would get to Steel's place if he needed her help with the baby. That was his biggest worry about moving away from her. He knew he'd need her when the baby came but how would she ever get to their new home in time? As Jackson tuned back into the conversation, he realized Steel asked him something. "I'm sorry, just thinking," he apologized. "What did you ask?"

"I asked if you have any other issues you want to bring up to Mystia?"

Jackson smiled. "I have tons of questions about my pregnancy but we can talk about that later." Turning to Mystia, he asked, "I'll need you when the baby is ready to be born. Is there a way I can have instant access to you once we move away?"

Mystia smiled, “I have already thought about that. I’m going to install a portal I can use to shuttle back and forth between here and your new home. I won’t be more than a few minutes away from you.”

Steel could feel his mate’s relief when he heard Mystia’s answer and it reminded him he needed to speak with his mother about having a doctor at the birth. And maybe setting up an operating and recovery room in his house just in case it was needed□he was determined his mate and pup would have everything possible to insure a safe delivery.

As soon as they returned home, he had to fill out the papers for Jackson to sign and then fax them off to the Universal Paranormal High Council. Once the complaint was filed, the Silver Point Alpha would receive a call informing him about it that would, he hoped, stop all actions against Jackson and his brothers. He wanted, no *needed,* his mate and pup to be safe. Steel stood when he saw Mystia and Jackson getting up and moved towards the door. A hug and a kiss from her, and they were on their way.

~/~/~/~/~

Steel drove to North Ridge, a mid-sized town about an hour south of where the Blackwood Pack lived. Jackson hadn’t been there for a number of years and was surprised at how much it had grown. As Steel parked at the supermarket, Jackson retrieved Dakota’s list from his pocket.

“You know, I would have gladly gone fishing for the list,” smirked Steel, after seeing his mate’s hand wiggle its way down the pocket of his skinny jeans.

“You behave yourself,” Jackson said, swatting Steel’s arm. “I don’t want to walk through the store with a raging hard-on.”

“Why not? I love that look on you,” leered Steel.

Ignoring his mate, Jackson got out of the Ranger Rover and grabbed a shopping cart. “If we split the list, we’ll be done in half the time,” Jackson suggested.

“Sounds good to me.”

Jackson headed to the dairy case first, while Steel hit the meat department. Jackson was enjoying himself as he went up and down the aisles, picking out items on the list. He decided to get extras since he wanted to make sure they had enough for Steel’s brother. Jackson figured the food would never be wasted considering how many wolves were now living at his pack house.

He hoped Slate would like him once they met. He didn’t want to be a point of contention between them, especially since Steel had been so wonderful and understanding about his need to lead and protect his brothers.

He had finished his half of the list and was looking for Steel, when he heard his mate’s voice coming from the next aisle. Heading for it, he suddenly realized the other voice sounded familiar but he couldn’t place it. He rounded the end of the aisle and came face to face with his worst nightmare—a member of the Silver Point Pack. He slowly began backing out of the aisle but before he made his escape, Steel looked up and saw him. Jackson’s eyes widened, shaking his head, sending a message to Steel through their mind link warning his mate about the guy he was talking to.

Panic crossed Steel’s face before he was able to school his features. Then grabbing the man’s arm just as he was turning to see what Steel was looking at, he said something to him, pulling him in the opposite direction.

Jackson's mind heard Steel command him to leave the cart near the checkout and go to the Rover immediately. He assured his mate he'd keep the Silver Point Pack member busy in the wine aisle until he heard he was safely inside the car.

Steel and the man he'd pulled into the wine aisle began to discuss the merits of various wines. Finally, when Jackson assured him he was okay and lying down on the back seat of the car, Steel took a deep breath in relief, and bid the man adieu.

After checking out, Steel rushed to load the car so he could get his mate out of town. What a bad-ass idea to come here; he should have headed east instead. *Shit, shit, and more shit*! He jumped into the Rover, locking all the doors. Shaken to the core at how close they'd come to putting his mate and unborn child in danger, he started the vehicle, carefully backing out of his parking spot. He looked at his mate through the rearview mirror, "Are you all right?"

"Yeah, I am. I don't think he saw me and I didn't see any other members on the way to the car," Jackson responded. "Why were you talking to a Silver Point Pack member and how do you know him?"

"Let me get out of town and then you can move up here, okay?" replied Steel, driving towards the outskirts of North Ridge.

After fifteen minutes had passed, Steel turned into a strip mall, stopping behind the stores. Putting the car in park, he turned to Jackson, "It's safe for you to move up front now."

Jackson sat up, looking out the windows. His mate had pulled in behind some dumpsters and no one was around, so he got out and slid in beside him. Turning to face him, Jackson waited for the explanation he'd been promised.

Steel thought about his father's warning about keeping secrets and now here it was, ready to bite him in the ass. "Babe, do you remember the day I found you at the side of the road?" asked Steel.

That wasn't what Jackson expected, but he decided to go along. "Sure, but there wasn't anybody with you."

"I know. But I had met someone in L.A. for lunch through a dating service for paranormals. I'd been looking for my fated mate for some time and I was getting desperate. So, when an acquaintance suggested the 'Out Of This World' dating service, I signed up. I was matched with several wolves and Khan—he was the man in the supermarket—was the last one I met with before I met you. He wasn't for me and I couldn't wait for lunch to be over."

"Okay, but I heard him say something about your father."

Oh shit, Steel was hoping to avoid telling his mate about meeting Khan on the Fox River Pack land. Well, better to just rip off the band-aid quickly. "When Dad and I went to see the land belonging to your pack we met Khan walking around on it. I asked what he was doing and he told me he was looking for a place to build a house. Honey, I never knew he was a member of the Silver Point Pack, I swear."

Jackson took it all in silently before asking, "I believe you, but why didn't you tell me you saw someone on our land?"

"Because I didn't want to worry you about it until I had more information. At that time, I didn't know Silver Point wanted to mine gold on the land," replied Steel.

"Don't give me that crap," Jackson said angrily. "I'm your Alpha, and you know what you did was wrong. I decide whether something is important to the pack, not you. So, stop the bullshit. I won't have you making decisions for me.

"You may be the dominant wolf in our personal relationship—and I have no problem submitting to you—but you are *not* the Alpha of the Blackwood Pack, so you need to get your head straight about your role in this pack," snapped Jackson.

"What's more, Steel, you put me in danger today." Jackson heard his mate gasp, but continued, "If you'd told me about Khan that day, I'd have told you he was my cousin. I don't know if he took part in the massacre but at the very least, he knew it was going to happen!"

Jackson liked some of his cousins but he didn't like most of the Silver Point Pack because he always sensed a streak of cruelty running through them. But who he liked or didn't was moot now, since nobody could be trusted in that pack anymore.

Steel was horrified□his mate was right. He'd put Jackson and his brothers in danger by not telling him about Khan. If he'd done what his father had advised and not kept quiet, none of this would have happened. It was only by pure luck his mate was able to get away before he was discovered. *What a clusterfuck! And I've no one to blame but myself.*

"You're right." he said, sighing heavily. "I'm sorry and I promise to tell you everything from now on, babe." He reached over and put his hand over his mate's hand, needing to feel close to Jackson. He hoped his mate would forgive him for his mistake.

Jackson was still fuming inside even though he knew Steel was just trying to protect him. But this was the closest he'd come to a member of the Silver Point Pack since the massacre and even though Khan didn't see him, the whole episode brought back the fears that had taken root in his heart after he heard about it.

What made it worse was that only yesterday he'd found out why Silver Point killed his family. His anger over their motives was still too fresh and hadn't settled yet. Jackson wondered if Khan participated in the killings; in his heart, he hoped not.

He, Kahn, and Logan were all about the same age and became close as they grew up. Jackson knew his cousin was supposed to be away at school when the massacre occurred but now wondered if Khan came home early to take part in it.

Even if Kahn wasn't one of the killers—did he know what was being planned? Jackson huffed. As if that mattered, because if Khan knew and did nothing to warn Jackson's father, then he was just as guilty as those who did the actual butchery.

As they drove on, Jackson intertwined his fingers with Steel's, drawing his mate's hand to his mouth and kissing it. He loved him with every fiber of his body, realizing if he continued to be angry over Steel's actions, he'd be guilty of hurting his mate over an innocent mistake.

His mate had apologized and Jackson hoped Steel learned his lesson about not keeping him in the dark. Turning, he smiled and looked at his mate. "Well, luckily we escaped by the hair on our chinny-chin-chins!" he giggled. Steel started to laugh and the tension broke.

Chapter 23

Steel appreciated his mate's effort to lighten the mood between them on the way home after what could have been a disaster. But the episode had strengthened his resolve to question everything that might endanger his mate and unborn pup. Driving up to the pack house, he felt the move to his land couldn't happen fast enough. He only hoped his mate thought the same.

Cody, Colton, and Carson were sitting on the porch drinking beers. Steel got out and opened Jackson's door for him. "You guys here to help carry in the mountain of food we got?" Steel joked. The brothers grinned at each other and Cody yelled back, "Nah, we thought we'd just watch you get your exercise today. Ya know, keep you strong for the bedroom activities we hear at night."

Jackson's ear tips turned pink and before Steel could reply, he said, "Don't worry, bros, we got this covered. I guess you need more chores to do if you have all this free time to sit around drinking beers in the middle of the afternoon." Jackson turned, reaching to take a bag from his mate, but before he could, the three brothers pushed them both aside, grabbing bags from the back of the Range Rover. "You guys go in," Cody said, "we got this."

~/~/~/~/~

Steel and Jackson were sitting in the den, waiting for everyone to come in for the short meeting. One by one, the brothers arrived, claiming their favorite places. When they were all seated, Jackson began.

"As you know, Steel has been investigating the Silver Point Pack, trying to figure out what was so valuable about our land they felt they had to kill for it. Well, he's found the answer." Jackson handed Logan copies of Slate's email with the application which he passed out to his brothers. Jackson waited while they read the documents. The reactions were swift in coming.

"Those sons of bitches!!!"

"Is this for real??"

"We have to kill them!!!"

"What the fuck???"

"Why???"

Jackson heard his brothers heatedly talking over and to each other. He gave them time to vent their emotions then, holding up his hands, said, "Enough." After they fell silent, he spoke. "I know how you feel but we're not going to kill them—at least not now. We wouldn't stand a chance against Silver Point—they're a much larger pack. Instead, I've decided on a different course of action.

"Tomorrow, I'll be faxing a complaint to the Universal Paranormal High Council against the Silver Point Pack for the massacre of the Fox River Pack. As soon as it's received, our uncle will get a call from the Council informing him of the complaint." Jackson looked at each of his brothers before saying, "That should make him back off about hunting us, at least until this is resolved." Pausing to see if his brothers had any questions and, when none were forthcoming, he continued. "In addition, according Slate's email, since he feels we're in even more danger than before, we'll be moving to Steel's compound. The house is big enough for all of us and he's going to hire a squad of enforcers to patrol his land so no intruders can get close to any of us."

Cody exchanged glances with Colton and Carson then asked, "Why can't we stay here and the enforcers patrol this land?"

Dakota broke in before Jackson could answer. "Is there a kitchen there outfitted like ours?"

Jackson answered Dakota first. "Yes, you'll find everything you need in Steel's kitchen." Then he hesitated slightly before going on, because he knew what he was about to say would affect Zane the most. "Cody, today while we were shopping, I almost ran into Khan, our cousin. And Steel tells me he and Maximus ran into him on the Fox River Pack land when they were there. While one time might be a coincidence, two times is a pattern—and one I don't like. Steel's land is further north and his house is surrounded by 200,000 acres which are fenced. That's a safer place for us until this mess is sorted out by the High Council."

As Zane heard his brother talk about running into a Silver Point pack member, his body started to shiver. Logan move close to him, putting his arm around him and murmured in his ear, "Zane, calm down. Steel and his family won't let anything happen to us."

"I know, but this just brings back feelings I had when I found out about the massacre, even though I've worked hard to bury that," whispered Zane.

Jackson looked over with a raised eyebrow at Logan. His brother was talking softly to Zane, probably trying to reassure him that everything would be all right. Damn his uncle! Damn him for making Zane worry about every change in his life when he should be footloose and fancy-free, having a good time. As Logan talked to Zane, Jackson could see some of the tension leave his brother's body; he was obviously reassured by what Logan was saying.

“When are we going to move?” asked Carson.

“Within the next few days,” said Jackson.

“Can we take our stuff with us?” asked Cody.

Mind-talking to his mate, Steel asked if he could answer this one, and after receiving approval, he answered Cody. “Yes, you can. Pack a bag with only the items you need for a couple of days and pack the rest of your things in boxes. After all of you are at my house, I’ll have a moving company pick up your stuff.”

“Okay, one other thing,” said Jackson. “Steel’s brother will be staying with us indefinitely at our new home in order to help with security.” He looked around and, seeing no more questions forthcoming, said, “Okay, goodnight then. I’ll see you all in the morning.”

Steel took his mate’s hand, pulling him toward him for a kiss. “Goodnight, everyone,” Steel said, ushering his mate out of the den and up to their bedroom.

~/~/~/~/~

Khan watched his father pace the room, anger radiating off him in waves. Josiah suddenly stopped in front of him. “Do you know for sure the wolf you scented was your cousin Jackson?”

“Yes, Dad, I’d know his scent anywhere. He’s with a guy I met for a date named Steel. But I told you, I don’t know where either of them went after they left the store. When I first met Steel in the store, I didn’t realize another wolf was there because Steel’s scent is so strong. But after he left the store, I could pick up the faint scent of Jackson. Both scents ended at the same spot in the parking lot,” explained Khan.

"I must find him because his brothers will be with him. At least we know he is still alive. Thanks, son, I'll take it from here," said the Alpha of the Silver Point Pack.

~/~/~/~/~

The complaint had been filled out by Steel and was awaiting Jackson's signature. Reading it over several times, he hesitated signing it, because once he did, everything would change. But would it be for the better? That was the question Jackson kept asking himself.

His brothers would be endangered because the document stated they were living. He and his unborn pup would be exposed to the evilness of his uncle, the one who ordered his death and the deaths of his brothers. Inhaling deeply, Jackson reached for his pen. In the end, there was no choice; he owed his brothers a chance at more than living a half-life, because when he thought about it, that wasn't any life at all.

His mate came in just as Jackson put down the pen. "Is it ready to fax off? I want it to get there before the end of the day."

"Yup, just signed it, so here you go," replied Jackson, handing the sheaf of papers to Steel. "When will you hear back from the High Council that the Alpha of Silver Point has been notified?"

"Hopefully, later today if they can reach him, otherwise probably tomorrow. Do you want to start packing now? My muscles are available for you to use any way you want," said Steel with a leer.

Jackson laughed. "Sure, let's pack. The sooner that's done, the sooner we can move and get settled in our new home."

Josiah angrily drummed his fingers on the desk while waiting for Rudy, his second in command. A series of staccato knocks on his door had him shouting, "Come in!"

Rudy entered, walking almost casually over to his Alpha's desk. He didn't have to wait long to find out why he was summoned. "Khan got a bead on Jackson but lost him in North Ridge. He was at a supermarket with a wolf named Steel but by the time Khan figured out his cousin was with the wolf, they'd both left in a car. I need you to find him and his brothers fast because I need the title to that land."

"Did Khan know in which direction they went?" asked Rudy.

"No, but they can't be far. I want all of them dead by next week. This fuck-up has to be fixed and I'm running out of patience," snarled Josiah.

"I need more men to search in order to meet your deadline," said Rudy.

"Use any many as you need. Just get the job done," barked Josiah.

It was moving day and Jackson was eager for everyone to get on the road. Steel organized a caravan of all the different vehicles the Blackwood Pack owned. Even Oracle and Maximus were enlisted to help. Jackson looked around his bedroom, remembering how he'd felt when the pack house was finally built and they were no longer living in tents. *Yeah, that was an experience but we all came through it and my pack is stronger for it.*

Picking up his suitcase, he headed downstairs only to be met by Steel who promptly took the suitcase from him. Jackson sighed; his mate was becoming more protective each passing day. Walking into the dining room, he was immediately assaulted by the smells of cooking bacon. He stopped short, feeling his stomach do a quick roll and then right itself. That was weird, thought Jackson, continuing to his chair at the head of the table.

Sitting down, he listened to his brothers' chatter floating over the table, most of which pertained to their new home. The only two that seemed a bit restrained were Carson and Zane but for very different reasons—Carson, because as an Alpha wolf, he was heading into a much stronger wolf's territory, and Zane because he just didn't like changes of any kind. But today, at least, both of them showed some excitement for what was about to happen.

Dakota brought in the rest of the food and everybody dug in. For the first time since he could remember, Jackson didn't take any bacon. In fact, every time he got a whiff of it, his stomach did the roll thing. Desperate for some meat, he heaped his plate with sausages instead, hoping his stomach would like those better. As a wolf, he never got sick, but something was off today. He managed to finish his breakfast, but just barely. He wondered if the move was causing his anxiety, and then huffed—of course it was. His brothers were going to be out in the open for the first time since they'd gone into hiding.

Once the stores of food were packed up and put into one of the cars, Jackson and his brothers stood in the den, surveying their home.

"I'm going to miss this place," said Cody, his brothers all murmuring in agreement.

"Well, I'm looking forward to my new kitchen," Dakota said excitedly, "Steel told me whatever it didn't have, I could get for it."

"Huh, I had to make that promise if I wanted to keep enjoying your delicious meals," joked Steel.

"Well, let's get this show on the road," said Jackson, moving to the front door. He felt sad his pup wouldn't be raised in the home he and his brothers built; it was a happy place because of the love they shared between them. He locked the door, giving the key to his mate.

Each brother got into the vehicle assigned to him; Jackson's was the one behind the truck Steel was driving. Maximus and Oracle were driving behind Jackson. The way his mate organized the caravan, Jackson had a Dire Wolf in front and two behind as protection. He considered it overkill but there was no way to dissuade Steel.

Chapter 24

Jackson's brothers got a look at their new home as the caravan drove through the security gate at Steel's compound. One by one, each brother parked his vehicle and got out, looks of amazement and wonder on their faces as they saw the size of their new home.

Smirking, Jackson understood completely, remembering how he'd felt when Steel first brought him here for their claiming. While Steel was giving his brothers a quick overview of his land, Jackson suddenly bent over, clutching his belly and throwing up his breakfast while moaning in pain.

Steel was at his side instantly, along with Colton. As his mate started to fall, Steel lifted Jackson up in his arms, rushing inside. Placing him on a sofa, Steel knelt down next to his mate and, holding his hand, asked, "*Mo chroí*, what's the matter? Are you in pain?"

Colton put his hand on Steel's shoulder. "Steel, let me see him."

Steel felt Colton trying to move him from his mate, but he wasn't going anywhere. Finally, Cody, Carson, and Dakota managed to shove Steel to the end of the sofa where he could continue to touch Jackson.

Colton knelt down, putting his hand on his brother's belly and pushing in on different spots. "Logan, grab my medical bag out of my car for me. Dakota, bring Jackson a glass of water and a cool wet towel." By this time, Oracle had joined the group and Colton turned to her. "How long is a Dire Wolf pregnancy? I tried to research it but found nothing."

She leaned over the back of the sofa, put her hand on Jackson's belly and answered, "It runs about six months—faster than a human pregnancy because the fetus grows more rapidly. Jackson is about a month into his pregnancy, and…" she said, continuing to examine him, "everything feels as it should."

"That's my conclusion," Colton said, turning to Steel, "has Jackson experienced any morning sickness yet?"

"I don't know, I don't think so," answered Steel.

"Colton," rasped Jackson. "I can answer your questions."

Dakota came back into the room with a glass of water and a wet towel at the same time Colton's medical bag arrived with Logan. Colton grabbed a thermometer from his bag, sticking it into Jackson's mouth. "Don't talk," he ordered, taking the water and towel from Dakota. Removing the thermometer from Jackson's mouth, he looked at the reading, pronouncing, "Your temperature is normal," and pushed Jackson down when he tried to sit up. "First, I need some answers, bro, before I let you get up," he said. "Have you vomited since you got pregnant?"

"No, but my stomach felt queasy at breakfast this morning," answered Jackson.

"Babe, why didn't you tell me?" Steel asked.

Jackson heard the hurt in his voice. "Because it passed and I didn't want to worry you about it."

"But I need to know everything you feel during your pregnancy so I can be prepared, *mo chroí*, that's my job," said Steel.

Jackson knew his mate was right, but damn, it would be hard since he was so used to handling everything by himself. "I promise from this point on, you'll know everything, even the unpleasant stuff," Jackson said, lifting his mate's hand to his lips and kissing it. Then he looked at his brother. "So, what's your diagnosis?"

Colton smiled. "I think you've had what is commonly known as morning sickness but it can happen at any time during the day. Oracle and I agree your pup is fine and all you need to do is take it easy for the rest of the day."

Steel pushed Jackson down when he started to sit up. Growling, "'Rest today,' is what your brother ordered and I will handle everything else. I only want to see you on your feet when you need to use the bathroom and then only with me by your side. Got it?"

Jackson loved it when his mate went all dominant on him in the bedroom but now it seemed he liked it at other times as well. "Got it. Do nothing and bathroom breaks only if you accompany me," he said, smiling.

"Okay then, good to know you can follow instructions," smirked Steel. He stood up and looked at everyone else. "I've assigned all of you bedrooms. After you see them and want to switch with anyone, go ahead. If there's a problem with a particular room, let me know. We're all in the North Wing on the second floor. I saved the South Wing for the enforcers," he said, handing out room assignments. "Mom and Dad, I gave you a downstairs guest suite with its own sitting room so I hope that's okay."

The brothers studied the map Steel had drawn for finding their bedroom assignments.

"Well, go find your rooms," commanded Steel.

Watching his brothers excitedly tease each other about who was next to whom, Jackson laughed as a mass of bodies rushed by them in a mad dash to see who got to their bedroom first. Steel's parents followed more slowly. Chuckling at the antics of his brothers as they raced to be first to claim their room, he said to Steel, "My brothers will never change when it comes to competitiveness—I think it's ingrained in their DNA somehow."

Steel sat down on the coffee table, giving his mate a sip of water, then cleaned his face with the wet cloth. His hand reached out to hold Jackson's while his eyes focused with love on his mate. "I was scared, *mo chroí*, when you threw up and were in pain—so scared that something was wrong with you and our pup."

"I'm sorry," said Jackson. "I should have told you I was feeling sick at breakfast, but then it went away and I really didn't want to worry you on a day when you had so many other worries."

"I understand, but I'm going to insist from now on you let me be the judge of what I want to worry about."

"Promise," vowed Jackson.

~/~/~/~/~

It had been a couple of days since Jackson vomited and he soon learned that his morning sickness came like clockwork at lunchtime every day. Steel had taken to stuffing him with food at dinner, hoping he'd have enough to last him until the next evening. Other than that, and an over-abundance of concern by his mate about every move he made, Jackson was feeling better except for being tired, probably the aftermath of the move and making a decision about what to do about the Silver Point Pack's actions.

Today the moving van would arrive and Jackson was looking forward to having his things once more in place around him. Steel made him promise not to unpack anything; all he had to do was to tell Steel where to put the items in the boxes. He could certainly get used to this pampering being heaped on him. Rolling over, he studied his mate while he was sleeping and could not resist licking the side of his beautiful jaw. Steel stirred, opened one eye, blurrily saw his mate and bestowed on Jackson the most beautiful just-awake smile Jackson had ever seen. Licking his mate's lips and pushing in a little, Jackson was trying to make Steel open his mouth so he could thrust his tongue in to scoop up his essence.

Steel rolled over onto his back, dragging Jackson on top of him. Opening his mouth, he sucked Jackson's tongue inside his mouth, and ran his hands over his mate's body, touching every special spot he knew would cause arousal in his mate. Jackson was moaning as his excitement grew, humping Steel's cock. Steel, in turn, reached down between their bodies for Jackson's cock, stroking it while giving occasional twists below the tip.

Steel could feel the need and passion grow in his mate as he sped up, sucking Jackson's tongue and matching it to the speed of his hand. Reaching down between Jackson's cheeks, he ran his fingertip over the puckered skin of his mate's hole before pushing in to find his special gland. Then, Jackson's body stiffened, yelling Steel's name as his cock exploded, cum gushing over Steel's hand and onto his stomach.

Steel gently rolled Jackson on his back, grabbing his t-shirt from the floor to clean them off. Then, lying next to Jackson, Steel's hand gravitated to his mate's belly, covering it as to protect the growing pup from harm. "You know, I think your belly has a slight rise to it," murmured Steel, rubbing it gently.

"You think?" Jackson asked, his hand moving down to rest on Steel's.

"Yup, and I can't wait to see your belly big and round with our pup," whispered Steel.

"Yeah, well, I remember how often my mother's back ached during the last months of her pregnancies, so I'm not sure I'm eager for that," grumbled Jackson.

"Ahh, *mo chroí*, I promise to give you a backrub anytime—in addition to something else to make you smile," crooned Steel, nuzzling Jackson's neck.

"Oh, and what would that something be?" asked Jackson, coyly.

"You'll just have to wait and see. Something for you to look forward to," his mate chuckled. Just then they heard someone knocking on their bedroom door. "Yeah, who is it?" yelled Steel.

"Logan. The moving truck has arrived. Are you coming down or do you want me to handle it?"

Steel looked at Jackson who nodded and then yelled back, "We'll be down in a few minutes, but go ahead and start, Logan."

They heard Logan walk down the hall and Steel broke up laughing. "I'll bet he was unanimously elected to come up here to deliver the news about the truck."

"Why would you say that?"

"Well, honey, I'm sure they all heard you come and I sure as hell wouldn't want to be the one disturbing the good time some guys were having," chuckled Steel.

Jackson's cheeks heated; he was so out of it when he came, he never even grasped that his brothers and—*oh shit*—that Steel's parents also heard him. Turning and burying his head in Steel's neck, he mumbled he was never going to show his face downstairs again. Steel laughed, pulling Jackson into a hug before getting out of bed. "Come on, get up or I'll send your brothers up here with your boxes and you can explain why you're still in bed."

"That's just downright mean," Jackson pouted, getting out of bed and heading to the bathroom.

Steel called after him, "Well, a person's just got to do what a person's got to do."

Turning, Jackson stuck out his tongue, before scurrying into the bathroom.

Chuckling and following his mate, Steel said, "If you need something to do with that tongue, I know just the thing."

~/~/~/~/~

The Silver Point Alpha picked up his phone after checking his caller ID, snarling, "You better have good news for me. I got the High Council breathing down my neck."

"What do they want?" asked Rudy.

"I'm not sure, but I've been ducking their calls for over a week. And if it's anything to do with Fox River, I don't want to talk to them until after you've taken care of the problem. So, what's the news? Have you found them?"

"Not yet. I've checked all the towns south, east, and west of North Ridge and turned up nothing. Me and the boys are heading north next. I'll find them, boss, because it's the only place left to search."

"Make sure you do," barked Josiah, slamming the receiver down. He had a fairly good idea why the High

Council was calling. His stupid nephew finally found his cojones and made a complaint. *Well, fuck him!* He'd be damned if Jackson was going to keep what rightfully would have been Josiah's if his brother, Striker, had done the right thing and made him the Alpha after their father died. But no, his asshole brother had the audacity to tell him he'd forfeited his rights once their father won Josiah's challenge. One more week was all he could give Rudy before he had to return the High Council's call.

~/~/~/~/~

Everything had been unpacked and put away in their bedroom and Jackson was exhausted. He now thought it was due to his pregnancy but wasn't sure, which was worrying him. Turning to his mate who was organizing their clothes in the dresser, he said, "I think we should sit down with your mother and Colton to find out what to expect with this pregnancy."

Steel stopped, looking at him with a worried expression. "Why, is something wrong?"

"No babe, I've wanted to do this for some time and since everyone is settled, I think it's time. I know Colton has quite a few questions and while he's been researching for answers, he told me yesterday he hasn't had much luck," replied Jackson. "He may be the only one here at the time of the birth so he should have all the knowledge he can so I have a healthy pup."

Steel nodded his assent. "Okay, I also want to ask my mother about a doctor who can be on call for the birth, so how about tomorrow morning, before your morning sickness hits?"

Nodding, Jackson lay down on the bed, falling asleep immediately. Steel looked over at his mate with a frown on his face, worried about how tired Jackson had been lately. Tomorrow, he was going to ask Colton to help him set up a mini hospital in the house just in case his mate needed it.

Chapter 25

Rudy knew his Alpha was going to be pissed when he told Josiah he found the pack house deserted and no new leads. Well, no sense in calling Josiah with the bad news. He yelled to his boys to head back to the vehicles they'd left parked five miles away. Shifting one by one, they ran off leaving only him.

He wanted one more look to see if he missed any clues as to the brothers' whereabouts. The house contained only Jackson's scent, which puzzled Rudy, but something else worried him more. Walking through it, he came to a bedroom, and smelled not only Jackson, but the presence of another wolf. In fact, the house contained three unknown wolf scents which caused the hackles on Rudy's neck to rise just thinking about it. The three were from the same pack but he couldn't identify it. The scent that alarmed him most, though, was Jackson's, because if he wasn't mistaken, Jackson had mated with one of the three unknown wolves. "Shit, shit, shit," cursed Rudy, heading outside, knowing his Alpha wouldn't like this news at all.

Khan came into Josiah's office, worry written all over his face. "Dad, a representative of the Universal Paranormal High Council is here and wants to see you immediately."

Josiah looked up at his son, knowing his time had run out. He could only hope Rudy had been successful and the Fox River brothers were dead. He stood up and said, "Show him in and shut the door when you leave."

The High Council representative greeted Josiah with, "Alpha Silver Point, I presume. I'm Wolfgrim Morris of the Universal Paranormal High Council."

"A pleasure to meet you, Mr. Morris. Just call me Josiah and please have a seat," he said, sitting down behind his desk, waiting for the man to speak.

"I couldn't get hold of you by phone which is why I've come to see you since time is of the essence."

"That sounds important. What is it you want to see me about?"

"A very serious complaint has been filed against you by the Blackwood Pack…"

"Blackwood Pack??? Wait a minute! I've never had any dealings with a Blackwood Pack. In fact, I don't even know who this pack is. Are you sure the complaint is against the Silver Point Pack?"

"The Blackwood Pack consists of seven brothers who were previously part of the Fox River Pack. Their complaint alleges the Silver Point Pack committed a heinous act against their former pack. I have a copy of the complaint for your records," he said, leaning forward and placing some papers on Josiah's desk.

"The accusations in it are detailed and you have 60 days in which to file an answer with the Universal Paranormal High Council. Also, please consider this as putting you and your pack on notice; if harm befalls any member of the Blackwood Pack, you and your pack will be held responsible for it—whether or not any of you personally caused the harm." Morris then stood up. "Good day, Alpha," he said, walking out.

His mate was sleeping when Steel left the room to seek his mother and Colton. He found Jackson's brother in the library, reading one of the many books there.

Colton looked up as Steel approached, waiting to see what his brother-in-law wanted.

"Good morning," said Steel, sitting down. "I need your help in a matter concerning Jackson."

Startled, Colton asked, "Is my brother okay?"

"Yes, sorry, I didn't mean to alarm you. What I want to do is to set up a mini hospital in case Jackson needs it during the birth of our pup. I just want to be prepared for the worst, though I hope it'll never happen. Can you tell me what should be in it?" Steel asked.

"Sure," agreed Colton, "but remember, I'm not a doctor and haven't even finished my nursing degree yet. I can give you a list but I'd feel better if you had a doctor look it over."

"I'm planning to ask my mother for a name of a doctor who'd be on call for the birth," Steel said, and then quickly added, "I don't have any doubts about your abilities; Jackson has sung praises about your healing skills repeatedly and I know he trusts you implicitly."

Colton was inwardly pleased at the compliment but reiterated, "I appreciate your faith in me but I want what's best for my brother and that's a doctor handling the birth of your pup."

Nodding in agreement, Steel said, "Jackson wants to ask my mother some questions about his pregnancy and thought you'd like to sit in on the meeting. It would be your chance to get answers to any questions you might have."

Colton's face lit up with a wide smile, already thinking about questions to ask. "Gosh, thanks, I'd appreciate that. When are you getting together?"

"I have to find my mother to see what she's planned today, but I'd like to do it as soon as Jackson is up and before his morning sickness kicks in. Okay with you?"

"Yup, I'll start writing down my questions now."

~/~/~/~/~

Sitting next to Steel, Jackson interlaced his fingers with his mate's while waiting for Oracle to join them. He looked over at his brother whose lips were moving as he reviewed the questions he wanted to ask.

During his shower this morning, Jackson noticed his normally flat stomach was now very slightly rounded—visual proof that he was really pregnant. And at that moment, with the water streaming down on him, a sharp and deep yearning coursed through his heart for his unborn pup. Caressing his wet belly, he realized he already loved his baby with his entire being and would do anything to protect it from harm. His knees buckled at the revelation, and he had to lean against the shower wall to steady himself.

Now, looking up, he watched Oracle sit down across from them. Her gentle smile greeted Jackson. "You are looking fine this morning, dear."

"Thanks, I feel pretty good but I tire easily which is very unusual for me. I'm hoping it's only the pregnancy responsible for that." He could feel his mate squeezing his hand and, through their mind-link, chastising him for not telling him. Jackson looked at Steel, murmuring, "I was going to tell you last night but I fell asleep."

"Yes," he heard Oracle say, "the pregnancy is causing your tiredness and it will disappear after two months, as will the morning sickness. The rest of the pregnancy should be easy, other than some water retention and back pain. There aren't many problems with a Dire Wolf pregnancy, but it will take a toll on your body."

Colton asked, "In what way?"

"A Dire Wolf pup," explained Oracle, "will be larger than a Timber Wolf pup and your body will struggle to provide everything the growing pup will need. Don't be shocked at the amount of food you consume once you are past the morning sickness stage. And of course, you will not be able to shift during the last two months as it would be very dangerous for the pup."

"What will I need to help Jackson with the birth?" asked Colton.

"Jackson will not be able to give birth in the normal way because a Dire Wolf pup is almost twice the size of a Timber Wolf pup. He'll need a Caesarian delivery when the baby is ready to be born," Oracle replied.

Colton, shocked, looking at Jackson, said, "Bro, I'm not qualified to operate. You're going to need a doctor for this."

Steel spoke up. "Mom, do you know a doctor who'd agree to stay here for the last few months of Jackson's pregnancy?"

Oracle thought for a minute. "Hmm, I think so, but let me make some calls first. Any more questions?"

Colton replied, "No, not right now, but I may have more later. I think the most important thing for me is to focus on working with a doctor to set up the mini hospital that Steel wants. So, let me know when you've found a doctor."

Jackson's mind was in turmoil about everything Oracle told them. Steel was worried, listening to his mate's thoughts. Wrapping his arm around his mate's shoulders to pull Jackson into his chest, Steel gave him reassuring caresses.

Bending down, Oracle kissed Jackson's cheek. "We'll take care of you, Jackson. The best advice I can give is just take it easy for now."

Feeling numb and alone, Jackson watched Colton and Oracle leave the library. Then, without warning, Steel scooped him into his arms, settling him on his lap. Safe within the circle of Steel's arms, Jackson buried his head against his mate's chest listening to the strong, steady heartbeat and inhaling his addictive scent, which calmed him considerably. Suddenly, this was very real to Jackson, almost frighteningly so. But that thought was fleeting—he knew that wasn't him. He faced problems head-on and that's what he'd do now.

Thinking about what he'd learned, he turned to Steel. "Did you know I'd need a Caesarian? Is that why you want to set up a hospital?"

"No, *mo chroí,*" answered Steel. "I decided to do it prior to this meeting. I wanted to be prepared for anything. I asked Colton this morning to give me a list of equipment we should have."

Feeling his heart swell with love for his mate, Jackson recognized Steel had been working all along to make sure he and their pup would be safe, even before knowing he'd need the procedure. "I love you so much, my love," Jackson said, lifting his lips to kiss Steel.

~/~/~/~/~

Rudy knocked on Alpha Silver Point's office door, waiting for permission to enter. He wasn't in any hurry because he knew Josiah, his Alpha, would become incensed when he heard what Rudy learned.

"Come in," barked Josiah.

Opening the door, Rudy saw him sitting at his desk, scowling as he read a document. Rudy closed the door and sat in a chair opposite Josiah's desk, steeling himself for the rage he knew would be directed at him.

Josiah exhaled loudly, looking up at Rudy, his trusted second-in-command. "Well, did you get it done?" he snarled.

"I found where they've been hiding, but they're not there anymore," replied Rudy.

Josiah sat there, his face turning red as anger coursed through his body. "Any idea where they went?"

"Nope. I searched the house several times and didn't find any clues as to their whereabouts. But I did scent three other wolves. I don't know which pack the three wolves belong to but I'm pretty sure one of them mated with Jackson."

Josiah sat back in his chair, staring at Rudy. "Get Khan in here. I need to ask him a question."

As Rudy headed out to find his Alpha's son, Josiah felt fear start to swallow him as he thought back to what his Shaman had foreseen. *No*! He wouldn't allow that to happen and he'd kill Jackson and his brothers before they killed him. There just wasn't any other option. The Shaman was quite clear about it and Josiah saw that prediction coming true if what Rudy said was correct. He slammed his massive fist on the desktop, cursing himself for not trying harder to find and kill those brothers before they alerted the High Council. Well, Jackson better not count him out yet, because he wasn't about to give up on everything he'd worked so hard for.

They'd soon find Josiah's elite fighting force was far superior to anything the seven puny brothers could come up with.

Khan knocked and then entered. "You wanted to see me, Father?"

"Yes, tell me who the guy was you met in the supermarket. You went out on a date with him?" Josiah asked, barely disguising his disgust. Khan claimed he was gay but Josiah refused to acknowledge it publicly. He knew it was just a stage and his eldest son would grow out of it because when he took over the Alpha position one day, he'd need to mate with a female to continue the line.

"Yes, I dated him once," Kahn answered. "I don't know a lot about Steel because he didn't talk very much during our date. When I met him again on the Fox River Pack land …"

"Wait! You met him on the Fox River Pack land? What was he doing there? Tell me!" he barked.

Looking at his father strangely, Khan wondered why his comment would upset him so much. "Yes, I met Steel and his father. Steel thought they were on public land. When I told them it wasn't, they left."

Josiah narrowed his eyes, doing an imaginary eye roll at the stupidity of his son. But instead of chastising Khan, which would just shut him down, he asked, "What about the supermarket?"

"I told you, I bumped into him, we exchanged pleasantries and then he pulled me over to the wine display where we talked about our favorites. Why?"

"When you scented Jackson, did you notice anything strange?" pushed Josiah.

"Well, at first I didn't realize it was Jackson because my wolf kept scenting a pregnant wolf. But as I continued to track the wolf through the store, I guess my wolf was wrong because it was Jackson," replied Khan.

"Thanks for the clarification. Tell Rudy to come in now," Josiah said.

Watching his son walk out of the room, he dropped his hands to his lap to hide their shaking. Shit, Jackson had mated and was now pregnant. He didn't know how that could happen with a male Alpha wolf, but his Shaman warned him Jackson must be killed before that happened.

If Josiah were honest, he'd never given much credence to the ramblings of his medicine man. *What normal person would? How could a male Alpha wolf become pregnant?* Josiah huffed; he still didn't believe it but just in case, Jackson and his mate must be killed at once. *Fuck the High Council!*

Chapter 26

Steel was becoming frantic. Two weeks had passed since the complaint was made to the High Council yet not a word from them came back about their notifying the Silver Point Pack. Fearing for his mate's safety, he decided to call them and demand an update. He also had to make decisions about hiring enforcers.

His property was very well protected electronically but he also wanted a fighting force at his disposal. He was reading through a list of candidates Slate sent him when Oracle glided into his office. Tossing the list on his desk, he glanced up at his mother. "Good morning, Mom, what's up?"

"Have you heard back from the High Council yet?"

"No, I plan to call them today. It's been over two weeks and they should have reported back to me by now," Steel growled.

"That's a good idea, sweetie" Then she added, "I have the name of a doctor who will be available to stay here for the last two months of Jackson's pregnancy and then for a month after the baby is born to make sure no problems arise."

"Thanks, Mom."

"Sweetie, nothing is too good for my first grandchild," Oracle said, a wide smile lighting up her face. "His name is Dr. Ian Wallace and here's his contact information."

"I'll get right on this. Colton has given me his equipment list but he wants a doctor to look it over first," said Steel.

"How's Jackson feeling?"

"He's sleeping right now. The tiredness is taking its toll on him but I think the morning sickness is getting better so hopefully an end to both is in sight," Steel sighed.

"Yes, it is coming to an end so just hang on for a little while longer," assured Oracle, bending down, kissing Steel's cheek.

"Oh, one more thing, Mom, I want to surprise Jackson before he begins to show too much. With all this Silver Point pack business, I haven't been able to romance him the way he deserves. So, I need a favor. Can you arrange for the helicopter to be at my disposal? I want to whisk my mate away for a babymoon."

"Oh, what a lovely idea!" exclaimed Oracle, smiling broadly. "Consider it done," she said and then, kissing Steel's cheek again, left his office.

Steel knew exactly what he wanted to do for Jackson's babymoon; he was sure his mate would love it. Of course, it had to be a surprise so when it was revealed, his mate would have a teary 'Oh Babe' moment. Deep down, Steel knew the babymoon would mean as much to him as it would to his mate but before he made reservations, he'd wait until Jackson's morning sickness and tiredness abated so they both could enjoy it.

~/~/~/~/~

Fuming as the pack's attorney reviewed the complaint against Silver Point, Josiah tapped his fingers in an endless beat, waiting for the lawyer's advice. He'd told Rudy to keep looking for Jackson, his mate, and his brothers despite the High Council's warning. He'd thought about how to get around the ban on harming members of the Blackwood Pack and the first step of his plan was the reason Boris Calhoun was sitting in his office.

"Well, is there a way to contest the complaint so the High Council declines to investigate it?" snarled Josiah, impatiently.

"The Complaint is well put together and seems to have all the elements necessary for the High Council to launch an investigation," Boris said, before pausing at Josiah's growl. "However, the one point I see as a problem for the Blackwood Pack is, they don't have an eyewitness to testify it was Silver Point Pack who committed the crime. The complaint gives circumstantial evidence but contains no concrete proof to support their claim your pack is responsible."

Josiah let out his breath. "So how would I go about challenging it?"

"Demand they produce an eyewitness who can clearly identify who killed the Fox River Pack," Boris explained. "If they can't do that, then insist the accusation be withdrawn."

Josiah smiled darkly. "Thank you, Boris. I'll do as you suggest. And thanks, also, for coming out at such short notice."

Boris stood and shook Josiah's hand before walking out of his office. Josiah then summoned Rudy to his office.

"I want you to find out where those boys are and once you locate them call me immediately, is that understood?"

"Yes," said Rudy, somewhat puzzled. "But you've already told me to find them. What's different this time?"

"This time, I don't want any action taken against them unless I personally give you the okay. You'll kill them only on my word, understand?" growled Josiah. "Are you clear on my instructions?"

"Yes," answered Rudy.

~/~/~/~/~

Jackson was dreaming of a toddler whose silky black hair kept falling into his eyes as he played hide and seek with Steel. Reaching out to catch him when he ran past, Jackson's eyes shot open when Steel murmured, "What are you dreaming about? Our pup again?"

Steel was rewarded with a slow, sleepy smile from Jackson as his mate turned into his arms.

Jackson yawned before he asked, "What time is it?" wondering how long he'd slept.

"Late enough that you slept through your morning sickness," answered Steel.

"Well, that's a blessing," chortled Jackson.

Swatting his mate's ass, Steel said, "Smartass," reaching down to Jackson's belly. Caressing his mate's tiny baby bump, he said, "Dakota made you a late lunch so it's time to get out of bed and eat something for that growing pup."

Jackson rolled out of bed. "Good, because my stomach is growling and I feel like I could eat a whole deer," he said. Then, pausing at the door, he announced, "Last one in the shower has to blow me," giggling as his mate jumped quickly out of bed, making a mad dash for the bathroom. But Jackson got there first and, with a leer on his face, he sassed, "Make it slow and tight, babe. I want to feel it all the way to my toes."

Steel loved his teasing mate but it had been a while since he saw this side of him. Between the vomiting and tiredness, the pregnancy was taking a hard toll on Jackson's body and, on top of that, Steel knew the emotional stress of the Silver Point kill order weighed heavily on Jackson's mind. So, it was a welcome surprise that Jackson was in a playful mood, and damned if Steel wasn't ready to play.

He walked into the shower, seeing Jackson's perfect bubble butt staring up at him as his mate bent forward wiggling his ass, tempting Steel to do more than a blow job. He groaned as his cock hardened, realizing Jackson was preparing himself for Steel. *Hot*

fucking damn, his lover was making sure Steel was going to enjoy this just as much as Jackson did.

Steel's hand reached for his hard, leaking cock—tugging it slowly and lazily, in no hurry to rush this along—while gazing at Jackson's fingers going just as slowly in and out of his perfect, pink puckered rose. He could hear the gasps and other sounds coming from his mate as their need grew. Steel loved all the sounds Jackson made but especially those gasping moans that brought him to the verge of coming every time.

Deciding not to waste an opportunity like this, Steel brushed Jackson's fingers away, growling, "Mine," replacing them in one thrust with his aching cock. Bottoming out in his mate, Steel stilled, giving Jackson time to get used to the fullness in him. "Move, now!" demanded Jackson. With one hand on his mate's hip to hold him in place, Steel reached around with his other, wrapping his fingers around Jackson's stiff cock, gripping it, stroking it slowly, giving little twists to the tip each time he reached it.

Jackson was alternately in heaven or being driven insane by all the sensations tingling through his body. When he asked for it slow and hard, he never dreamed Steel knew how to deliver it so perfectly; he was now in danger of melting from the heat his mate was generating in him. All rational thought had left him, instead incoherent whimpers, moans, and gasps steadily streamed from his lips as he tried to remain standing.

As his mate's legs began to give out, Steel wrapped his arm around Jackson to hold him up. He knew his slow and hard thrusts were pushing Jackson to the heights of frustration, keeping him from coming. As his mate grew more frustrated, he knew Jackson's orgasm would reach new heights when Steel finally allowed it. He loved hearing his mate begging for relief—the endless stream of disjointed, slurred words and sounds erupted from Jackson's throat as Steel continued to thrust into Jackson's tight hole. Looking down and watching his cock disappear into Jackson, he felt his balls start to tighten at the sight, signaling he was ready, so he sped up.

Jack-hammering into his mate's pucker, Steel also increased his strokes on Jackson's cock. Faster and faster, harder and harder, until Steel's hips were a blur of motion as he was driven to finish. Crying out, Jackson's orgasm finally found freedom, exploding out the end of his cock, his ass clenching down on Steel's rod, causing a chain reaction as a tsunami of cum flooded his insides. Steel roared out Jackson's name; his incisors emerged and he bit down on his mate's neck once again, drinking the blood that rushed into his mouth. Withdrawing his teeth slowly, Steel licked the bite to help it heal.

Leaning on his mate's back, Steel's breathing was erratic as he came down from the height of his passion.

Standing up slowly, he lifted Jackson up against his chest. Wrapping both arms tightly around his mate, he nuzzled his nose in the hollow of Jackson's neck, before licking the bite again. He listened to Jackson's heart, still beating in double time as his mate drew in ragged, deep breaths, trying to still his body.

They stood like that for a while as the water cascaded over their bodies, taking with it all the visible signs of their lovemaking. Finally, when their bodies had calmed down, they washed each other silently, lovingly caressing each other.

After rinsing off, Steel dried himself, grabbed a heated towel, sat down, then lifted Jackson onto his lap. Slowly drying his mate's body, he continued to press kisses all over his chest, neck, and face. And when his mate was dry, Steel hugged Jackson tightly, whispering into his ear, "I love you, now and forever, and that won't even be enough time, *mo chroí.* You are my heart, my soul, my everything."

~/~/~/~/~

Jackson felt better than he had in a long time after eating the large, late lunch Dakota made for him. Now, sitting next to Steel in his office, he waited for the call to the High Council to be answered. After several rings, a voice said, "Wolfgrim Morris here."

Steel replied, "Mr. Morris, I'm Steel Valentin, mate to Jackson, the Alpha of Blackwood Pack. I have you on speaker phone and Jackson is sitting next to me."

"Hello Mr. Morris, I'm Alpha Blackwood," said Jackson.

"Hello Alpha. Let me get straight to the point. I was unable to reach Alpha Silver Point by phone for several weeks…"

"How come?" asked Steel.

"I don't know why he wasn't available to take my call. I was only told there was an emergency in his pack. Since time was of the essence, I decided to personally visit Silver Point Pack so I could give the Alpha the Complaint and the official Warning. This has been accomplished," Morris explained.

"What's an official warning?" asked Jackson.

"When a complaint has been filed against a pack, the High Council gives an official warning to that pack about not harming any member of the complaining pack," explained Morris.

Steel looked at Jackson. "What comes next?"

"The Silver Point Pack has sixty days to file an answer to the Complaint," replied Morris.

"Okay, so right now it's a waiting game until they answer?" asked Jackson.

"That is correct. When I receive their answer, I will forward a copy to you. Until then, there is nothing to be done," Morris explained.

"Thank you for the update. Good-bye, Mr. Morris," said Steel.

"Good-bye," added Jackson.

"Good-bye Alpha Blackwood, Mr. Valentin," replied Morris.

Hanging up the phone, Steel contemplated the discussion. The High Council knew that Silver Point Pack had been officially warned and therefore would assume no harm would come to Jackson and his brothers. Steel wasn't so sure. Silver Point Pack had already shown they were dishonorable.

What made their actions all the more sinister was the night they'd picked for the massacre—a new moon, the darkest night of the month. And then, if he added their killing of innocents—women and children—there was no other conclusion Steel could reach; he could not trust them.

Breaking the silence Jackson asked, "What do you think, babe, will my uncle behave himself and rescind the kill order on us?" He had his own ideas but wanted to hear Steel's thoughts first.

"I would like to think so, but in reality, no, I don't trust them. Silver Point would kill all of you first and then beg forgiveness from the High Council," replied Steel. "But I have an idea I want to run past my father and brother first. I think we can force them to obey the High Council's warning and rescind the kill order if their Alpha realizes there may be some unpleasant consequences if he doesn't."

Chapter 27

Colton went over his final list several times to make sure it was as complete as he could make it. The first list he submitted was perfect, but Steel asked him to add more patient rooms to the mini hospital he was setting up on the lower floor, hence the need for a new list. He was meeting with Steel shortly and wanted to be fully prepared, ready to answer any questions his brother-in-law might have. He regretted he hadn't completed the final year of his nursing program but it was what it was. He wasn't alone in lost dreams. After the massacre, all his brothers had to give up their dreams as well when they went into hiding.

He *had* managed to take some classes online in the past few years, but not enough to earn his RN degree. That could put him at a decided disadvantage with the doctor Steel hired since some doctors were notorious for treating nurses badly because they didn't have an MD after their name. But not having one never bothered Colton. Nurses, he was convinced, had more hands-on contact with sick people and could help them recover faster because they were the ones patients most often trusted and turned to for help.

He didn't know who this doctor would be but made up his mind he wasn't going to be pushed around or talked down to simply because he lacked a degree on his wall. His brother was relying on him. Walking toward Steel's office, Colton could feel his wolf pacing. Hmm, guess it was time for another run.

His wolf's uneasiness ignored, he knocked on the door, waiting for a response. In the past, he'd have entered after knocking but that was before his brother mated.

He'd learned the hard way after Steel came on the scene never to do that. As it was, the picture of his brother sucking Steel's cock would forever be etched in his mind and he wasn't keen on adding to that file.

"Come in," Steel called. Entering the room, he saw Jackson sitting next to his brother-in-law. Steel kissed his mate, then turning to Colton, "Have you brought the list of equipment we'll need?"

"Yes," said Colton, sitting down and handing Steel the list. "As I've said before, the doctor you hired should give final approval but the one piece of equipment you should buy immediately is the ultrasound machine. I've been trained to operate it and Jackson will need a number of these tests throughout his pregnancy."

"Why?" asked Jackson.

"To see if the baby is progressing as it should, alert us to any potential problems, and also give you the sex of the pup—if you choose to know it—before the birth," replied Colton.

"The sex of the pup? But I already know it's a boy," said Jackson.

"Really? And how did you find that out?" smirked Colton.

Jackson's cheeks flamed red and Steel interrupted the brothers. "I don't have a problem, but as you suggested, I'll fax Dr. Wallace to get his input."

Colton expected Steel to consult the doctor; he was just startled that the call would be done while he was present. He watched as Steel scribbled some notes on the list before faxing it to the doctor. "I asked Dr. Wallace to call as soon as he's reviewed the list."

Nodding, Colton checked Jackson over. "You look good today. How are you feeling, bro? Has the morning sickness abated at least a little bit?"

"Actually, I feel great today," Jackson said with a big smile.

"Good, maybe you're nearing the end of morning sickness and extreme fatigue," said Colton. Just then, the phone on the desk rang and Steel picked up the receiver. "Hello… ahh, Dr. Wallace, just a minute, I'm going to put you on speaker," he said, pushing a button and Colton heard the doctor for the first time.

"Hello, hello, can you hear me?" said a voice sending shivers down Colton's back.

"Yes, Dr. Wallace…"

"Call me Ian, please."

"Hello Ian, I'm Steel. Jackson, my mate, and his brother Colton are with me. I faxed you a list of equipment Colton made. He recommended I buy the ultra sound machine immediately so he can see if everything is all right with the baby. Before I do that, I just wanted your approval."

"Who put together this list?"

"I did," replied Colton.

"Do you have medical training…"

Oh yeah, there he was, the snot-nosed, know-it-all doctor who thought only he knew anything. "I completed three and a half years of nursing school," Colton said angrily. He saw his brother look at him with raised eyebrows, as if to ask what Colton's problem was. *Shit, I need to cool my emotions.*

Ian heard the anger in Colton's voice and was puzzled. What had he done to arouse those feelings in this man? "I'm sorry, I didn't mean to imply anything by my question. I was impressed with the thoroughness of the list, wondering how you knew so much."

Yup, it was now official, I'm an asshole. Shit. He over-reacted, jumping to the wrong conclusion. *Dammit to hell,* he needed to get his head on straight but every time Ian spoke, he was put on edge. The results of his thoughtless reaction were right there for all to see as Colton said, "I'm sorry, Dr. Wallace… my apologies. Do you have any questions or additions to the list?"

Ian felt Colton didn't like him after hearing the tone of Colton's answer, though he didn't know why. He was sure he never met the young man but that didn't seem to matter; it appeared he had been judged and found lacking by him. *Should I just back out of this assignment, although it is a fascinating case?* He'd never heard of an Alpha/Omega hybrid before which is why he'd jumped to say "yes" when Oracle called him. But Colton was Jackson's brother and Ian didn't want Jackson's care compromised by any friction that might develop. *Shit, now my wolf is snarling. What the fuck…???*

"The equipment list is very complete and I was quite impressed by it. I know many doctors who couldn't do as well."

"Good to know," said Steel. "What about Colton's idea of buying the ultrasound machine right away?"

"I agree with that. I believe Jackson is about two months pregnant?"

"Yes," replied Steel.

"Then Jackson should have an ultrasound done as soon as possible. Colton, have you been trained to give the test?" asked Ian.

"Yes, I've done a lot of them."

"Would you please send me a copy of each result so I can keep a file on his progress?" asked Ian.

"Sure, no problem."

"Okay," said Steel. "I'll put in an order for all of the equipment and ask the supplier to rush the ultrasound machine as soon as possible. Is there anything else we need to address?"

"I'm finished for the time being," said Ian. "Oh wait… Colton if you have any notes you've been keeping on Jackson, would you please forward copies of them to me when you get a chance?"

"I'll do it immediately," replied Colton.

"Thanks. Good-bye, for now."

A chorus of "good-byes" sounded just before Steel hung up the phone.

Colton got up. "Well, if there's nothing else, I'll go get my notes for Dr. Wallace."

Jackson spoke up. "Sit down, Colton. You want to tell me why you got so pissed off at the good doctor?"

Colton looked down at his fidgeting fingers. Dammit, he knew his brother would want some answers since it was so unlike him to lose his temper. All during their childhood, Colton was always the calm one, never angry at any of his siblings. So yeah, Jackson would notice his stupid anger at the doctor. "Sorry about that," he mumbled. "I just jumped to the wrong conclusion. It won't happen again."

Steel asked, "Will you be able to work with him without any drama? I don't want Jackson to be put in the middle of spats between his brother and his doctor."

Colton nodded his head in assent as he looked up at Steel. "Don't worry, the doctor and me… we're on the same page. There won't be any friction."

"Are you sure? Because I can find another doctor," said Steel.

Colton nodded. "I promise. Is that all?"

Jackson smiled at his brother. "Yes, and thanks Colton. I appreciate all your help."

Colton walked over to his brother, bending down to hug him, whispering in his ear, "I love you, bro, and I'm so happy to be part of the coolest pregnancy ever." He straightened up, smiling at Steel. "Let me know where you're going to set up the hospital and I'll start getting the rooms ready."

~/~/~/~/~

Slate's phone was ringing again and he knew exactly who the asshole on the other end was. Josiah, Alpha of the Silver Point Pack was trying to reach him about a waiver on the title issue. *Fuck that!* This must be the sixth call in the last two days. Slate would've answered it sooner but he was trying to buy Steel all the time he could until the proverbial shit hit the fan. And by the sound of it, that time wasn't too far off.

Better call his brother to see what he wanted Slate to do. As he dialed, his thoughts once again reverted to Steel's luck in finding a mate. Well, maybe not so much luck as having the grit to keep looking. While he was happy for his brother, Slate wasn't ready to settle down just yet even though his mother was nudging him in that direction. No, he was having too much fun finding a different man in every port—*oops*—make that in every city while traveling all over the world. Maybe if he entered his *toirchigh* period like Steel, he might be more focused, but right now, he was free to be a man whore and wasn't ready yet to give up that title.

"Steel here."

"Well, hello to you too, brother. Not getting enough since Jackson got pregnant?" chortled Slate.

"Fuck off," Steel replied with a laugh. "What's up, little brother—and I do mean little—where it counts."

"Did your mate ever say you have a streak of meanness in you?"

"My mate loves me and only tells me how good I am in bed. Too bad you'll never hear that from your mate," said Steel smugly.

"Okay, okay, brother—enough with the barbs or I'll tell your mate on you."

"That is *so* not fair. Wait until you find your mate and you'll see what I mean," Steel said, laughing lightly. "Now that that's over, what did you want to talk to me about?"

Slate's voice became serious "Alpha Silver Point has been calling me a number of times during the last several days but I haven't picked up. He's left messages on voicemail so I know what he wants."

"And what *does* he want?" asked Steel in a deadly calm voice.

Slate knew when his brother used that voice, he was very angry. "He wants me to give him a waiver on our requirement for him to produce a title to the Fox River property and release the money for his mining operation on the land." Slate paused, waiting for the explosion he knew would be coming.

"That fucking asshole!" Yup, there it was, Slate thought, as Steel erupted.

"He's being investigated by the High Council and he knows the brothers are alive. He's either got a lot of nerve or he's the stupidest prick alive." Steel was seeing red and his anger threatened to consume him. *That sonofabitch—I'll see him dead before he ever gets his filthy hands on the land. That land is my pup's legacy.*

Slate said, "I understand what you're saying but I don't get why the Alpha would want to proceed on the mining project when he may be found guilty and sentenced to death? It doesn't make sense on the face of it, but my gut tells me he thinks he'll have the land—and soon."

"But how?" asked Steel. "He's been put under official notice he can't harm anyone in the Blackwood Pack while the investigation is underway."

"How ironclad is the complaint?" asked Slate.

"Pretty tight as far as I can see," said Steel. "The only problem is it lacks eyewitnesses. But even without that, I don't believe the High Council will dismiss the complaint before investigating it."

"Well," said Slate, "I'll tell Josiah I've submitted his request to the Board and my hands are tied until they decide. In the meantime, show the complaint to Penn," he suggested, referring to their attorney.

"Thanks, I'll do that," said Steel, then asked, "When will you be here? My mate is eager to meet you."

"I've been delayed due to a health crisis I have to handle concerning Mexican Wolf shifters. Wolves in Mexico are getting attacked, many of them badly injured. So, unless you need me right now, I have to solve that problem first," said Slate.

"Do you know who's attacking them?"

"No, I'm heading down there tomorrow for a firsthand look," replied Slate.

"Be careful," cautioned Steel. "Call me if you need anything."

"Will do. Say hello to Mom, Dad, and Jackson for me. Talk to you later," Slate said before hanging up.

Steel sat deep in thought about what Alpha Silver Point was up to. He knew Silver Point wouldn't back down, but what they'd do remained a mystery. He had a back-up plan that would force the Alpha to retreat and stop threatening his mate and his brothers if the warning from the High Council didn't do it. Steel just didn't want to play the card too soon. He turned his thoughts to the crisis in Mexico. That certainly took priority right now over Steel's problem with Silver Point though he was disappointed his brother's visit would be delayed.

Steel sighed. Might as well do what Slate suggested so he placed a call to their attorney.

"Penn Anderson."

"Penn, its Steel. How's everything?"

"I heard you got mated. So, no more Friday night tail chasing? Just Slate and me from now on, huh? Poor baby, your fun days are over," teased Penn.

"Hardy har, har. I have everything I've ever wanted and don't miss those days at all," Steel said, grinning. "Someday you and Slate will find your fated mates and it will be the end of the 'Wolf Man Whore Club' forever."

"Never! So, what's up?"

"My mate filed a complaint against the Silver Point Pack with the Universal Paranormal High Council. It's a long story and I won't waste your time now because it's all in the complaint."

"Has the Alpha of that pack been notified of the complaint and has he been given the warning?"

"Yes, the representative warned him in person," replied Steel.

"Okay, so what's the problem?" asked Penn.

"I received word today about some of the Alpha's actions and wonder how strong our complaint is and if there's some way for Silver Point to get it dismissed. I'd like you to look it over for any defects which could be used by them in their defense," said Steel.

"No problem. Send it over and I'll call you as soon as I've a chance to review it," said Penn.

"Thanks. Later dude," Steel said, hanging up. After he emailed the complaint to Penn, he thought about the many wild nights the three of them enjoyed through the years. Yeah, he had been a man whore—not that he would ever tell his mate that. He and his brother met Penn at school and were best friends ever since. They immediately clicked: together they spent their younger years fucking any piece of ass that caught their interest. Now those days *were* over for Steel, but he had no regrets. That was then. His life now was so much better with a mate he loved and a pup on the way.

Chapter 28

Seated in his office, Steel watched Jackson walk toward him. He carefully searched his mate's face and studied his body to see how he was handling the pregnancy.

"Hey babe, you're looking good. How are you feeling?" he asked.

"Great, lover," said Jackson leaning down to kiss Steel's jaw while placing his hand on the bulge in his mate's pants.

"Love you," Steel moaned, as Jackson palmed his hard cock, swiveling the office chair until he stood between his mate's legs.

"I have a gift for you," purred Jackson, kneeling and unzipping Steel's pants. Fishing out Steel's thick, long cock, he slowly stroked it, marveling at the feel of the iron rod beneath the velvet skin. Then Jackson's pink tongue darted out to lap up the pre-cum dripping from the slit.

Running his tongue down the length of Steel's cock and up again, his right hand kept stroking while his left massaged his mate's balls. Howling moans erupted from Steel's throat as he feverishly finger-raked his mate's hair. Tightening his lips around Steel's tip, Jackson butterflied his tongue into his mate's slit, scooping up the dripping, slick nectar.

Steel began breathing heavily, his head fell back, but Jackson wasn't finished. Deep throating Steel's cock to the hilt in one motion, he then stopped. Steel protested, his hips starting to hump his mate's face. But Jackson quickly gripped Steel's hips to immobilize them while slowly sliding his mouth up his mate's cock.

With Steel's cock-tip in his mouth, he looked up to see his mate's eyes half closed. Whimpers and moans streaming from his mate's throat made Jackson quickly slide Steel's cock down his throat while one of his fingers searched for the puckered bud waiting to be plucked.

As his tempo of sucking and licking Steel's cock increased, Jackson's finger wormed its way up his ass, searching for the magic spot to rocket his lover to the stars. Steel was desperate to come, surrendering to the assault on his senses, when Jackson's finger finally found its mark.

Roaring out his mate's name, Steel's eyes rolled back in his head as his cum squirted deep into Jackson's throat. Soaring through the stars, one thought kept racing through his mind—when it came to blow jobs, no one ever deep-throated him like Jackson. Back on earth, Steel heard the erratic beating of his heart, wondering if it might explode. Focusing on his mate, he was mesmerized by that wicked pink tongue, eagerly at work cleaning his cock, lapping up the remaining traces of his cum.

No longer willing to wait, he pulled his mate onto his lap, kissing Jackson's swollen red lips, his tongue gently parting them as it found its way into his mouth. Steel groaned as his tongue sought out and found tasty traces of his essence in his mate's mouth. Continuing to explore, licking everywhere before he gently ended his kiss, he finally rested his forehead on Jackson's. "I loved your gift," he whispered.

"I knew you would," replied Jackson smugly.

"Oh, you did, did you?" Steel challenged, tickling his mate's ribs.

"Stop it," Jackson gasped between bursts of giggles.

Steel's hand stopped, his hand moving to Jackson's baby bump. "Okay, I'll pick it up later when I have you at my mercy," he leered. "So, aside from the ecstatic pleasure you gave me, what did you need me for?"

"Well, I came to see you about the night of the full moon."

"Yes-s-s-s?" mumbled Steel, nuzzling his mate's neck, licking and sucking to mark him.

"Babe, pay attention, the full moon. Remember?"

"What about it?" asked Steel, seemingly lost in his cuddling.

"I wanted to go for a pack run on the full moon. We haven't done it for a while and I want to explore your land..."

"Our land," corrected Steel.

"Okay, our land. There'll only be a few more full moons when I'll still be able to shift. And I think my brothers really need to let their wolves out and stretch their legs with a good long run as a pack."

"Okay," Steel mumbled, while continuing to mark his mate, leaving a trail of hickeys on Jackson's neck and shoulders.

"Are you listening to me?"

Steel paused, and with a wry smile, looked at his mate. "Yes, you want to go on a full moon pack run because you think it'll be good for your brothers and you won't be able to shift in a couple of more months. Did I miss anything?"

Batting Steel's chest, Jackson grinned. "You think you're so damned clever, don't you?"

"If the shoe fits..."

"Enough! Well, what do you think about a pack run?"

"I'm for it. Personally, I can't wait to see your wolf. So, set it up. I agree—it'll help settle everyone down," said Steel, resuming his marking mission.

~/~/~/~/~

Hanging up after talking to Steel, Slate sat looking at the phone. Gods, he hated Josiah already and he didn't even know him. He felt sorry for a pack that had to follow a sadistic killer. Slate would bet anything—because he knew he would win—Josiah ruled his pack by fear. Well, better just get this over with, thought Slate. Placing the call, he waited for Josiah to pick up.

"Hello, Alpha Silver Point speaking," Josiah barked, answering on his personal phone.

"Alpha? I'm Slate Valentin, calling you back about your request to waive the requirement of producing a title to the land."

"Mr. Valentin, thank you for returning my call. Yes, about the waiver—as you know, pack land is usually titled to the Alpha. Since I'm only the brother of the deceased Alpha and not a direct descendant, I'd have to go to court to have the title changed to my name and it would take at least six more months," said Josiah.

"I don't see the problem in doing it that way, Alpha."

"Well, if I have to ask the Court to transfer the title, my pack would suffer because it would take longer until I'd be able to set up a mining operation. We need to start sooner rather than later because we're in bad shape and need the gold to buy food and other necessities," whined Josiah.

Slate was disgusted with Josiah's tone of voice and his pathetic attempt to manipulate him by using hunger as a weapon. “Alpha, I can’t make this decision myself. The only option is for me to bring it up to the Board and ask them to approve your request.”

“I appreciate that, Mr. Valentin. If you need anything else from me about the request, please let me know,” Josiah said.

“I’ll do that,” said Slate and hung up the phone. He had a strong urge to take a shower to wash off the filth that Josiah had contaminated him with.

~/~/~/~/~

Announcing at dinner there’d be a full moon pack run the next night, Jackson decreed attendance mandatory. He invited Oracle and Maximus to join them. “I know it’ll be a treat for Steel to have the chance to run with you again,” he told them.

Oracle looked at Maximus who gave a slight nod, and answered, “Thank you, Jackson. We have not had a run in our wolves for some time now—it will be a treat to do it with Steel.”

“I was also going to invite Slate, but he hasn’t arrived yet. Do you know when he’ll be joining us?” asked Jackson.

Steel answered, “I spoke with him this afternoon and his trip has been delayed because of a crisis in Mexico. As soon as it gets resolved, he’ll be coming.”

“Oh, was that before or after I saw you this afternoon?” teased Jackson.

A faint pink blush washed over Steel’s face, and he decided no answer was the best answer. Shit, Jackson’s question brought up the image of his mate on his knees sucking Steel’s brains out through his cock. His blush grew deeper and it wasn’t helped when his mate surreptitiously placed his hand on Steel's groin, giving it a squeeze. Steel was rendered speechless as his cock hardened in response to Jackson's touch.

Maximus broke the silence. "Colton, I understand you're in charge of outfitting the hospital downstairs."

"Well, not in charge actually, I'm assisting Dr. Wallace," replied Colton.

"Ian is a good man," said Maximus, "in fact, one of the best. Jackson couldn't be in better hands. When is he going to arrive?"

"I think in another two months. In the meantime, Steel has ordered the equipment and I'll set it up when it comes so everything will be ready for the doctor," Colton answered.

Steel heard only half of what his father and Colton were discussing but he owed his father a debt of gratitude for diverting attention away from him. Jackson removed his hand but Steel was left with very tight pants; his hard-on refusing to go down. Someone was speaking but it wasn't until Jackson nudged him that Steel realized he'd been asked a question. "I'm sorry. What was that?"

"I asked if you knew when the ultrasound machine would be arriving?" said Colton.

"Ahhh… in two days," Steel managed to say, deciding his mate would pay tonight for wreaking havoc on his cock.

Colton turned to Jackson. "How about we schedule your first ultrasound for Friday then?

"Will you be able to see my nephew?" asked Dakota.

"Maybe the baby will be your niece," smirked Cody.

"*Your* niece too, you know," retorted Dakota.

"Actually, the baby will be *ours*, no matter what it turns out to be," Logan said. Then turning to Colton, "Will you be able to determine the pup's sex this Friday?"

Colton thought for a moment. "Maybe. This is my first Dire Wolf pregnancy so I can't give you an answer until I see what stage the baby's development is at," he replied.

"I'm putting 40 bucks on it being a boy," called Zane from the end of the table.

"Forty on a girl," responded Carson.

Listening to his brothers shouting out their bets on the sex of his pup made Jackson happy that they'd all accepted his pregnancy. And it seemed they were just as excited about having a new Blackwood Pack member.

~/~/~/~/~

Gazing from their bedroom window at the clear, darkening sky, Jackson contemplated the view. He loved the way Steel's house was oriented. The views were spectacular and at night, in bed, he and Steel were bathed in moonlight. He looked forward to the run tonight which, hopefully, would include mating with Steel in their wolf forms. That would be the height of pleasure as their wolves could fully express their animal instincts.

Moving his hand to his belly, absentmindedly caressing his pup, Jackson was sure his morning sickness was over and his overwhelming tiredness had subsided. He was looking forward to seeing his baby on Friday during the first ultrasound session. Jackson was so deep in thought, he never heard Steel enter.

Wrapping his arms around Jackson, Steel pulled him back against his chest.

"I love you," Jackson murmured, turning his head for a kiss.

Gently kissing his mate, hugging him tighter to him as one hand moved down to their pup, Steel asked, "How are you feeling, babe?"

"Funny, I was just thinking about how good I felt—no more barfing, more energy, I think my pregnancy has turned a page," replied Jackson.

"Well, I have a present for you since you've passed the pain-in-the-ass stage."

"Really?" Jackson's face lit up with a sweet smile. "I love getting presents. That was my favorite thing about the Long Night Moon Festival. In fact, I always bought myself a gift and wrapped it just to make sure there was one for me to open."

"You did *not* do that. You're just making it up, right?" Steel asked, grinning.

"No, really! When I bought gifts for my family, I always bought one for myself. And then I would wrap and unwrap it several times before we all opened our presents. I really miss it now that my parents and younger siblings are gone," he said sadly.

"I'm sorry babe," Steel whispered in Jackson's ear. "But I promise we'll make new traditions with our pup and families so you can replace the sad ones with happy ones."

Turning around in his mate's arms, Jackson snuggled into his chest. The sound of Steel's strong and steady heart beat made him relax. Secure in his mate's arms, he played with Steel's nipple, "So, what's my present?"

"Ummm, babe, I recommend you stop that or we won't make it to the run tonight," Steel groaned.

"Party pooper," giggled Jackson, removing his fingers.

"Ahhh, later babe, I promise," Steel smirked, continuing, "since you're feeling better, I want to take you on a babymoon."

Jackson couldn't believe it. *A babymoon!* He'd dreamt about it but wasn't sure how his mate would feel. Time away for just the two of them and no day-to-day worries or problems to interfere. *What a treat!*

Raising his head, he grabbed Steel's face, planting a loud, lip-smacking kiss on his startled mate.

"I take it you approve," Steel chuckled, while Jackson kissed him all over his face and neck.

"Hell, yes!"

"We have to go soon, because once you start showing more, it will be hard to explain to humans."

"Oh, where are we going?" Jackson asked, pausing his kissing assault.

"That, *mo chroí,* is a surprise."

Chapter 29

Once outside, Jackson and Steel saw the large, deep-yellow, full moon hanging low in the dark sky. "My parents have shifted and are waiting for us in the woods," said Steel.

This news pleased Jackson as he didn't think he was ready to see his mother-in-law naked just yet or vice versa. He giggled at his modesty but really, he knew he just wasn't ready.

Steel nudged him, "What's so funny?"

"I'll tell you later, babe," answered Jackson standing on the top step, looking down at his brothers who had gathered below.

"Okay, guys, Steel's going to lead us tonight since he knows the land. So, let's have some fun," Jackson said, joining his brothers. "Start shifting."

One by one, the brothers shifted; Jackson was the last. Steel gasped as he saw seven snow white wolves looking at him, all as large as the biggest Alpha he ever met. White wolves! Seven of them! All from the same pack! What were the odds? Steel didn't even want to figure that one out—even one white wolf was such a rarity that a wolf could live a very long life and never see one. Steel's eyes narrowed and knew he'd be having a conversation about this with his mother. Suddenly, Jackson's wolf pressed its nose into his hand, whining and wondering why he hadn't shifted. Steel knelt down, scratching him behind the ears, and rubbed its nose. "Your wolf is so beautiful, babe," Steel murmured to his lover before shifting.

A massive wolf, with black tipped silver-grey fur, emerged, prompting Jackson to step back along with his brothers at the display before them. Whining at the presence of this massive wolf, Jackson's brothers nervously scuffed their paws on the ground. Acting quickly to quell his brothers' concerns, Jackson confronted Steel, demanding his submission by grabbing his snout in his teeth and dragging it toward the ground.

At first, Steel's wolf resisted but then quickly acquiesced, exposing his neck in submission. Jackson let go, licked his mate and then howled. Joining in, his brothers and Steel sang the song of wolves, echoing through the trees and rising to the moon.

Suddenly, Steel took off, running toward a special place in his forest. Following quickly, Jackson and the rest of his brothers tagged along behind him. Steel saw his parents standing at the side of the trail as he ran past and they joined the pack. Onward, up the mountain, Steel led the pack, the sounds of the forest stilling as the wolves ran through it.

Panting and huffing, the pack followed Steel, reveling in their run under the full moon. Near the mountaintop, the pine needle carpeted forest floor gave way to bare ground and rock, the trees thinned and the wolves had a clear view of the night sky.

Jackson followed closely behind his mate, savoring the cool night air rushing through his fur—he never wanted this night to end. So much had happened since the pack's last full moon run, Jackson found it hard to believe. He could smell his mate in front of him—the scent that would drive him crazy for the rest of his days. And a pup on the way! Oh, he could hardly wait until their pup could run with them—a beautiful silver-grey pup, nipping at his heels, in an effort to make Jackson run faster. And Steel behind their pup, guarding him from threats. Jackson had no doubts after seeing Steel's wolf he'd always be able to protect their pup. Nope, no doubts at all.

Slowing down after about an hour, the pack reached an outcropping of rock near the top of the mountain. From here, Steel always felt he could touch the stars. The wolves all milled about before flopping on the ground, breathing hard. Jackson lay next to Steel, resting his head on his paws, fascinated by the stars above moving lazily across the night sky.

Seeing those stars reflected in his mate's eyes, Steel knew he'd never forget this night. Being this close to Jackson caused his cock to harden and he dearly wanted to fuck his mate's wolf. First, though, he needed to get rid of the pack; he didn't need an audience. Shifting, Steel stood, "Dad, would you lead the pack down the mountain? I'd like to spend some time up here with Jackson."

Logan shifted suddenly, asking Jackson, "Is it a problem if we run some other trails?"

Steel looked at his mate and waited for Jackson's response through their mind link.

That's fine with me. Is there anything they should be aware of?

No babe, my land is safe.

Okay, but they must stay together.

Jackson nodded his approval. Steel said to Logan, "Just stay together. Have fun."

Logan shifted back as his brothers got up. Steel's parents also rose and followed the boys back down the trail. Turning to his mate's wolf, Steel asked, "Please, would you shift, babe?"

Jackson felt the pain of disappointment; he'd really wanted his wolf to be claimed by Steel's wolf. Hesitating, but then shifting, he stood before his lover. Gathering Jackson into his arms, Steel held his mate against his chest, allowing his heat to keep Jackson warm. "I wanted to ask you if I... I mean, could my wolf make love to your wolf? I've been dreaming of doing that ever since we claimed each other."

Jackson was stunned; that was the last thing he'd expected when Steel asked him to shift. Facing his mate, he said softly, "We're on the same page. I hoped you'd claim me as a wolf tonight."

"Thank you, babe. You know, this is my favorite spot. The stars feel close enough to pick one out of the sky to give to you…the light of my life," Steel said, kissing his mate passionately. "This is the spot my wolf wants to claim yours, under the light of a thousand stars," crooned Steel. Stepping back, he said, "Shift for me, babe."

Jackson's wolf appeared again. Kneeling and throwing his arms around the pure white beauty, Steel buried his face into its neck ruff. He inhaled deeply, loving the scent. Then, rubbing his hands all over the wolf's body, he hummed his approval of his strong and muscled mate.

Steel shifted into his Dire Wolf. Standing in front of his mate, he watched as Jackson's wolf lowered himself until his belly was touching the ground. Whimpering, Jackson's wolf inched forward in a submissive pose, yielding to his mate.

This was the very private moment between the two Jackson hadn't wanted his brothers to witness. At the beginning of the night, Steel submitted to him, showing the brothers Jackson was the Alpha of the pack. But now, it was he, willingly submitting to his dominant mate. Jackson wasn't sure what would happen in the future. Deep down, he felt Steel would make a better Alpha, especially after the pup came. But for the time being, he was content to fulfill the role. Jackson flipped over, exposing his belly.

Steel lowered his head, licking his mate's face before licking and rubbing his scent over the rest of Jackson.

Rolling over and lifting his hindquarters, Jackson moved his tail aside to entice his mate to mount him.

Steel's cock slid into his mate with ease. His body heated up, his blood boiled, and he grew large in Jackson. His orgasm approaching, Steel's snout burrowed through Jackson's snowy-white fur until, reaching his mate's skin, he bit down hard on his neck, claiming Jackson's wolf.

Feeling Steel's teeth, Jackson's wolf howled; his cock erupted, spurting cum over his fur and onto the ground. Steel's howl united with Jackson's as his seed filled his mate. Joined together, the two wolf spirits danced on the winds of night.

~/~/~/~/~

The morning after the Full Moon Night run, Steel asked his mother to join him in his office. While waiting for her, he thought about what he'd discovered about Jackson and his brothers on their run. Seven white wolves, seven brothers, all saved from a massacre. He wondered if their uncle Josiah knew these brothers were white wolves and the significance of it. If he knew, then Steel understood why he not only wanted the Fox River Pack land but also wanted them dead.

"Hi sweetie, how is Jackson feeling?" asked Oracle, sweeping into his office.

Watching his mother's graceful movements as she glided around his desk, Steel could only describe her as "other worldly." Hugging each other, he replied, "Jackson's fine. You've been keeping something about my mate and his brothers from me, mother."

Oracle sat down opposite Steel, eyeing him intently, and asked. "Why would you think that?"

"Mom, I saw seven very large white wolves stand before me last night. Seven white wolves who are Jackson and his brothers. You know how rare white wolves are and why. That alone makes my mate's brothers a target for every greedy, immoral, and untrustworthy wolf out there who wants to get their hands on one. Jeez, and I'm bringing an unknown doctor into my house to work with Colton."

"Ian is okay. Do you think I would have just anyone take care of Jackson and my grandbaby? At least give me more credit than that," she huffed.

"Still, you know it would devastate Jackson if anything happened to his brothers. You should have warned me so I'd be able to take more steps to protect them."

"Steel, look at me. I am the Oracle. I am the voice of the Fates on earth. I know they saved Jackson and his brothers from the massacre. They have told me these seven brothers are very special to the future of wolves and that is why they escaped death. The only danger I know of is from Silver Point Pack. You are handling it. So, do not worry about what you perceive as possible danger."

He knew his mother, as Oracle, could only speak the truth about the welfare of Jackson's brothers. Steel gave a deep sigh, and then asked, “Will you let me know if the Fates tell you about any danger?”

“I promise.”

“So, can they all the bear pups like Jackson? Or does each have a different power?” asked Steel, curious about the brothers’ gifts.

“I haven’t been told that yet. All I know is they have been selected by the Fates for reasons known only to them at this time. We will have to wait and see,” Oracle said.

Steel sat back. “Okay, but you know waiting is not my strong suit.”

“Oh, I know,” laughed Oracle.

Chapter 30

Colton was waiting for Jackson and Steel in the examining room he'd set up for the ultrasound. Steel certainly hadn't skimped on equipment for the mini hospital. Everything was the best money could buy.

He was pleased Steel allowed him to pick the rooms he wanted for the hospital. This room was painted in a soothing light aqua, complimented by beautiful beiges and warm wood doors, giving it a sense of tranquility. He knew it would help alleviate any anxiety Jackson might have during subsequent examinations.

It was hard to believe he was once more working in a hospital, even though it was a private one with only one patient, but still, Colton was doing a happy dance in his mind. When his family was killed and he went into hiding, Colton felt his goal of being a nurse died the same day. Now, it was a different world and he was walking on cloud nine because he had a real patient to care for.

"Hi, Colton," Jackson said, entering with Steel on his heels. "Wow, this is so cool! Did you do this?"

"Yeah, I chose room colors so everything would be perfect for you."

"Well done. I love it. So, do I need to undress for this test?"

"No, just lie down on the table and open your jeans so I have access to your belly. Raise your t-shirt, too." Jackson complied as Colton rolled his chair over along with the ultrasound machine.

"This test won't hurt. First, I'll rub some gel on your belly," Colton said, squirting and rubbing the emollient on Jackson's bump.

"What's that for?" asked Steel, who stood at Jackson's head.

"The gel creates an airtight bond between the wand and skin so the sound waves pass directly to what we want a picture of—in this case, Jackson's baby," explained Colton, pleased to be using his medical knowledge at last." Then he said, "Steel, would you please lower the lights?"

"This switch?"

"Yeah, just move it to the middle," replied Colton, turning on the ultrasound.

"Then if you stand on that side of Jackson, you'll be able to see the screen."

Once at Jackson's side, Steel reached out to hold his mate's hand. Jackson turned, smiling at Steel while softly mouthing the words, "I love you." Grinning, Steel squeezed Jackson's hand as Colton lowered the wand to his mate's belly, slowly moving it until suddenly, a loud thumping sound was heard. "That's your pup's heartbeat. Nice and strong," Colton announced.

Jackson knew his pup's heartbeat because he'd heard the low, soft, muffled thumps for a while now—they'd lulled him to sleep many a night and the sound comforted him. Still, it surprised him now how much he loved hearing it amplified, drumming out a steady beat.

Colton continued moving the wand as he fiddled with the machine. Then he said, "There's your pup."

"Where? What are we looking at?" asked Steel "I don't see anything."

"Here, see? Here's the baby and there's its heartbeat," said Colton, pointing to the screen. "I'll print out a picture for you."

"Can you tell whether we're having a boy or a girl?" asked Jackson.

"Nope, the baby is not cooperating today. Maybe next time. I just need to do some measurements for Dr. Wallace and you're finished," Colton replied.

Steel and Jackson looked at the first picture of their pup, smiling at each other. "I guess this is the real deal, huh?" said Jackson.

"As real is it gets," answered Steel.

"All done for today," Colton said, wiping the gel off Jackson's belly.

Reaching out for Jackson's arm to steady him as he got off the table, Steel was determined no harm would befall either his mate or pup at this point in time—or ever.

"So, now what?" Jackson asked Colton.

"I'll need you back next week at the same time for the next ultrasound. Once I write up my findings, I'll send them off to Dr. Wallace and we'll wait to see what he orders. As far as I can tell, everything is looking good."

"You don't see any reason Jackson can't go on a mini vacation, right?" asked Steel.

"No, I don't, but it really isn't up to me. I'll ask the doctor if it's all right, okay?"

"Yeah, that's fine. Let me know what he says," replied Steel.

After Jackson and Steel were gone, Colton took the information and pictures he'd made of Jackson's baby into his small office next door.

He was pleased with what he saw and everything seemed normal. Jackson and Steel made such a great couple and they were so much in love. Colton admired Steel's protectiveness of his brother and their pup. But that wasn't a journey Colton was planning to take anytime soon. He was determined to finish nursing school, get his degree, and then find a job in his chosen field.

Ever since he was a young child, he knew that medicine was in his future. Cody and Carson always teased him about healing every sick animal he came across. But he couldn't help it; the need to help was so deeply ingrained in him, it could never be torn from his soul.

For the last few years, he was limited to injured animals he found in the forest. But now he'd gotten the greatest gift from his brother—someone who needed his knowledge and skills to have a healthy pup.

He put aside his musings, forcing himself to do the report for Dr. Wallace, not wanting to give the good doctor any reason to scold him for not sending the patient's test results promptly.

~/~/~/~/~

Spending the morning in his study, Jackson was catching up on the pack's affairs he'd fallen behind on due to the side effects of his pregnancy. But now, these having passed, he was full of energy more than ever. Doing the bookkeeping, he realized Steel had been paying for most of the pack's expenses. That had to stop. Hearing a knock, Jackson said, "Come in!" and watched as Logan sauntered over to him.

"Hi bro, what's up?" he asked.

After taking a seat, Logan studied Jackson. "You're looking good."

"You know what I'm getting tired of? Is everyone asking me how are you feeling or doing or whatever other crap they can come up with."

"Hey, I didn't ask you that!"

Jackson sighed. "No, you didn't, but you examined me as if I were some kind of bug under a microscope."

"Fair enough. I'll try to refrain from looking at you anymore."

"Fuck off," smiled Jackson. "So, what did you want to see me about?"

"I've been wondering how long we're going to be staying here."

"Is there a problem about Steel's home? Do the boys have any issues?" asked Jackson.

"No, no, nothing like that. It's just that this house doesn't feel like a home, you know, it's all cold and impersonal. I redecorated my bedroom and I did some of our brothers' bedrooms, but I was hoping you might talk to Steel about letting me loose on the great room and some other areas of the house. What do you think?"

"I think it's a great idea. I'll ask him today and get back to you."

"Also, what are you going to do about a room for the pup?"

"Shit, I haven't even thought about that. I just wanted to survive my morning sickness and exhaustion."

"I'd be happy to use my skills to design a nursery. I've already done some research and made a list of what would be needed," offered Logan.

"I'd love your input," exclaimed Jackson "I'll put the subject on the agenda when I talk with Steel."

"And finally, what about clothes for the pup? Have you thought of what you'll need? Or more like it, have you thought of it at all?" chortled Logan.

"Ha, ha. You know I've been a little preoccupied, oh brother of mine. But I'm not worried, because if I know you, all that has been taken care of already," Jackson said, smirking at Logan.

"You think you know everything, don't you? Well, maybe someday I won't have your back"

"Never, brother, never."

"Yeah, yeah. You're right. I'll always have your back. So, kidding aside, what about baby clothes?"

"I haven't a clue so I'm hoping you've been on top of this," said Jackson.

Handing Jackson a list, Logan said, "I've included everything you need for the pup from birth to about six months. You might want Oracle to look at it because I'm not sure how fast a Dire Pup grows."

Jackson's eyes widened, looking at the list. Jerking his head up, he eyed Logan. "Shit, you're kidding me, right? Why all these clothes? How the hell is a pup going to need twenty onesies? What the hell is a onesie anyway?"

"You're going to be a father and you don't know what a onesie is? Jackson, you need to get your head on straight. I'll tell you what. Instead of bitching to me about the stuff on the list, ask Mystia or Oracle. Then follow their advice. But no matter who you talk to, we need to do something about getting ready for your baby."

Jackson knew his brother was right, but had avoided thinking about it until he knew the baby was okay. No longer having that as an excuse—because his pup was doing well—it certainly was time to talk to Mystia or Oracle about it.

"You're right," sighed Jackson. "I'll take care of it. Hey, you want to see a picture of the pup Colton took when we did the ultrasound last week?"

"Absolutely! You had it and never told me? Bastard! You owe me," said Logan, smiling while taking the picture from Jackson. "Do you know if it's a boy or a girl yet?"

"No. Colton thinks maybe we'll know this week."

"What do you want?"

"Me? Just a healthy baby. This is all so new to me I still worry about it, even though Mystia assures me it'll be okay—but..."

"Hey dude," Logan said softly, "I'd believe Mystia if I were you. She knows stuff—if you know what I mean." He handed the picture back to Jackson.

"Yeah, I know," Jackson said quietly, "but it's still hard to be strong every minute of every day. I worry about everything. I never thought I could get pregnant. Then I found out I could have a pup. And now I'm worried as hell I'll lose him or her, as the case may be. Crazy, right?"

"You know, Jackson," said Logan softly, "I'd feel the same way. Have you talked to Steel about your feelings?"

"I haven't because they seem so foolish. You know—like I should be able to deal with them because I'm Alpha. I just don't want Steel to think less of me."

"Bullshit. Talk to him, Jackson. Steel would never make you feel anything except important to him," said Logan.

"Yeah, I guess you're right. I know it inside my heart but I can't seem to wrap my head around it."

"Your pregnancy hormones are ruling you, bro. Talk to Colton about how you feel if you don't want to talk to Steel," urged Logan.

"Okay, okay. I see Colton tomorrow and I'll ask him then."

"Good. Let me know what Steel says about my decorating requests," said Logan. Standing, he looked at Jackson for a moment and then left the study.

Jackson knew Logan was right. He needed to talk to someone and he'd feel more comfortable with Colton right now. Ever since he saw the ultrasound picture, Jackson had fallen in love with their pup. He wondered if Steel felt the same way.

"Yes, I do," said Steel, walking in to hug and kiss his mate. "And what is this I heard about you worrying about something happening to the baby?"

Jackson kissed his mate back, "Who told you? I only mentioned this to Logan a few minutes ago and I know he didn't tell you."

"*Mo chroí*, you have been broadcasting your thoughts to me for the last few minutes. That's why I came to see you so we could talk about your worries."

"Oh," Jackson turned a deep shade of pink. "I didn't realize I was doing it."

"I'm happy you did. Babe, talk to me. What are you worried about?"

Steel lifted Jackson up from his desk chair, sat down in it, and pulled his mate onto his lap so they were face to face

Bending his head down so it was against Steel's chest, Jackson was embarrassed he'd inadvertently mind-linked his worries to his mate. Now, talking to Colton seemed pointless because his mate already knew.

"I'm afraid something will happen to our pup... I'm in love with the pup, so much, and this is all so new… I mean, I'm the only Alpha/Omega hybrid and what if something goes wrong? I can't lose that pup because when I heard the heartbeat, I fell in love… I am a mess…" Jackson rambled on.

Steel lovingly held his mate and rubbed Jackson's back soothingly. He let Jackson get it all out, the worries and the fears, and he just listened. Steel knew these feelings were real to his mate and even though he felt everything would be fine, that didn't lessen the importance of Jackson's concerns. After a while, Jackson fell silent, exhaling loudly.

"I guess you think I'm weak for having these feelings, huh?" Jackson finally said, voicing his biggest fear.

"Babe, I think you're amazingly strong and I couldn't be prouder to have you as my mate and to follow you as my Alpha. Never think otherwise. If I were in your shoes, I don't know if I could handle a complete upheaval of my life and my understanding of who I thought I was as well as you have," replied Steel.

"Really?" asked Jackson, and then hated the way it made him sound so needy.

"Really, babe. You know, I think the pregnancy hormones running rampant through your body right now are responsible for at least part of your worries. Why don't you ask Colton what you can expect?" offered Steel.

"I'll do that," said Jackson, now calmer. Then, "Have I told you lately how much I love you?"

Steel gave Jackson a kiss, "No, not since this morning when you were screaming my name as I fucked you."

Jackson, grinning at the memory, sassed, "Well, that was far too long ago." Reaching for his mate's lips, he licked at them until they parted. Then he thrust his tongue in, seeking his mate's in a dance of love.

Breathless from the heat of the kiss, Jackson pulled back and said, "I… Love… You..." punctuating each word with a kiss.

Hugging his mate tightly, Steel inhaled Jackson's special scent. "I love you, too, babe, you're my everything," seizing Jackson's lips in a devil-take-all kiss.

"Wow," Jackson said breathlessly after the kiss ended

Steel chuckled, "Yeah, I agree. So, mate-of-mine, is there anything else you want to talk to me about?"

Loving his mate, who could bring him to the edge of insanity with just a kiss, he paused to get his rioting emotions under control. Then he remembered what Logan wanted, and turning to pick up the baby clothes list from his desk, he handed it to Steel.

"What's this?"

"That, my father-to-be, is what Logan thinks our pup needs in the way of clothes."

"All of this? Really? He's kidding, right?"

Jackson huffed out a short laugh. "Yup, that was pretty much my reaction, but Logan said if I didn't believe him, I should check it out with Mystia or your mother."

"Okaaay. Shit. What Logan is really telling us is we're fucked as far as thinking he over exaggerated what's needed. Why does a baby need so many clothes?"

"Oh," teased Jackson, "Logan also said to check with your mother as to how fast a Dire pup will grow because he might need bigger sizes."

Shaking his head in disbelief, "Now I understand how you feel. This just got very real to me," Steel murmured.

"Oh babe..." Jackson said, in a sing-songy voice, "there's more."

"More?" asked Steel.

"Logan told me we needed to do the nursery and wondered if we'd done anything about it."

"Nursery?" Steel asked faintly. "Oh shit."

"Yup, that's how I felt too. I'm *so* glad we are *so* in tune with each other," sniggered Jackson. "However, Logan came up with a solution. He offered to design the nursery for us if we just tell him which bedroom we want it to be in."

Finally, Steel thought, a solution for at least one thing concerning the pup. He asked Jackson, "Ahhh, how do *you* feel about Logan doing that? Is it okay with you?"

"I was going to tease you about this," laughed Jackson, "but after seeing the look on your face, I think not."

"What do you mean 'the look on my face?'" asked Steel indignantly.

"We-l-l-l-l-l, you have a look of sheer panic on your face," snorted Jackson.

Steel opened his mouth, and then shut it, narrowing his eyes. "Hey, this is all new to me. I'm still suffering from the shock of seeing the clothes list."

Jackson laughed again. "I know… right? Anyway, to answer your question, if Logan wants to design our pup's nursery, it's fine with me. Did you know he was studying interior design before the massacre?"

"No… is he any good?"

Swatting Steel's chest, Jackson snapped, "Of course he's good. He's my brother so how could he be anything else?"

"*Mea culpa*," Steel said, grinning. "Right, why would I even think to ask that?"

"Logan's amazing. Once we'd built our pack house, Logan designed and decorated the interior. He's done his bedroom here, as well as some for my brothers. You should check 'em out."

"Babe, if you're okay with Logan doing the nursery, it's fine with me," said Steel. "I just wanted to make sure he didn't pressure you to do it."

"No," said Jackson. "His ideas are so amazing; I know you'll love them."

"Good. Now we only have the clothes list to do. I'll run that past my mother and see what she has to say," said Steel.

"Oh, and one last thing. Logan would like to redesign the great room and dining room so they have more coziness. He said the way they are now makes him feel like he's in a hotel."

Thinking for a minute, Steel said, "You know, he's right. I never felt like this house was a 'home' and I want that for the baby. So, tell him to go ahead and have fun."

Jackson showed his appreciation by attacking Steel's lips with his own.

Chapter 31

Jimmy watched the shifter gas up his truck and knew the guy was trouble. As he vacillated between alerting Mystia or handling this himself, he sniffed again just to make sure he smelled Silver Point Pack. Yup, the guy belonged to that pack and he would bet anything he was an enforcer. He watched as the guy looked up behind Jimmy's place to where the Blackwood Pack house stood and that clinched it—this dude was hunting today.

Dylon knew he was being watched but couldn't spot who it was. He looked up the mountain. Nope, nothing there. He slipped on his sunglasses and then saw Jimmy. Now, why was that old wolf staring at him? And fidgeting—like he might know who Dylon was. He topped off his tank, put the nozzle back, and decided to pay in person instead of at the pump. Maybe the old wolf knew something.

This was an easy assignment Rudy had given him. Dylon was new to the Silver Point Pack and was still learning pack politics. He'd left his old pack soon after he became an enforcer there because his job required shaking down or threatening pack members the Alpha wanted targeted. His parents hadn't raised him to be a thug; to Dylon, being an enforcer meant keeping the pack safe from outside enemies—not harassing members of the pack who hadn't committed crimes.

Rudy told him they were tracking a band of brothers who killed his Alpha's brother and others in the brother's pack. They found where the killers were hiding but failed to execute them because they'd fled. So, Rudy sent him back here to see if he could pick up the trail. He headed inside to pay for his gas and maybe, if he got lucky, the old wolf would know something. "Hi," Dylon said as he walked up to the counter, fishing his wallet from his pocket. "How much do I owe for the gas?"

Jimmy told him and as Dylon handed over the cash, he nonchalantly asked, "Hey, I'm looking for an old friend named Jackson. Do you know him?"

Jimmy pressed a button under the counter before he replied, "Maybe, depends on what his last name is."

"Well, can I speak plainly here? I know you're a wolf, as am I, so let me just say Jackson is a member of the Blackwood Pack. Do you know them?"

"Who are you, young man?"

"I'm sorry, I'm Dylon and as I said, Jackson's an old friend of mine."

"Is that so?"

Dylon's eyes narrowed. The old wolf hadn't given him any information and avoided giving answers to his questions. His gut told him something wasn't right. He glanced around, his eyes settling on a business license taped to the wall behind the counter. Owner: Jimmy Blackwood. *Fuck!* Dylon now knew why he felt something was fishy and his eyes narrowed as they swiveled back to Jimmy. "I think you know exactly who I'm looking for, don't you, Jimmy? Are you going to tell me where he is or do I have to convince you to help me?"

Suddenly, Dylon heard a melodious female voice behind him. "Now why would such a handsome man want to do that to someone clearly not a threat?"

"Mind your own business," he snarled, turning around. And in a split second, Dylon knew he'd made a big mistake as the witch waved her hands and he felt himself falling, but could not shift. The witch had paralyzed him. Jimmy quickly moved around the counter, caught Dylon, and laid him gently on the floor. The last thing Dylon remembered was thinking how sad his parents would be about his death.

Jimmy looked up at Mystia. "What are you going to do now?"

"I want to talk to him," Mystia replied.

"Okaaay, about what?"

"You'll see. Move aside so I can teleport him into your office."

Jimmy got up from his kneeling position next to Dylon, moving away. He watched as Mystia waved her hand over the prone body, and then headed back to his office where he found Dylon sitting in a chair.

"Jimmy, I want you to record my interview with this shifter."

"His name is Dylon," Jimmy said.

He took out his smartphone and set it to record mode as Dylon slowly woke up.

When he came to, Dylon became aware of the two people—no, make that a wolf shifter and a witch—standing before him. *Damn!* He had to get out of here, report back to Rudy and come back with reinforcements. He tried to get up but found he was still frozen. Snarling, Dylon said, "Let me go. You have no right to hold me!"

"I have every right," said Mystia, "You lied to my mate and threatened him. Now, I'm going to ask some questions and you will answer them truthfully."

"I don't have..." Dylon started to say, as Mystia waved her hand and murmured the words of a spell. "...yes, madam, I will answer truthfully."

"Jimmy, start recording," Mystia said, before continuing. "Dylon, are you an enforcer for the Silver Point Pack?"

"Yes"

"Why did you stop at this place?"

"I needed gas."

"Why did you ask about a person name Jackson?"

"I'm looking for him."

"Why?"

"Because Rudy sent me to find out where he is."

"Who's Rudy?"

"He's Alpha Silver Point's second-in-command."

"Why is Rudy looking for Jackson?"

"To kill him."

"Kill just Jackson?"

"No, Jackson's brothers, too."

"Who have you killed so far since becoming an enforcer for the Silver Point Pack?"

"Nobody."

Mystia looked over at Jimmy to make sure he was recording, and then asked Dylon, "Is there a kill order out on Jackson and his brothers?"

"Yes, they are enemies of the Silver Point Pack."

"Who put out the kill order?"

"I-I-I don't know, the Alpha? Rudy just told me that there was a kill order on Jackson and his brothers."

Mystia turned to Jimmy, indicating he should stop recording. Once he had turned his phone off, Jimmy asked, "What now?"

"Now Dylon is going to leave here and he will remember only that he did not find anything of interest," said Mystia as she did one more spell over him before teleporting him to his truck.

As they watched Dylon drive away, Jimmy asked Mystia, "Why did you want me to record him? We already knew all that."

"Yes, we did, but the video will be useful for those who don't."

Steel found his mother in the solarium reading one of the many books in his library. Sitting down in one of the large, plush, club chairs next to hers—as he waited for an acknowledgment—his thoughts drifted to Logan and his incredible design ability. He'd already told Jackson he had no objections to Logan doing the nursery, great room, and dining room, but now he had another design project for Logan to do. It would have to be kept secret and Steel just hoped Logan would agree.

Oracle inserted a bookmark, closed the book and looked at her son. "I assume you want to see me about something, sweetie?" Oracle asked.

Steel handed his mother the list of baby clothes Logan prepared. "Logan gave us this list a couple of days ago and said it's what the pup will need for his first six months."

Oracle glanced at it. "Okay, what do you want me to do?"

"Wait, are you telling me we'll need all these clothes for a baby who is going to sleep most of the day?"

"Ah-hh-h, you think the list is excessive, is that it?"

"Well, yes. Look at it. Don't you think it's a bit too much?"

"Not really, I think it is quite conservative. If I had done the list, there would be plenty more on it. But maybe Logan was careful about spending your money," replied Oracle.

Steel's mouth flopped open as he processed what his mother said. More clothes? Bending forward, he buried his face in his hands so his mother could not see his panic. This was too much. *Don't I have enough to worry about just keeping my mate safe? Now I will have a helpless baby. What if I screw up? Hurt the baby? Shit, shit, shit.* Oracle set the list down and leaned forward. Steel felt his mother take his hands away from his face as she said softly, "What is the real problem here, sweetie? Why are you so upset about the clothes?"

Steel looked at his mother, sighing. Trust her to know him.

"I freaked out when Jackson handed me this list. Then he talked about a nursery and suddenly I panicked because I'm not ready to be a father. What if I screw up or hurt my pup? Ever since I saw that list, I've been freaking out. I'm trying to hide it from Jackson because he's also freaking out with his own worries and fears."

Oracle took her son's hands in hers, "Look at me, Steel. Every new parent feels exactly as you do. We all worry something will happen to our babies. We never want to let them out of our sight. And we all think we will be the worst parents and screw up our kids so they will hate us forever."

"Did you feel this way? Did Dad?"

Oracle chuckled. "Someday, I'll tell you all the stupid and dumb things we did as new parents. But you know what? You and Slate survived and even thrived. You know why? Because we loved you with our whole hearts. And love overrides a lot of dumb things new parents do. So, my advice? Don't worry. You and Jackson will be great parents, trust me. And besides, you have Mystia and me as backups if you ever truly fuck up."

"Mother! Jeeze, when did *you* start using that language?"

Oracle laughed. "Oh sweetie, I've never stopped but just never did it around you. Now, do you want me to take care of the clothes list?"

"I thought Jackson and I could do it—or at least start—when we're on the babymoon. I looked online and bookmarked some stores that sell stuff that's on the list and I'm sure he'll enjoy doing it but if not, it's all yours."

"When are you going on the babymoon?"

"I'm hoping we'll go next week"

"Does Jackson know about it yet?"

"Yup, but not where I'm taking him. And before you ask—no, I'm not telling anyone because I want it to be a total surprise," Steel said, grinning at his mother before getting up and walking toward the door of the solarium.

"Wait. Where are you going?"

"Uh, uh. I know when it's better to retreat than stay and get interrogated," Steel called over his shoulder.

~/~/~/~/~

Today, Jackson hoped they would find out the sex of the pup. Not that he really cared, but he hoped it was a boy, for Steel's sake. His mate stood by his side as he lay down on the examining table with his hand resting on his baby bump, noticing it was a little bit bigger than the week before. Jackson was trying to imagine how he would look with a big belly when he heard his mate say, "You will be beautiful."

Damn. "Was I broadcasting again?" Jackson asked. "It's a little creepy how you know what I'm thinking."

"Babe, as your pregnancy progresses, I will be able to hear more of your thoughts. I think it's a protection mechanism in case you're in trouble."

"You forgot to tell me that," said Jackson petulantly, not sure how he felt about *that* side effect of his pregnancy.

"How's the father-to-be feeling today?" asked Colton, entering the room, forestalling any response from Steel to Jackson.

"I'm fine," he said curtly.

Colton looked at Steel after hearing the unhappy tone in Jackson's voice. Steel shook his head almost unnoticeably.

Colton nodded once in return. "Well, let's see if your pup wants to show us anything today," he said, moving the ultrasound machine over to Jackson. After he prepped his brother's belly, Colton turned on the ultrasound, pressing the wand to the baby bump. Colton moved it around, taking a series of pictures for Dr.

Wallace and then said, "Okay, everything seems to be fine. The pup is growing nicely. Do you want to know its sex?"

Jackson looked at his mate and nodded. Steel said, "That would be great."

Colton moved the wand again, pointing to the screen. "It's a boy!" he shouted with excitement.

Jackson could feel tears fill his eyes, looking at his mate with joy. "A boy! Babe, we're having a boy!" he exclaimed, taking Steel's hand and kissing it.

Steel could feel his mate's joy mirroring his, basking in the knowledge that he would be a father to a little Dire boy pup and then a thought flashed in his head causing him to exclaim, "We need a name! Our pup needs a name!"

"Babe, we have time," laughed Jackson, his former gloomy mood now gone.

~/~/~/~/~

Slate looked at Jimmy's video several times before emailing it to Steel. It was good, but it didn't give irrefutable proof the Silver Point Pack actually did the massacre and that's what Penn, their attorney, needed. Penn made that point clear after he'd reviewed the complaint, confirming Steel was correct about the weakness in it any good lawyer would exploit.

However, a new possibility opened up after the tape showed up in Slate's mail. Steel came up with the basics, Penn refined it, and now it was time for Slate to implement it. That meant talking to that jackass of an Alpha again and he wasn't happy about it. But it was a small price to pay if it helped Steel protect his mate.

Slate dialed Alpha Silver Point's number, drumming his fingers as the phone rang.

"Hello," snarled Josiah, "Alpha Silver Point."

"Hello, Alpha Silver Point. This is Slate Valentin," he said, waiting for it to sink in who it was the Alpha snarled at.

There was a moment of silence and then, "Mr. Valentin, sorry about my tone. I was busy with pack matters and forgot my manners for a moment," said a chagrined Josiah.

Slate inwardly chuckled. "I received a video and after showing it to the Board, they instructed me to call you."

"Video of what?" asked Josiah cautiously.

"It shows one of your enforcers talking about a kill order you or your second-in-command has out on some shifters."

Josiah paused, worried about what else might be on the video regarding the massacre. "Is that all that's on it?"

Slate ignored the question. "The Board would like to know why this kill order was issued. The enforcer said Jackson and his brothers were enemies of your pack. What have they done? Were they notified of the charges?"

"Wait a minute, Mr. Valentin, this is pack business and doesn't concern your company..."

"That's where you're wrong, Alpha. The company's bylaws require us to assess each pack to make sure all laws mandated by the Universal Paranormal High Council are strictly followed before we can release any money to the pack. You have a kill order out on the shifters. I'm asking if you have proof they've received notice of their crimes against your pack? It's a simple 'yes' or 'no' answer."

Josiah inhaled sharply and then finally replied, "We were unable to find them to serve them notice."

"In order for the Board to consider your request to waive the right to provide proof of title to the land in question, the kill order will have to be rescinded immediately," Slate said, and then shot the next harpoon. "I'll need a sworn statement from you that the kill order has been rescinded as well as sworn statements from your enforcers that they know about it."

Slate paused before continuing, "Once I have those documents, I will inform the Board so they can convene a meeting to consider your request for the waiver."

"Certainly, I understand. I'll get them to you in the next few days," replied Josiah.

"Finally, the Board has authorized me to give you a Dire Warning in this matter."

"What's a 'Dire Warning'?" asked Josiah.

"If we find out at any time from this point forward that you or any members of your pack, in any way, shape, or form, did not follow the laws of the Universal Paranormal High Council, a Dire Wolf will issue a challenge to you—a fight to the death, Alpha, for the sole purpose of taking control of your pack. This will be the only Dire Warning you will receive, so govern yourself accordingly."

"What Dire Wolf?" Josiah exclaimed. "They've been extinct for hundreds of years!"

"No, I assure you they are very much alive. Thank you for your cooperation. I look forward to hearing from you. Good-bye, Alpha," Slate said, hanging up.

Slate slumped back in his chair, exhaling heavily. *Gods, how I managed to speak to that asshole with a civil tongue is beyond me.* After calming down, he placed a call to Steel and Penn informing them of the outcome.

Chapter 32

"Jackson, are you ready yet?" yelled Steel from the bottom of the stairs. He was eager to get going because it was finally time to romance his mate with the fantastic babymoon he'd planned. For the first time since he met Jackson, there wasn't a kill order hanging over his mate. And if he had anything to say about it, there never would be again.

Slate had received the documents from the Silver Point Pack and Penn filed them with the High Council to begin building a case against their Alpha. Penn also assured Jackson and Steel the High Council would punish Silver Point Alpha if, for some reason, he broke the rules concerning the kill order. That last piece of information didn't give Steel the total comfort he wanted but at least his mate could now appear openly in public and not worry about being hunted. He knew there still would be a battle in the future, but he would take the peace right now while his mate was pregnant.

"Be down in a minute," Jackson called. He was packing the last few items in his suitcase while Logan sat on the bed. "Do you have any questions about the nursery you need to ask me before I leave?" Jackson asked his brother.

"No, I've told you, I'll be busy on a different project while you're gone," Logan replied. "I'll have plenty of time to do the nursery after you get back from your babymoon. Any idea where Steel is taking you?"

"Nope, he won't tell me. I tried everything. Why, last night when I was…"

"No, no, no, TMI, TMI," blurted out Logan as he covered his ears. "I do *not* need to know anything that goes on in your bedroom, understand?"

Jackson burst out laughing, then smirked. "Got it. Anyway, to answer your question, no I haven't a clue. Lordy, that man can keep a secret like nobody's business. All I know is we're leaving here by helicopter."

"Wow, I haven't ever flown in one of those."

"Me either. But I'm looking forward to it. Listen, I told our brothers that you're in charge while I'm gone. If you have any problems, call Mystia. She'll make sure the boys toe the line."

"I'll be fine, we'll be fine. Stop worrying and go have a good time. You deserve it. I'll be waiting to get a full report from you when you get back—minus any bedroom information," Logan said, grinning.

"Jackson, babe, please hurry," shouted Steel impatiently.

"You'd better go or your mate will come up here and drag you down," snickered Logan. "Let me carry your suitcase for you."

As they walked down the hall, Jackson put his arm around his twin's waist, pulling him in for a one-armed hug and murmuring, "I love you, bro, and thanks for all your help and support."

"I love you too," Logan replied. "Just promise me you'll enjoy yourself and not worry about anything else."

"I'll try," answered Jackson as they descended the stairs.

Steel looked up at Jackson coming down the stairs. The love Steel felt for his mate overwhelmed him. He reached out for Jackson's hand, pulling him to his chest, leaning down to caress Jackson's soft, pliable lips with his own. "You look gorgeous. Let's hope I don't have to fight off advances from other men."

Jackson deepened the kiss and when his mate's lips opened a sliver, he thrust his tongue in, entwining it with Steel's. Everyone around them was forgotten as the soul mates got lost in their love for each other. Steel started grinding his hard cock against his mate's as they breathlessly consumed each other's mouths. Jackson felt the heat rising in his body, wanting to be taken by Steel when something penetrated his lust fog—the clearing of several throats.

Jackson's teeth sunk into Steel's lower lip, holding it as he separated from him. Finally, he released it, looking with passion-filled eyes at his mate, whispering, "Till later, babe."

Shit, Steel realized he was so lost in the need for his mate he would have fucked him in front of everyone. He looked around, seeing various smiles, grins, leers, and smirks from his parents and Jackson's brothers, and felt a blush fall over his cheeks. "I—ahh, think we're ready to leave now," Steel mumbled, reaching for his mate's hand.

The couple was smothered with "good-byes" all the way to a clearing near the house where the chopper sat. Noticing how small it was, Jackson nervously asked Steel, "Are we going to be safe in that—that thing? Maybe we should drive."

"Babe, it's very safe. And it's bigger than you think—it seats seven passengers and we use it all the time. So, trust me, *mo chroí,* I would not have you and our pup flying in an unsafe helicopter. Come on," Steel said, pulling Jackson toward the man who was standing next to it.

"Hi, Robert, good to see you again," Steel said, shaking the man's hand. "This is my mate, Jackson."

"Glad to see *you,* sir," Robert replied, looking at Jackson. "Very happy to meet Mr. Valentin's mate, sir."

"Please, call me Jackson."

"Have you ever flown in a helicopter, Jackson?" asked Robert.

"No."

"Well, this baby is one of the best there is," he said, opening the passenger door and beckoning them to climb aboard.

Steel helped Jackson into the helicopter, directing his mate to one of the seats facing forward. He buckled Jackson in, giving him a headset to put on. Once Jackson was set, Steel sat down next to him as Robert closed the passenger door and climbed into the cockpit.

Jackson heard the engine power up and as the blades started to rotate, slowly at first, then reaching full speed, he realized the need for the headset; he wouldn't hear anything over that noise. Suddenly, he heard Steel's voice in his ears, "Are you okay, babe?" He realized all, well, most of his fear had dissipated and he was eager to get up in the air. Jackson answered Steel by nodding his head and then saw Steel pointing to the microphone on Jackson's headset. "We use the headsets to talk while we're in the air or else we can't hear each other."

"Got it," Jackson said, "I'm good to go," Startled as he felt the helicopter lift off the ground. He looked out the window and saw his brothers who were looking up at him, squinting in the sunlight. He waved at them as the pilot turned, heading away from the house. Jackson was enthralled with the view from his window. He'd never flown in a helicopter before so he didn't know what to expect. Even if he tried to imagine it, he wouldn't have been close to the thrill he was experiencing.

Jackson followed Steel's finger as he pointed out different mountains, rivers, towns, and highways to him. He was amazed his mate knew exactly where they were, even while in the air, because Jackson was totally lost. After they'd been flying for a while, Jackson finally looked at Steel who had a big smile on his face. "What are you smiling at?"

"You, my love. I love watching you enjoying things."

Jackson felt his cheeks turning pink. "I guess you think I'm naïve."

"Oh, no, babe, I don't think that at all. I feel so lucky that I get to do these things with you first," assured Steel, who was rewarded with a blinding smile from Jackson. "Look out there, what do you see?"

Jackson focused on what Steel was pointing to, gasping when he realized where they were heading. His head snapped back to Steel's face, yelling, "San Francisco! Really??? I always wanted to go there. How did you know?" Turning back to look at the skyline as it continued to get closer, he brought Steel's hand to his lips, kissing it with a loud smack.

Jackson heard Robert address Steel. "Sir, we will be landing in about ten minutes. The car is waiting for you."

"Thanks," replied Steel. He grinned at Jackson who was bouncing his legs in excitement.

Steel had planned activities he thought his mate would especially like, including a special surprise for their final night in San Francisco. Romance was foremost in mind as he picked each restaurant, place to visit, or hotel to stay at for this trip. He wanted his mate to be both wowed and wooed and to feel all of Steel's love.

"Are you ready for the start of your babymoon?" asked Steel as the helicopter started its descent to the heliport in downtown San Francisco.

"Yes, babe. I love you for doing this for me," said Jackson, awed his mate had gone to such lengths to please him.

"You know, I'm going to enjoy this too," admitted Steel, "because I'll be with you, my love."

Jackson blew Steel a kiss as they landed. When the rotors wound down, he and Steel took off their headsets and unbuckled their harnesses before stepping out onto terra firma—or at least what passed for it on the roof of a tall building. Steel took his mate's hand, walking towards a door. Robert followed with their suitcases. A short knock and a man opened it to let them inside.

"Mr. Valentin, I'm James," he said, introducing himself. "When you are ready for your return trip, please call me. The car is downstairs in front of the building, waiting for you and your husband."

"Thank you, James," said Steel.

James took the suitcases from Robert leading the way down one short flight of stairs to an elevator. After entering a security code on the keypad, he said, "It'll be here in a minute."

But Steel wasn't ready to wait. He started to nibble at Jackson's ear lobe after pulling his mate to his side, causing Jackson's cock to rise. When Steel ignored his mate's poke in the ribs, Jackson retaliated by palming his mate's cock which immediately hardened, causing Steel to bite down on Jackson's earlobe in an effort to stop his mate from rubbing. Luckily, before his teeth pierced Jackson's ear, a ding announced the arrival of the elevator. James moved aside, ushering Jackson and Steel inside.

Steel pushed Jackson against the back of the elevator, both facing forward. Jackson felt Steel's hand stretch the hidden elastic waistband of his new maternity pants, his fingers sliding down inside between his cheeks, searching for his puckered rose. He had no defense against Steel's game; his cock pushed against the constraints of his pants and his breath became ragged, trying to control the need for his mate that was consuming his body. When Steel's finger found and then breached him, Jackson could no longer hold back a whimper.

It caused James to look around at them, but finding nothing unusual, he turned forward again. Jackson had never done anything like this in an elevator but it was one of the hottest things that ever happened to him. Just as the elevator reached the ground floor, Steel removed his hand and raised his fingers to his nose. Jackson saw him inhale his scent, then gasped as Steel put them into his mouth, sucking them. *Holy Fucking Damn!* Jackson knew he was in so much trouble watching the blissful expression cross his mate's face. "Hurry, I need to be fucked right now," Jackson whispered to his mate.

Steel chuckled, leading his mate to the waiting car where Jackson's eyes widened looking at the chauffeur holding open the rear door. Steel helped him in, sliding in next to him. After the chauffeur closed their door, he got in behind the wheel and started the car.

As they drove off, Jackson surveyed luxurious interior and inhaled the intoxicating scent of English leather.

Steel, watching his mate's reaction, smiled, "It's a Bentley," while palming Jackson's cock.

Yup, it was now official. Public displays of cock teasing turn me on. His cock was now as hard as it had ever been and just as he thought he was going cream his pants, Steel leaned over, whispering in his ear, "You are not allowed to come unless I give you permission."

Jackson narrowed his eyes at his mate's command. *Shit*! He was so close to coming, he wasn't sure if he could hold off. Then Steel murmured, "If you do come without permission, you *will* be punished."

Clenching his fists, Jackson felt his claws extend, poking into his palms. *Fuck*, he knew his teeth had dropped because he could taste blood. Jackson was literally shaking with the effort to control both his shift and orgasm. And then, just as he thought he would lose the battle, the car stopped in front of a hotel.

Steel removed his hand from Jackson's cock, hissing, "Good boy. In a few minutes, you'll get your reward."

Jackson concentrated on retracting his claws and teeth as Steel got out of the car. Grabbing his mate's hand, Steel pulled him out of the Bentley. Standing up, he was greeted by the hotel manager who shook their hands. "Welcome to the St. George, Mr. and Mr. Valentin. I hope your flight was good and, if you'll please follow me, I'll show you to your suite."

Steel took Jackson's hand, following the hotel manager through the lobby. Jackson had never seen anything like it. Sleek, modern, and sophisticated came to his mind immediately. Oh, Logan would love this, he mused, taking in the grey striated marble floor, mirrored reception desk, and pale grey and soft taupe chairs scattered around the lobby. From the black marbled walls to the floor-to-ceiling glass windows everything was monochromatic except for accents of color from large murals of ancient Rome. Eventually arriving at a private elevator, they were whisked upward to their floor.

Getting out, the hotel manager handed Steel a key and said, "This is a private elevator for this suite only." Walking over to a set of gleaming wooden double doors and, with the click of a keycard, the manager opened them, standing aside.

Steel led Jackson into a living room with floor-to-ceiling windows framing a sweeping panorama of San Francisco Bay. Jackson stopped short. His heart nearly stopped. Steel and the hotel manager were talking, but he heard nothing. He was simply overwhelmed by everything. *Oh, my gods, wait until Logan hears about this!*

Chapter 33

Jackson heard the door to the suite lock; suddenly Steel was behind him, his mate's hard cock nestling between his cheeks.

"Now, where were we?" queried Steel, reaching down to unzip Jackson's pants. He pulled out his mate's cock, slowly tugging it, using Jackson's pre-cum as a lubricant. "Well, I see someone was a good boy," Steel crooned into Jackson's ear. "Too bad... I was so looking forward to punishing you. I'll have to save that for another time."

Jackson moaned, unable to do anything except tremble in his mate's arms. The sensations of Steel's hand on his cock, his mate's iron rod grinding against his ass, along with the promise of a future punishment was too much for Jackson to bear. Shouting Steel's name, he shot his cum all over his mate's hand. Breathing in short gasps, he leaned back against Steel's chest, thankful his mate had a firm grip on him since his legs were trembling violently and he was in danger of falling.

Steel lifted Jackson into his arms, carrying him to the bedroom.

Jackson felt himself lowered gently onto the bed, his mate murmuring words of love.

Then, Steel took off his mate's shoes and pants before getting a warm, wet washcloth from the bathroom, running it over Jackson's cock and belly. He leaned down, pushing Jackson's shirt up over his baby bump before kissing and licking every inch of it. Rising to his feet, he undid Jackson's light-blue, button-down, pulling his mate's arms from the sleeves, one at a time, before removing his shirt. Finally, he stood back, his eyes examining Jackson from head to toe, noting with pleasure that his mate's cock was ready to play some more.

Jackson stared up at Steel's face which was filled with heat, desire, and lust. Shivering at the intense emotion he saw there; he wanted his mate to fuck him so hard and so fast he'd feel it tomorrow. Jackson bit his lower lip, lazily stroking his newly hardened cock while continuing to gaze at his mate's face. With his other hand, he gripped Steel's cock, stroking it in time to his own. Jackson saw Steel's eyes darken to obsidian as they bore into his. Trembling at the series of growls rising from his mate's chest, Jackson knew he was going to get the fuck of a lifetime.

Tossing a bottle of lube he'd placed on the nightstand onto the bed, Steel followed, kneeling between Jackson's legs. Pushing aside his mate's hands, he commanded, "This is mine tonight!" His hand circling Jackson's cock with his fingers, teasing it with soft, easy strokes.

Jackson began to thrust his hips trying to gain the friction and speed he needed to come again.

Steel would have none of that. Using one hand to still Jackson's hips, he rasped, "Stop moving or you won't come tonight, understand?" Stopping the tease of his mate's cock, he could see Jackson was beside himself—his need so desperate he could only toss his head from side to side as he tried to answer.

But Steel remained frozen, demanding a verbal answer from Jackson. Finally, when his mate sobbed a faint, "Yes, I understand," Steel resumed his cock teasing while lowering his mouth to Jackson's balls. He sucked and circled them with his tongue until he ended up at

Jackson's puckered hole, rimming it before stiffening his tongue and breaching it. As he tongued-fucked his mate, he synchronized his thrusts with the movement of his hand on Jackson's cock.

Jackson was keening as he held still, his body demanding more but his mate unwilling to give it to him right now. Looking for relief from the passion consuming his body and soul, Jackson's head kept tossing and his hands grasped the coverlet. Finally, he was reduced to begging, calling out, "Steel, please, have mercy on me!" Then, nearly senseless, he became overcome by his feelings of need and lust, unable to do anything more than shout out his mate's name over and over. Finally, his mate gave him what he so badly needed. Jackson felt his legs being bent up and Steel's cock thrusting into him in one long push. He let out a wild cry that resounded throughout the room.

Halting briefly, Steel gazed at his mate, watching the pleasure roll across the face he loved so much. He pulled out until just his tip was inside, then pushed hard back in. His mate grunted, then yelled, "More! Harder!" Steel ratcheted up the speed of his thrusts. With his cock in the tight channel of his mate, he was consumed with pleasure and knew he'd never get enough of it. Steel became a fucking machine, pounding his mate so hard the bed started to move. But he didn't slow down—he wanted his mate to savor this all day tomorrow. He wanted to mark his mate in the most intimate way possible between two men. Tomorrow, he wanted to see his mate wince each time he sat down, reminding him of their lovemaking tonight.

Steel felt his balls tighten and tingle signaling he was ready to come. He reached down for his mate's cock, stroking it hard and fast, whispering in his ear, "Come for me."

Jackson howled as his cock shot out globs of white cream onto his chest and face. Steel howled in unison with his mate, shooting his passion deep into Jackson. Collapsing on Jackson's chest, Steel was careful to keep most of his weight supported by his arms and off his mate's belly. Slowly they came back to earth; their breathing slowed, rapid heartbeats subsided and Steel, pulling out of Jackson, rolled over on his side, and drew his mate into his arms. There, side-by-side, the lovers fell into a deep sleep.

~/~/~/~/~

Steel awoke first, his arms wrapped around Jackson and one of his legs between his mate's. Sniffing deeply, he caught the scent of last night's lovemaking encrusted on their bodies—gods, he loved that smell. The session had taken it all out of them both. They'd slept through the night, never even waking to grab dinner. *But fuck, it was worth it.* The Fates gave him the perfect mate and once again he thought how lucky he was—taking the shortcut home; it was the best decision he'd ever made. Yup, as soon as he spotted Jackson that day, he knew that man was perfect for him.

"You're perfect for me, too, and yes, I'm really glad you took the shortcut and found me," Jackson said sleepily, reading Steel's mind.

"Hey babe, good morning. Did I wake you?"

"Well, actually," Jackson said, rolling over to face his mate, "it was your growling stomach that woke me. And then I realized I was very hungry, in fact, I'm starving. You're falling down on your mate responsibilities."

"Oh, really?" Steel asked, tickling Jackson.

"No, no," giggled Jackson, "not this morning. I'll take it back. Please, stop," he said, struggling to avoid Steel's tickles. "I take it back! You are a superb mate, really," he said, finally rolling away from his mate's wicked fingers.

Jackson sat up on the edge of the bed, looking down at his chest. "Ugg, dried cum. I need a shower," he declared, heading for the bathroom. "Are you joining me?" he asked with a wink, before disappearing through the door.

~/~/~/~/~

After their shower, Steel padded into the living room to await the arrival of their breakfast he'd ordered from room service. After it was delivered, he shouted, "Chow time!"

Jackson emerged from the bedroom, smiling with delight at the big spread on the dining room table. "Hey, thanks, babe. I think I'm moving into my 'eat a cow at every meal' phase because I could devour most of this.

"Eat as much as you want," Steel said. "I can always order more." He set down the newspaper he was reading, passing Jackson the scrambled eggs, pancakes, bacon, sausages, and sliced breakfast ham. As his mate heaped his plate with lots of meat and scrambled eggs, Steel poured orange juice and coffee for them. Soon the only sound in the room was the clink of silverware against plates.

After Jackson finished, his mate poured more coffee for them. "Well, are you ready for your first day in San Francisco?" Steel asked.

"Yup. What do you have planned?"

"This morning, I thought we would do a little shopping."

"Shopping? Like shopping-shopping?"

Steel laughed, "Yes, babe. Shopping for our pup. There are some great baby stores in this city and I thought you might want to take a bite out of the clothes list my mother told me was 'modest'."

Jackson smiled brightly. Oh yeah, he was up for that kind of shopping with his mate—wait—what was that about the list... "Modest? Your mother thinks the pup should have more clothes?"

"Yes, she thought Logan may have been careful about spending my money when he made the list," Steel said, chuckling.

"Fuck, I can see this kid will have enough clothes to start his own store if we follow her advice. Let's just stick to the original list."

"Okay, then let's go."

~/~/~/~/~

Steel watched Jackson shop for their pup, enjoying his mate's enthusiasm for everything with a wolf on it as the shopping bags began to fill. His personal favorites were the onesies—yes, they found out what onesies were—with wolf sayings on them. Jackson bought several that said *Wolf Pack's Newest Member*, *Raised by Wolves*, and his personal favorite, *Throw me to the Wolves and I will Return Leading the Pack.* Steel had a sneaking suspicion the pup would be leading all of them from the moment he was born.

Jackson squealed, holding up a small t-shirt that said *Wolf Pack Pup*, exclaiming, "Look, babe, here are matching t-shirts for us!" and held up a much larger one that read *Wolf Pack Alpha.* He was enthralled by all the baby clothes he saw. This was the third store Steel had taken him to and it was the best. The saleslady suggested items Logan hadn't included; Jackson hoped his brother would never realize that because he'd tease Jackson mercilessly about buying so much.

Steel saw his mate tiring and stepped in to stop the shopping frenzy. "Babe, it's noon and this wolf needs his food."

"Oh, right, I didn't realize the time."

Steel paid and asked that everything be sent to the St. George. Then taking Jackson's hand, he led him out to the waiting car. "The Pier House, please," Steel told the driver.

Jackson rested his head against Steel's shoulder, thinking about all the wonderful clothes he'd found for their pup. He enjoyed the shopping trip more than he ever thought. He closed his eyes for a second before hearing, "Wake up, babe, we're here."

Jackson looked around. He saw a low, white, wooden building with bright blue trim. Steel said a few words to the driver before helping his mate out. Entering the restaurant, he admired the causal sea shanty décor as Steel steered him to a waterside table on the outside deck. Ignoring Steel's invitation to sit, Jackson stood there, transfixed by the view.

"Babe, sit down," said Steel. Jackson finally sat and closed his mouth as Steel chuckled. "Thought you might enjoy eating out here today because of the sunny weather."

"I love it. Look at all the sailboats on the bay. And the ferries and cruise ships, holy cow, look at all of this," Jackson said, waving his hand toward the bay. "And look! There's a dolphin!"

Steel loved seeing his mate so happy and excited. Jackson's life wasn't easy before he came along and he vowed to make the rest of it better; it seemed he was off to a good start. He perused the menu, thinking about what his mate would like. "Babe, do you want me to order for you?" he asked.

But Jackson's eyes were still firmly fixed on the water scene in front of them. "Yeah, that's fine," he mumbled.

~/~/~/~/~

The food was great, the view fantastic, and the company delightful making lunch a dream come true mused Jackson. Steel led him to Chinatown after lunch where he was overwhelmed by the throngs of people walking the streets. Strolling along, his mate held his hand as they looked at the unique architecture, people-watched, and window shopped the odd and unique shops.

Jackson stumbled into an old book store, buying some books to give to Logan, Colton, and Dakota as gifts. After stopping at the Golden Gate Bakery for a couple of egg custard tarts□which they devoured on the spot□Steel then bought them a bag of cookies from the Golden Gate Fortune Cookie Factory. But Jackson didn't need cookies to foretell his future; he already knew and it was all good.

Finally, his mate led him to a side street where the car was waiting to take them back to the hotel. As they wove through traffic, Steel asked, "Did you have a good day, babe?"

"Loved it. Loved everything about it. Thanks so much, lover. It was better than anything I could ever dream of," he said, sighing, snuggling up against his mate.

Chapter 34

Jackson turned over, feeling a twinge in his ass. Steel fucked him into the mattress again last night after they ate at a very romantic restaurant. He turned over, seeing the time—shit, ten in the morning! He grabbed Steel's arm, shaking him. "Wake up, babe! It's late! We're missing the day! Come on! Last one in the shower gets a blow job," Jackson shrieked, jumping up and running to the bathroom.

Steel groaned, rolling over, burying his head in the pillow. He could use another couple of hours sleep. *Blow job? Is that what my mate said? He's going to give me a blow job? On my morning wood? Yessir, I'm all for that—fuck sleep! A blow job was much better than sleep.* Steel tumbled out of bed, rushing to the gigantic shower in their bathroom. He stopped short, seeing his mate tugging on his cock and looking at Steel with an evil grin. *What was that about?* Didn't matter once his eyes focused on what his mate was toying with. Steel stepped in, grabbing Jackson's cock that was now stretching towards him. His mate had lathered it up with shower gel and Steel got right to work, stroking it.

Jackson's eyes rolled back in his head as he fell against the shower wall. A steady stream of sobs and moans left his throat as Steel picked up speed. Jackson felt his body ready itself for the pleasure of coming. A sharp cry, "Steel!" and Jackson's cum shot all over his mate's hand. When he finally came back down to earth, he watched as Steel licked cum from his hand, smiling wickedly.

Steel pushed Jackson down on his knees. His mate smiled up at him before taking Steel's cock in his mouth. Jackson's plump lips squeezed his mate's cock, sucking it into his throat. Slowly pulling back, his teeth lightly scraped Steel's shaft until they reached the ridge under the head of it. Swirling his tongue over the tip and corkscrewing it into Steel's slit, Jackson repeatedly scooped up Steel's pre-cum. Suddenly, his mate gave a low growl and, sucking Steel's cock down his throat, beckoned him to take control.

Gripping Jackson's hair, Steel held his mate still while he pumped his cock into Jackson's mouth repeatedly. He would never get enough of his mate's full, cock-sucking, red lips and felt his blood starting to boil. Balls drawn tight, his jack-hammering hips caused his need to rise until he was at the tipping point. And then it happened—Jackson's finger pierced his hole, finding his prostate. Steel roared, and screamed Jackson's name as his cum shot down his mate's throat. He came and came, longer than he ever had but Jackson eagerly swallowed it all. When his cock finally slipped from Jackson's mouth, Steel watched with half-closed eyes as his mate's pink tongue licked it clean.

Jackson stood up, wrapping his arms around his mate. "I'm yours now and until the end of time, babe, and I love you with my whole heart, body, and soul," he whispered into Steel's ear.

Tears filled Steel's eyes when he heard his mate's vow. Everything that came before in his life paled in comparison to the bright light Jackson brought to his world. He gently kissed his mate, wrapping him in his arms, whispering, "You are my everything. My life was so dreary until you painted it the colors of the rainbow…every day, every hour, every minute. And if that wasn't enough, you gave me a pup…a life to cherish and guide and watch as he becomes a man. I'll never be able to thank you enough but I swear I'll spend the rest of my life trying."

~/~/~/~/~

Tonight was their last night in San Francisco, and Jackson was getting ready for the big surprise Steel arranged for him. He couldn't imagine how his mate could top himself since Jackson was pretty sure they'd done everything already. He went over it in his mind like a slow-motion replay, savoring each moment of it.

They'd hung side-by-side out of an open-air cable car, taken a boat ride on Stow Lake, had a picnic lunch overlooking the Golden Gate Bridge during a three-mile hike in Land's End, dined at the Cliff House, ridden a ferry to Alcatraz, walked through the Aquarium of the Bay, and meandered around Fisherman's Wharf and Chinatown.

And then there was the kiss they shared at Twin Peaks with the marvelous view of San Francisco, the Bay Bridge and Oakland as a backdrop. Finally, last night, Steel took him to the Foreign Cinema Restaurant, giving a new meaning to a "dinner and a movie" date. What more could there be? Whatever it was, he knew this much—it would require formal wear because Steel had ordered tuxedos for them.

"Having trouble?" Steel laughed, watching Jackson struggle with his bowtie. After his third try, Steel strolled over, "Let me, babe." Jackson huffed in frustration, giving himself over to his mate's ministrations.

"There… you look gorgeous," Steel grinned, as Jackson put on the black jacket.

He took his mate's hand, leading Jackson down to the waiting car. Inside, Steel gave the driver a nod after they were settled. As they accelerated into the evening traffic, Jackson marveled at the vibrant city, wondering what Steel had in store for him. He glanced at his mate, whose eyes laser-locked on him with an intensity he'd never before seen. Shivers went down his back, as he could only guess what that look meant. Without wavering in his gaze, Steel lifted Jackson's hand to his mouth and kissed it gently. Jackson knew then this would be a night he'd remember forever.

The car stopped in front of a hotel and Steel's hand never let go of his mate's after helping him out of the back seat. Smiling at Jackson, he led him to an elevator where, once inside, he pushed the top button. During the elevator ride, Steel eyed his mate steadily, causing Jackson to squirm with desire but Steel wanted to give Jackson even more tonight. When the elevator finally stopped and the doors opened, Steel saw his mate's eyes flick away from his, looking into the restaurant.

Jackson gasped at the stunning view through the floor to ceiling windows and then, as if mesmerized, slowly left the elevator, following Steel and the maître d' to their table next to one of them. Once seated, Jackson gazed wide-eyed at his mate. "Oh, my gods, this is beyond 'wow.' Babe, the view is fantastic! How can I eat when I don't know where to look first?"

"I wanted you to see the lights start to twinkle below us when dusk falls on this beautiful golden city. I felt it would be a perfect end to our babymoon."

"It couldn't be better. I can't believe how perfect this is. Love you babe, so much," uttered Jackson, his eyes roaming over the darkening city.

The evening was as special as Steel hoped it would be. They watched as night fell, thousands of stars shimmering at their feet. During dinner, the conversation flowed easily between them as if they'd been together all their lives. Steel felt a sense of peace envelop him, watching a multitude of expressions cross his mate's face while they talked. He knew then, that no matter what problems they might face in the future, so long as Jackson was by his side, it would be okay. When they'd finished and he'd paid the bill, he asked, "Ready for your final surprise, lover?"

"There's more?" exclaimed Jackson. "Okay, mate of mine, it better be huge, if you plan to top this."

"Trust me, *mo chroí.*"

They stood to leave, but not until Jackson had a long, last look around, did they take the elevator down to the waiting Bentley. Once inside, Jackson leaned against his mate, wallowing in the scent he and his wolf loved. His eyes were half closed, blurring the city lights speeding past them. His mate's nose was buried in his hair, nuzzling it. Jackson suddenly felt his baby move. He seized Steel's hand, pressing it to his belly.

"What's the matter, *mo chroí*?"

"Wait a moment. There! Did you feel it?"

"Was that the baby?" Steel whispered in Jackson's ear.

He nodded. "Yes, it was. Did you feel him? There he is again!"

Steel placed his large hands over Jackson's belly and waited. "He's kicking again!" Steel exclaimed softly.

Jackson turned to his mate and, after a long, deep kiss, Steel whispered, "That's our pup." His eyes misted up with joy.

"Yes, it is, my lover," Jackson whispered back.

Steel was so wrapped up with his mate and pup it wasn't until the car stopped that he realized they'd arrived. Another elevator ride, during which Steel kept his arms wrapped around his mate, his hands resting on Jackson's belly, brought them to an archway framed by heavy, crimson, velvet drapes.

Jackson noticed they were standing in a dance club, high above the city and, like the restaurant where they'd dined, the club boasted a stunning, panoramic view of San Francisco.

When they were seated next to a window, Steel ordered a desert for two and coffee. Jackson's eyes wandered over the city lights below, marveling at how vast San Francisco was.

The waiter arrived with their dessert and Jackson drew a sharp breath. There before him was a chocolate drizzle-covered, mini strawberry cake with a chocolate dipped strawberry perched on top—his favorite dessert. He smiled, delighted, gazing at his mate. "Babe, I love you," was all he could manage to say, but that said it all.

Steel forked into the luscious cake, bringing a piece of it up to his mate's lips. Jackson opened his mouth, moaning as his lips closed around the fork. Steel's eye darkened with pleasure at the sound and fed his mate another bite. Jackson couldn't let his mate miss out on the best dessert on the planet so he offered a piece of the heavenly cake to Steel. Their cake slowly disappeared as they indulged each other with the city's lighted skyline as a backdrop.

When they'd finished, the hostess appeared, bending down to whisper in Steel's ear. He nodded. "We're ready."

Lifting an eyebrow at his mate, Jackson asked, "Ready for what?"

Steel smiled, offering his hand to Jackson, who took it, rising and looking quizzically at his mate. Steel answered, "My surprise."

Steel led Jackson over to a dark corner of the club. "For you, my love," he crooned in his mate's ear before leading him onto the dance floor. Steel embraced Jackson by looping his arms around his waist, holding him tightly. He felt his mate's hard cock pressing against him.

At first Jackson saw a faint glow, growing stronger as hundreds of fairy lights twinkled above them, reminding him of the thousands of stars in the night sky when their wolves mated. Then his nose sniffed the scent of roses. He searched for the source and finally saw that the dance floor was carpeted with red rose petals—so many their scents twined up and wrapped around the two lovers.

When the first strains of music started, Jackson instantly recognized the song. It was his favorite, *Thinking Out Loud,* and somehow his mate had found out. As the orchestra played, Steel started moving to the music in a slow and sensuous dance. Jackson rested his head on Steel's chest, his mate's heart beat echoing throughout his body. Steel bent his head down, singing the words of the song to Jackson, softly and oh so personally, just for him alone.

Listening to his mate's voice, Jackson thought back to everything that happened to him since that fateful day Steel stopped to help him; he was overcome with love for the man who saved him and fulfilled dreams he didn't even know he had.

Jackson looked up at his mate, giving him a loving smile. As Steel continued to sing to him, Jackson was overwhelmed by the love his mate felt for him, reflected in those words and he knew for as long as they lived, he would always be loved, protected, and cherished. Jackson had finally found his forever.

Epilogue

After Dr. Ian Wallace read it, he set aside the latest report from Colton, Jackson's brother who'd been training to be a nurse. He'd been impressed from the very beginning when Steel sent him the equipment list Colton compiled and Ian looked forward to meeting the man. Well, to be honest, Colton's voice had sent his wolf into a tizzy. It'd been a long time since his wolf felt anything and Ian was unsure what that meant. But he was curious to find out…

~~~~~~~~~~~~~~~~~~~~~~~~~~~~~~

TO MY READERS

I hope you enjoyed reading *Dire Warning* as much as I did writing it. If you liked it, please consider leaving a review at Amazon, if you purchased it there or borrowed it through KU, and also at other sites. There's been a sharp increase in book pirating lately and authors in all genres have been affected by it to the point that many can no longer afford to write. I am a full-time author and any small part you can play to help me reach and attract new readers would be greatly appreciated.

Hugs and Kisses,

Mary

If you'd like to find out more about the Blackwood Pack, here's the place to go: the Blog on my website, *maryrundle.com* where you'll find posts written by Jackson, Steel, and the others.
~~~~~~~~~~~~~~~~~~~~~~~~~~~~~~

They have lots to share with you: insights into their feelings and issues, what they're doing, and their plans for the future. They'll also reveal some great backstory stuff that didn't make it into the book. And who knows? They may even take questions from you, the reader. So, click on over and catch up on what your favorites have to say.

Turn the Page for a Sneak Peak of Book Two Blackwood Pack: Raphael's Power

Colton looked up and saw the cloudless, blue sky through the holes in the rocks. He'd lost all sense of time after his fall. Trying to stay awake but failing, he knew he was in deep trouble. Wallowing in darkness punctuated by brief periods of awareness, he became increasingly disorientated. "Tell my brothers I love them," he whispered, as he lost consciousness again...

Chapter 1

Almost two months earlier...

Colton stuck his head into Jackson and Steel's bedroom where Logan was admiring the results of his decorating job. "Hey, bro, come on! The helicopter will be landing in a few minutes."

Logan turned around, smiling. "Yeah, I'm coming." Looking around once more, he knew Jackson would love his efforts. Steel hired him to redo their bedroom while they were in San Francisco on their babymoon. "Make it romantic and serene," Steel said, responding to Logan's questions. Everyone was astonished when Jackson finally found his fated mate and discovered he was a very rare Alpha/Omega hybrid who could bear pups, chosen to mate with Steel, one of the last Dire Wolves on earth. Though the mating was blessed by the Fates, not all of Jackson's six brothers welcomed the news about their Alpha having a baby. It was rough in the beginning but now they were eager to greet the soon-to-arrive new member of the Blackwood Pack.

Colton headed downstairs to welcome the couple back. He thought about the last few years, beginning with the massacre of the Fox River Pack that wiped out his parents and younger siblings. He and his six brothers were in Vegas partying at the end of the school year when word reached them. Jackson took control, getting them to a place of safety.

As the eldest, Jackson was now the Alpha of the newly formed Blackwood Pack. Other members were Logan, Jackson's fraternal twin, the triplets, Cody, Colton, and Carson and Dakota and Zane. The pack had expanded when Steel claimed Jackson and now included the last four Dire Wolves on earth—Steel, his brother Slate, and their parents, Maximus and Oracle.

One of the fallouts from the massacre was that their educational goals screeched to a halt. And for Colton, that meant he never finished nursing school. One year short. *Just one fucking year*—and he would have received his degree. He'd since picked up a few online courses but was still short of the credits he needed. Before Jackson became pregnant, his nursing skills were confined to sick or injured animals found in the woods surrounding their old pack house.

But now, Jackson's pregnancy gave Colton a real patient to use his knowledge and skills on. Eager to see the expectant father, he bolted down the rest of the stairs, joining his brothers on the porch.

Zane shouted, "There they are!" Joined by Steel's parents, Colton and his brothers scanned the sky as the chopper grew larger and noisier, finally landing.

Waiting for the blades to stop, Steel emerged first, helping Jackson out. "Hey guys, I need a hand with some bags," shouted Jackson, waving his brothers over. Colton studied Jackson. What he saw pleased him. His brother's face was calm, his body relaxed, his spirits high—just what the doctor, or in this case, the nurse ordered. Colton hugged his brother and then Steel. "Did you guys have a good time?"

"Oh, my gods, we had a fantastic time," boasted Jackson. "I took lots of pictures so maybe we should do a picture-night."

Steel passed the bags to Colton and the other brothers. When Jackson reached for one, Steel admonished, "No, babe, I don't want you carrying anything." Jackson rolled his eyes behind Steel's back making them all laugh.

"Are you doing that thing again?" asked Steel.

"What thing?"

"You know the eye roll thingy you do."

Jackson reached over, kissing Steel, "You know I love you, babe."

"Holy crap, did you guys buy out all the stores in San Francisco?" Logan asked, as Steel kept passing shopping bags to the brothers.

"What the hell you bitchin' about? *You* gave us the list of baby clothes we needed," smirked Jackson.

Logan and the brothers started their hike back to the house while Steel greeted his parents. Oracle hugged her son, then asked Jackson, "How's the little one?"

A wide smile crossed his face. "We felt him move for the first-time last night, didn't we, babe?"

"Yup, it was amazing, Mom."

Oracle hugged Jackson, murmuring, "You look radiant. I will take it that the babymoon was good?"

Jackson nodded as he looked lovingly at his mate. "It was the best."

Steel asked Maximus, "Did you hear anything more from Slate about the kill order on our pack?"

"Nope, I think the Dire Warning did its job."

"Come on, let's go eat. I'm starving," announced Jackson.

Laughing, the four of them walked toward the house.

~/~/~/~/~

Evening found everyone relaxing in the great room as Jackson showed their babymoon pictures on the huge TV screen. Listening to his brother describe the trip, the urge to travel swept over Colton. His goal, after becoming a nurse, was to join Frontline Doctors, to serve where the need was greatest. Colton sighed heavily. *Well, it doesn't mean it won't happen.* After all, he was a Timber Wolf shifter and they lived a long time.

He knew Jackson would never allow him to volunteer until the mess with the Silver Point Pack was resolved. Steel's brother Slate had made progress when he forced Colton's uncle—the Alpha of Silver Point Pack—to rescind the kill-on-sight order for Colton and his brothers. But it was only temporary. He shook his head. Who would have thought his uncle would order a massacre that orphaned Colton and his brothers? No one… The day Jackson's friend Jimmy called, telling them what happened, would be forever etched in his memory.

Nightmares plagued Colton for months, imagining his family's pain and suffering that awful night. It went against everything Colton dedicated his life to prevent. Growing up, it was he who his brothers and sisters relied on to take care of their cuts and scrapes, yet he wasn't there when they needed him most. And *that* was something he couldn't forgive himself for. He never talked to Jackson about it because his brother had enough on his plate just making sure the seven of them survived.

Yup, his brother had risen to the task at hand, providing a roof over their heads and food for their bellies. Just for that, Jackson deserved all the happiness in the world. He knew some of his brothers were jealous of Jackson finding his mate and discovering he could have a baby but he wasn't. Nope, his eyes were clearly focused on the attainment of his goal. *Mate? No, not right now. Maybe sometime in the far-off future—sure, that would be nice.* But right now, he had more important things to do and nothing was going to stop him from achieving them.

Cody nudged him. "What?" he asked.

"Jackson asked you a question," murmured Cody.

"Oh, sorry. What did you say?" Colton asked Jackson.

"I asked if you had talked to Dr. Wallace while we were gone."

"Uhm, yes. He ordered some blood tests along with the weekly ultrasound," said Colton. "We can do that in the next few days. No hurry."

Jackson smirked. "Well, that's good to know, but did he tell you when he'd be arriving?"

Colton's face turned pink. "Oh. Sometime at the end of this month."

Logan came to his rescue, asking Steel if he was ready to show Jackson the surprise he ordered.

"Babe, another surprise? You are spoiling me. What is it?" asked Jackson, smiling.

Steel stood, pulling Jackson into his arms. "Well, do you want me to tell you or show you?"

"Show me…no, tell me…no, tell me first *then* show me!"

Everyone began to laugh. "Did my brother ever tell you he used to buy himself a gift for the Long Night Moon Festival?" asked Logan.

"Hush," shushed Jackson. "Don't give my childhood secrets away."

Steel said, "I know about it, babe. Remember, you told me."

"Yeah, but your parents didn't know," pouted Jackson.

"Oh no, you leave us out of this," said Maximus. "We'll pretend we didn't hear anything about your secret gift buying vice," he laughed, as everyone cracked up again.

Jackson smiled. "What's my surprise?"

"Well, I'll let Logan tell you since he's responsible for it."

Jackson looked at Logan. "Well?"

"It seems you bragged about my interior design skills so your mate hired me to redo your bedroom while you were away."

"What? Really?" exclaimed Jackson, wrapping his arms around Steel's neck, kissing him senseless before asking, "Wait, is that why you didn't let me go upstairs before?"

Steel replied, "I wanted to tell you first. And by the way, Logan, you did an outstanding job."

Smiling at Logan, Jackson said, "Come on. Show me what you did. Has everyone seen it?" A chorus of voices chimed in, claiming they helped in some way.

"Okay. Come on and you can tell me what each of you did."

~/~/~/~/~

Getting ready for bed, Colton looked around his room. He supposed he should let Logan do his magic in here but he'd declined his brother's offer. *Why? Who knows? No wait. That's not true.* He knew exactly why he rejected the redesign. He felt if he accepted, it would mean giving up on his dream. *Yup, that was dumb on my part.* Just seeing Jackson and Steel's beautiful bedroom tonight showed him what a mistake he made. Colton resolved to talk to Logan tomorrow.

He climbed into bed, pulling his cock from his briefs. Slowly tugging on it, he thought about the man consuming his thoughts since first hearing his voice. Dr. Ian Wallace. That did it! His cock went from 0 to 60 in three seconds.

Just thinking about that voice did it to him every night. He wondered what the man looked like. Mmm, maybe he should do a search on him and see what comes up. It would be nice to have a picture he could put to the voice. *Shit, maybe not. Nah, it would just make the man too real.* Right now, the fantasy worked just fine—except to his dismay, Ian invaded his dreams every night.

Colton's hand worked his cock, using his copious pre-cum as a lubricant, stroking it with just the right amount of pressure. Nearing completion, he twisted the shaft, striving to satisfy the endless need that now was his daily companion. As his cock exploded, soaking his hand and abs with cum, he roared Ian's name while his body shuddered with the pulses. Coming down from his high, Colton drew in deep breaths, waiting for his heartbeat to slow down. Shit, he did it again—calling out Ian's name when he came. He hoped everyone was asleep because how embarrassing would that be if his brothers heard him—they would rag him mercilessly.

After wiping himself off, he turned over to sleep. But it did not come easily. Pictures of Jackson and Steel's happiness and love kept flipping through his head. *Shit. Shit. Shit. No, I won't go there.* Colton refused to let his mind picture him and Ian as a happy couple. *No! No Way!* He was going to finish his degree and spend his life saving lives, not setting up house with a mate.

Colton punched his pillow, frustrated that his mind wouldn't stop thinking about Ian. Groaning, he sat up. *What the fuck.* This was getting worse every day. He knew even if he fell asleep now, his dreams would be filled with Ian. *How the fuck could that happen?* He didn't even know what Ian looked like, yet every night, Colton clearly saw him in his dreams. And shit, the multiple wet dreams he'd been having forced him to change his sheets every day. So far, Cody, who took care of the pack's laundry, hadn't mentioned it. But he would soon. And then what was Colton going to say? *Shit!*

He rose from his bed and was struck by the beauty of the trees swaying on the mountain behind the house as he looked out the window. It would soon be time for another full moon run. It was something he missed most after he and his brothers were forced into hiding. Even with the spell Mystia—Jimmy's wife—cast to protect them from being scented by other wolves, Jackson insisted they stay close to their pack house. But when they'd moved to Steel's place with 200,000 fenced-in acres and electronic surveillance, Jackson resumed the pack runs again.

Sighing, he knew he had to get some sleep. Lying down, he worked on clearing all thoughts from his brain by breathing deeply in and out, concentrating solely on the action of his lungs. Slowly, his body relaxed, finally succumbing as silence fell over the household. All asleep. Except two people.

Downstairs, Oracle listened to Colton's voice calling out Ian's name. Yes, he had been doing that more frequently. She turned over, facing Maximus who was leaning against the headboard reading the latest business reports from their son, Slate.

"Honey, did you hear that?"

"Mmm, hear what?"

"Colton."

"Uhm, yeah. Why?"

"Well, the Fates are at work again."

"What? You mean Colton? And who is it this time?" asked Maximus.

"Dr. Ian Wallace."

"Ian? But how? They never met—at least not yet."

"But they did talk on the phone, which was enough to trigger the mating pull."

"Ian's a good man. Colton could do worse."

"I agree. But Colton is fighting it."

"Why?"

"Because he has things he wants to do first."

"Ian won't stand in his way."

"I know that and so do you, but Colton will have to discover it for himself. The Fates have big plans for

Colton—so it is imperative that he claim his fated mate."

"You're enjoying all this, aren't you?"

"Of course. Rarely do I have a front row seat to the Fates' actions on earth. Yes, I know what they tell me, however, I am never where their decisions are being carried out. Oh, don't get me wrong, I love being an Oracle but I am finding out how wonderful it is to see the Fates in action."

Maximus set the reports on his night stand, rolled over and gathered his wife in his arms. "Have I told you lately how much I love you?" he whispered, nuzzling Oracle's neck before kissing her passionately. Only a deep sigh was heard in reply.

The Fates looked down at their Oracle and smiled. "This is a great match we made. Still in love after all these years."

About the Author

I never went to school to learn writing nor attended a writing workshop, but it didn't stop me from entering a writing contest and from that came my first book, Dire Warning. Readers loved it and I was on my way to chronicling the Blackwood Pack, seven brothers who are gay wolf shifters in search of their fated mates–stories about love at first sight with twists and turns, angst and humor, romance and adventure and, of course, happy endings.

My stories come to me as if they were being channeled by my characters, all of whom I love (except for a few villains). They are eager to recount their lives, loves and adventures and are not inhibited when it comes to revealing steamy details. I love the M/M paranormal genre because it gives my imagination a lot of territory in which to roam. My mind can really run wild and come up with some amazing stuff when it doesn't have to stay inside the box. Although my writing is sometimes raw—that's the way I like to tell my stories—readers love it and are clamoring for more. I currently live in the Northeast and love the beautiful change of seasons, my husband, and our quirky calico cat, though not necessarily in that order.

I would love to hear from any of my readers. You can catch up with me on any of my social media links below.

Facebook - https://www.facebook.com/maryrundle69

My Facebook Group - https://www.facebook.com/groups/171112140176036

Twitter - maryrundle69

Instagram - maryrundle69

Website - https://www.maryrundle.com

Email me directly at - maryrundle@maryrundle.com

Books by Mary Rundle

Blackwood Pack Series

Book 1   Dire Warning – Jackson and Steel

Book 2 – Raphael's Power   *Coming Soon*

Made in the USA
Monee, IL
27 May 2022